FOR LOVE OF
A PIRATE

Other novels by Anthony Esler

FORBIDDEN CITY

LORD LIBERTINE

HELLBANE

THE BLADE OF CASTLEMAYNE

FOR LOVE OF A PIRATE

by ANTHONY ESLER

WILLIAM MORROW AND COMPANY, INC.

NEW YORK   1978

Library of Congress Cataloging in Publication Data

Esler, Anthony.
   For love of a pirate.

   I. Title.
PZ4.E762Fm [PS3555.S52]   813'.5'4   78-17287
ISBN 0-688-03375-X

BOOK DESIGN   CARL WEISS

Printed in the United States of America.

First Edition

1 2 3 4 5 6 7 8 9 10

FOR LOVE OF A PIRATE

BOOK I

SWEET AND TWENTY

BOOK II

THIS SCOURGE WILL COME

55

FOR LOVE OF
A PIRATE

BOOK I

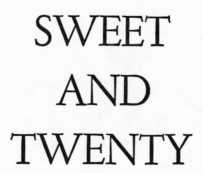

SWEET
AND
TWENTY

What is love? 'tis not hereafter;
Present mirth hath present laughter;
　What's to come is still unsure:
In delay there lies no plenty;
Then come kiss me, sweet and twenty,
　Youth's a stuff will not endure.

—WILLIAM SHAKESPEARE,
　Twelfth Night

CHAPTER

1

TAMAR DE LA BARCA WAS ASLEEP AND DREAMING. HER EYES moved beneath her lowered lids, and she murmured something to herself in the darkness. Her body shifted restlessly between the scented sheets.

It was purple flowers at first. Cascades of purple flowers spilling over the whitewashed wall above her, richly fragrant, filling her nostrils with a pleasure that was purely sensuous. Flowers above her bent head, and sun-bleached earth, cool with white dust, beneath her tanned bare knees as she played happily at the end of her father's garden. It was a familiar and beloved dream of childhood. For it had been years since Tamar had played bare-legged in the dust.

But something was changing now. The girl's head rolled uneasily on the bolster. Her lips parted in a muttered exclamation, and her small hand thrust out against the hangings of the tall four-poster bed.

The flowers were still there, their sensuous fragrance all around her. But other odors mingled with that of the flowers now, smells less familiar but even more sensually stimulating to the sleeping girl. The odor of leather and steel, the pomaded smell of a man's beard, the rough smell of his skin. For there was a man there now, standing in the shadow of the adobe wall. A shadowy figure himself in that thick shade, yet familiar too—a man she knew—

With a strange, unreal deliberation, he drew her to him, pressed her small body up against his own, and kissed her on the mouth.

She knew it was not really happening, knew that it could not really be happening to her. It must be a dream, she thought. But the velvet doublet with its jeweled ornamental buttons felt so concrete and real against her straining body. The large male mouth between the wiry moustache and the beard sent such waves of giddiness and desire radiating through her.

The girl moaned softly in the darkness, a sound like the surge and subsidence of white surf along a beach. It was a moan of pleasure, and one of the first ever to escape this young girl's lips.

She awoke quite suddenly, and the dream vanished at once from her consciousness. Only the faintest echoes of desire remained. Only a dim sense of warmth and half-forgotten excitement, that made the moment of awakening as pleasant as any other in the happy life of Tamar de la Barca, the only daughter of Don Gabriel de la Barca, Governor of Cuba in that year of grace 1597.

She awoke to a ringing of bells.

She knew them at once, of course. They were the bells of the Franciscan monastery in the town below, summoning the brothers to prayer. Tamar had been awakening to that familiar tintinnabulation rising through the still morning air for almost all the twenty years of her life.

Behind the peal of the Franciscans, the bells of the Domini- can house across the city began their somewhat more strident call to worship. The Dominicans were always just a shade behind their Franciscan rivals. Tamar smiled sleepily, imagining Father García heaving exasperatedly on his rope, trying manfully, as a good Christian should, not to resent the fact that Father Gonzalez at the Franciscans' had beaten him again.

The girl opened one eye speculatively. It was still dark. Then, somewhere down the hillside, cocks began to crow.

Sunday, the girl thought drowsily. And then, with a flash of expectation: *The carrack!*

The last echo of the bells faded into silence. The cocks fell silent too, waiting for the real dawn, a good hour away. Tamar nestled deeper into the bed and settled down to sleep at least that long herself.

* * *

Her real awakening came rather more abruptly and un-compromisingly when Marina jerked back the heavy hang-ings to let in the morning sun.

"Oh, Marina," the girl cried, covering her eyes against the glare. "It's too early!"

The old Indian woman said nothing. She padded across the room to fetch the basin of water and bring it to the stand beside the bed. Then she padded off again, into the adjoining chamber, to fetch the first installment of her lady-ship's clothing.

Tamar watched her duenna pass out through the door-way, her dark, hawklike features set in their usual expression of disapproval. Tamar tried to decide whether to be cross in her turn. Then she thought again: The carrack! She swung her legs out of bed in a flurry of white nightdress and darted across to the window.

There were no glass panes, only a wrought-iron grille between her and the warm June morning. She felt the dry breeze on her face as she looked out.

Immediately below her lay her father's walled garden, alive with many-colored flowers and fragrant, fruit-bearing trees. Beyond that was the green parkland, thick with grace-ful palms and tropical hardwoods, falling steeply away to-ward the red-tiled roofs of the city below. The girl's eye skipped quickly over the far-off dusty rooftops to the cathe-dral and the Plaza de Armas down by the water. Her gaze flicked on, across the low mass of the Fuerza—the old fort—and the newly built customs house beside the quay, out over the sparkling waters of the harbor.

The *Madre de Dios* was there, floating majestically a hun-dred yards or so off the quayside. They had warped her round from the dockyards during the night. Now she rode at anchor within easy reach of the main warehouses of Havana, taking on supplies and re-embarking her cargo. A steady stream of lighters and wherries plied between the quay and the ship, feeding her capacious holds.

Tamar stood rapt, gazing with awe and admiration at the

great ship which had swept, battered and leaking, into Havana harbor a month before. Careened, calked, refitted, she was now ready for sea once again. Within twenty-four hours she would take up her interrupted voyage home. But before she sailed—this very morning in fact—the Governor's daughter was to accompany her father and a handful of dignitaries aboard her. They were to be the lord admiral's guests, and even take lunch on board this giant of the seas. The girl's eyes sparkled with excitement. Such attractions were rare in this far provincial capital of New Spain.

"If my lady will wash," said the old duenna in her guttural Spanish, "she may perhaps be dressed in time for mass." Her tone indicated that she doubted it.

"Yes, Marina," said Tamar submissively, turning with a sigh away from the breeze and the blue sky. "But after church, will you come with us aboard the carrack?"

Marina's only answer was a disgusted grunt. In all her sixty years the Indian woman had never set foot upon one of the white-winged bird ships of the Spaniards. She was not likely to begin now.

Tamar plunged her face and hands into the basin. She came up gasping, reached for the towel her servant held out to her. "But truly, Marina, isn't it wonderful? The largest ship in the whole world, they say she is. And Admiral Mendoza is a famous old soldier, a great favorite of King Philip himself. It's quite the most exciting thing that's happened here since—since—" She gave up the hopeless search for a parallel and toweled her face vigorously.

Doña Tamar de la Barca was small and slender—too small, it almost seemed, for the high-ceilinged room, the thick hangings and heavy furniture. Slim-hipped, with small firm breasts, she was as lithe and active a young woman as she had been an active girl. But her black hair was more lustrous now, her small mouth softer and given to an occasional very attractive pout. Nor was she unaware of her own burgeoning beauty, as the cheerful self-satisfaction with which she settled down to let her servant dress her made clear.

Dressing was a tedious process for anyone so exalted as the daughter of the Governor of Cuba. It meant more than an hour of sitting or standing to her duenna's order, extending an arm or tilting her head on command, until she thought she would scream for boredom. Not many years ago, she might well have done so. Youthful energies beat high in her: she had been a hellish child to raise. But now she found the emergence of her own lovely self quite fascinating enough to carry her through the tedium. Even the extended tedium of dressing for Sunday church and a state visit afterward.

So the wiry old Indian woman bent and pinned and laced, and the girl was transformed step by step into the Governor's beautiful daughter, a credit to Don Gabriel and the cynosure of every young male eye in Havana.

She was certainly the most elegantly turned-out young woman in that sleepy little port city. Her petticoats and chemises were of the finest silk, her farthingale banded with the lightest and most flexible cane. The black satin gown she slipped on over these underpinnings was trimmed with silver thread. The thin wire upon which her hair was slowly and painfully dressed was silver too. The small velvet cap that crowned all gleamed with a fine patterning of pearls.

When it was done, she studied the result in her small hand glass with satisfaction. A simple provincial she might be, but surely no lady of the court could be more elegant! She wondered if Don Ricardo would notice the cap, her finest, worn for the first time in honor of the occasion. She was sure that Don Diego would not—and yet somehow, she realized, she actually liked him the better for that.

Being young and lovely and desired was very exciting for Tamar that summer, the first real summer of her young womanhood. And yet, as she slipped the silk handkerchief into her sleeve and accepted the scented gloves and the sunshade from Marina, she had to suppress a brief yearning for the freer garb of earlier, childish years. How much simpler life had been in those vanished days, when she had run bare-legged in a simple frock, free of farthingales and wire head-dresses and stiff black satin gowns.

Tamar's real name was not Tamar at all, but Doña Isabel Angela Serafina de la Barca y Sánchez. Tamar was a childish shortening of Tamerlane, the nickname given her at the barbarous age of eight by Señor Fuentes, her distracted Latin tutor. She could still remember that afternoon of storm and passion, and the balding, pale-faced pedagogue's lamentations over the wreckage of his little classroom. "Vandal! Scythian! Tartar!" he had raged, throwing up his hands at the ruin she had made. "She is a Genghis Khan, a Tamerlane! As God is my witness, a veritable Tamerlane!" Señor Fuentes had long since given up in despair and gone home to Spain. But the name he had given her, in her own abbreviated form, had stuck.

The name, and the reputation that went with it.

Doña Isabel—as her father's stiffer friends among the island aristocracy still called her—was certainly turning into a charming young woman. A worthy match for whatever Castilian grandee her father managed to marry her to. And yet—so some of the more censorious matrons murmured—there was still more than a touch of the little savage she had been behind those wicked black eyes of hers. And she was Tamar still to all their sons.

She had heard a shocking jest about herself—she was giggling over it yet—attributed to no less a notable than Don Geronimo Rojas, the portly head of the island's richest clan. "Our Tamar hasn't been tamed yet," Rojas had been heard to chuckle more than once. "Some young gentleman will take the wickedness out of her soon enough, I've no doubt." And then, with a gleam in his eye and a bobble of his multiple chins: "I hope it's the gentleman she marries!"

Tamar smiled at herself in the Venetian glass, wondering. Don Ricardo was Rojas's own nephew and would be a splendid match—if only her father got along better with the Rojases. Don Diego, on the other hand, would never do for a husband for the Governor of Cuba's daughter—even if he did have a body like a hunting cougar, and such strangely fascinating eyes!

Tamar de la Barca set down the glass and passed out of the room, on her way to another perfect day.

CHAPTER
2

THE SHIP WAS MONSTROUS.

Looking up at the *Madre de Dios* as the official party was rowed out to her, Tamar thought of what a whale must look like surrounded by shoals of lesser fish. For the great carrack was environed on every side by small boats. Lighters were still busy loading cargo. Boats full of citizens, gentlemen and ladies came out expressly to get a closer view. Tamar had seen a woodcut drawing of a whale, "that great Leviathan," in an old book somewhere, with swarms of lesser fry clustered about her. Surely, she thought now, the *Mother of God* was the Leviathan of the sea!

"She runs almost two hundred feet from bow to stern," the pompous mustachioed officer who had come to escort them aboard explained, "and forty feet across the beam. She displaces more than sixteen hundred tuns. She can carry more than a thousand people, passengers, crew and halberdiers."

"Remarkable!" said His Excellency Don Gabriel de la Barca heartily. "Amazing how the shipwright's craft has advanced, even in my time!" The Governor always spoke with energy and enthusiasm. There was a perpetual glow of perspiration on his pudgy cheeks, and he always smiled. "Don't you think it is remarkable, my dear?" he demanded of his daughter as the little ship's boat drew near.

The girl only nodded. She was counting the towering decks of the aftercastle, each more elaborately carved and painted than the one below. Four, five, six, seven—seven decks. And along four of them at least, rows of gunports stood open to reveal the ugly muzzles of cannon.

"What do you think, Don Diego?" the Governor demanded next of the hawk-faced young man beside him. "Isn't it the most amazing vessel you've ever seen?"

Don Diego Aguilar, the Commander of the Fuerza, nodded. He was a lean-waisted, wide-shouldered man in his thirties. His skin was unfashionably sunburned, but his steady, almost lashless eyes had a strange fascination for women. He habitually spoke very little. Today, however, he had a question. Not for the Governor, but for the self-important officer who had come for them in the longboat.

"Truly a monumental ship," said Don Diego. "But how does she handle in foul weather? Surely such a high-built craft must run some danger of capsizing in a storm?"

The ship's officer paled at the very thought. "Indeed," he replied, "there have been losses around the Cape. Due entirely to overloading in the East," he hastened to add. "But our admiral now, Don Fernando de Mendoza, he is a commander who *commands*—eh? When the fat villains at Goa tried to stack additional bales of silks on the deck itself—on the open deck itself, sir!—Don Fernando ordered them to get their goods over the side in one hour, or he'd have them pitched into the harbor! That's a commander for you. And a fine old soldier too," he added unctuously. "He fought at Lepanto—did you know that? And he's made the East India—Lisbon voyage three times before this. Three times, for all that seas and storms and corsairs can do!"

Seas and storms and corsairs, meditated His Excellency the Governor of Cuba. And the worst of these the corsairs, the pirates and privateers of all nations that swarmed across the waters of the world. God knew they were at least as thick here in New Spain as in the Indian Ocean. But so great a ship as this would be more than a match for any of them, he told himself. No Dutch, no French, no English freebooter would ever set foot upon the lofty decks of this monarch of the seas.

It was a comfort to him to think it, in these trying times.

They were nearly there now—Don Gabriel and Tamar de la Barca, Don Diego Aguilar and two or three other notables, with the ship's officer and half a dozen dark-skinned sailors leaning to the oars. Tamar craned her neck, gazing up at a forest of masts and spars that seemed to touch the sky. Then the shadow of the ship came over them, and the longboat scraped alongside.

"Sheathed in solid teak," said the officer proudly, resting a hand on the massive sea-wet planks. "Round shot would bounce off like peas!"

He steadied the boat at the foot of the ladder, and the official visitors debarked.

The climb up the ship's side was dizzying, frightening, and thoroughly delightful for Tamar. Step after step she clambered up, past row on row of black gun muzzles, with the bright green of the sea below and the railing high above. She knew her gown could not escape some soiling. Yet it was with a laugh of sheer exhilaration that she accepted Aguilar's hand at the rail and sprang onto the deck at last.

"Oh, Don Diego," she cried impulsively, "isn't it magnificent?"

She could scarcely have said what it was about the great carrack that set her heart to beating faster and made her breath come short. There was the sheer size of it, of course. There were the splendid rows of soldiers drawn up to welcome them in the ship's waist, halberds and arquebuses held rigidly vertical, breastplates and plumed morions gleaming. Above all, there was the massive power of this monster of the deep. A thousand men, a hundred heavy guns at least. Impregnable, unstoppable. No wonder Philip II, King of Spain and Portugal, trusted his richest Eastern treasures to her holds.

"My lady, may I present His Excellency Don Fernando. de Mendoza, Count of Olmedo, Knight of the Golden Fleece, Lord Admiral of the Malabar carracks—commander of this vessel!"

Tamar curtseyed properly to the tall old man who now bent over her hand. He had pale cheeks and the eyes of an eagle under his tufted brows. His hair was white, his moustache and goatee impeccably trimmed. His back was straight as a lance, and his hand was as strong as it had been when he was twenty.

Tamar quailed deliciously under his eye. And her admiration for her own father went up at once when he stepped forward to embrace this epitome of proud Castilian honor. For the portly provincial Governor and the lean old Admiral had known each other when they were both boys in Cádiz, half a century before.

Don Diego Aguilar was presented next. The broad-shouldered Commander of the Fuerza was half the Admiral's age and half a head shorter. His sun-darkened face and flat features had none of the pale Castilian fineness of the old warrior's. Yet there was something similar in their bearing, Tamar decided, watching them exchange stiff military bows. There was a fierceness about both of them, a restless dissatisfaction with peaceable times and quiet places that set the two of them off from every other man on the great ship's deck.

Tamar felt immensely proud to know them both.

But the Admiral would dine at the Governor's house that very night. And she would see Don Diego that very afternoon—if her father did not find out about it. And meanwhile, there was the ship! The Governor's daughter clasped her hands and spun around on her toes just as the last of the visiting dignitaries set foot upon the deck. Don Geronimo Rojas, vastly fat, puffing and mopping his brow, came first. He was followed by his grey-bearded brother, who was also the royal treasurer for the island colony of Cuba. Last of all came Don Geronimo's elegant young nephew, Don Ricardo de Olid.

"Oh, Don Ricardo!" the girl exclaimed. "Have you ever seen such a sight?" She spread her arms, encompassing the vessel entire, from looming forecastle to multitiered poop deck, from the crow's nest to the keel.

Don Ricardo smiled, showing perfect teeth beneath his crisp moustaches. He was a visitor on the island, come over that spring from Spain, and considerably more sophisticated than his provincial kin. He "talked court" like a Frenchman, wore a doublet of the latest Italian cut, wore boots of what he swore was English leather. And he had seen an East Indiaman before.

"She is a magnificent ship, my lady," he murmured. "Magnificently manned, magnificently commanded." He made a particularly elegant leg to Don Fernando de Mendoza. Only the cold perfection of the Admiral's answering salute revealed the old warrior's contempt for the courtier. Tamar did not notice it all.

Instead, she put her hand lightly on Don Ricardo's arm and led him slowly aft, exclaiming at every new wonder. "And look! Twice the size of those on any galleon of the Plate Fleet . . ."

They toured the officers' quarters aft, sumptuously furnished and decorated as was fitting aboard this queen of the Spanish seas. They climbed to the highest point of the poop deck and gazed down upon the harbor and the Plaza de Armas as from a precipitous mountain crag. They even descended into the cavelike holds to examine the newly restored cargos which the great carrack had brought halfway around the world. There were bolts and bales of silk from China and colorful cottons from India. There was cinnamon from Ceylon, nutmeg from the Celebes, ginger from Malabar and cloves from the far-off Moluccas. In the Admiral's own cabin, they had already been shown the vessel's most valuable cargo—small brassbound chests heaped with Indian emeralds, sapphires from Ceylon, rubies from Tibet.

Above all, Tamar heard once more the story of the voyage that had brought the *Madre de Dios* into this quiet haven, so far from the sea-lanes of the Atlantic.

The *Mother of God* was one of the half-dozen huge carracks to attempt the perilous journey from India to Portugal —the King of Spain's Portuguese provinces, as they were now —every year. She had sailed from Goa in December of the previous year. In company with four others, she had made her slow way across the Indian Ocean, around the southern tip of Africa, and up across the South Atlantic toward her rendezvous with convoying warships in the Azores. From there, with a fleet of galleons to protect them from pirates and privateers, Admiral Mendoza's five carracks should have sailed due east to Lisbon and the end of their twelve-thousand-mile voyage.

The other four had quite likely done precisely that. But not the flagship of the fleet. For a tremendous storm had struck the ponderous vessels almost within sight of the Azores, scattering them like chips across the sea. The *Madre de Dios* had been swept violently westward by screaming winds and seas higher than her own castles. For three days and nights the ship had driven before the gale, sails and even spars torn away, beams strained, planking twisting and splintering.

When the storm had abated at last, the proud carrack was a leaking, wallowing hulk, floating somewhere off the northeast coast of Brazil. Don Fernando had realized at once that they could not even make the Azores without repair, let alone Lisbon. He had thought first of putting into Bahía, but had decided to let the prevailing winds carry them on into the calm waters of the Caribbean, where the galleons that guarded the Plate Fleets might offer protection. And so it was that the great ship which had sailed halfway round the world came limping at last into Havana harbor on a smiling afternoon in May, six months out of Goa.

"And how did the men respond to the great storm, my lord admiral?" Tamar demanded, eager to savor this epic of Spanish heroism.

"The Lascars and the slaves wept and wailed," replied Don Fernando. "The Spanish and the Portuguese consigned their souls to God and did their duty. And I"—the ghost of a smile touched his lips—"I was most abominably sick the whole time."

Governor de la Barca laughed deprecatingly, and Tamar gave the Admiral her most radiant smile. She stood between

Don Diego and Don Ricardo with a hand on each young man's arm.

"And now," said the officious ensign who had brought them out from shore, "if you would care to partake of some refreshment in my lord admiral's cabin?"

The soldiers drawn up in the waist stood rigidly at attention, sweating in their helmets and steel corselets, until the door had closed behind the official visitors. Then, at a brusque signal from their officer, they broke ranks and sought what shade and refreshment there was until they should be needed for the farewell ceremonies. Meantime, a Portuguese lieutenant stepped to the rail and waved to the swarms of lightermen resting patiently on their oars in the broiling sun. Other working officers appeared, and a flood of half-naked East Indians poured across the deck. Wooden cranes were swung round, hatches uncovered. In minutes, the serious business of loading salt pork and dried fish, cassava bread, oil and water and wine, was under way once more.

3

THE TWO LATHERED MOUNTS LABORED NECK TO NECK UP THE slope in the glare of the afternoon sun. Tamar's bay and Aguilar's black mare were evenly matched, given the disparity in the weight of the two riders. They climbed toward the summit together, horses and riders alike eager for the touch of breeze that awaited them there.

The dry touch of the trade wind brushed their cheeks as they rode out on the rounded hilltop at last.

"I was so sure the wind would change today," the girl said, sighing, and she looked up at a hot blue sky without a cloud. "The ground is so parched, and the animals. The rains must come soon."

Aguilar nodded but said nothing. He was silent that day, as usual. His eyes were gazing out to sea beyond the distant harbor. Tamar glanced over at him and decided that taciturnity was one of his charms, along with his strange eyes. A soldier should be taciturn, she thought. Babblers are no good doers.

"It may yet change before the day is out," she added more brightly. "The wind. And then the rains will come."

Aguilar nodded, silent still.

They made a handsome couple, sitting their horses easily there on the hilltop. The girl, riding sidesaddle, wore a lighter gown than she had that morning. She had dispensed with the farthingale, but she still wore quite enough petticoats for decency's sake, and her hair was still piled high upon her head. The lace at collar and wrist was wilting under the Cuban sun, and her cheeks were flushed. For this daring afternoon's escape, she had left her sunshade at home.

The man beside her wore a brick-red doublet and hose and high leather boots. A long cup-hilted rapier hung at his side. The simple clothing went well with his ruddy complexion and broad-shouldered military bearing. His eyes surveyed the valley before them as if they were sweeping a battlefield.

It was a peaceful scene enough. It was a region of rolling hills and gentle valleys west of Havana, dotted with browsing herds of cattle, scored here and there with lines and clusters of royal palms. In a dell off to their left, they glimpsed the tree-lined avenue and white buildings of one of the Rojas *estancias*, with its croplands and cluster of palm-thatched Indian *bohíos*. At the far end of the valley, back along the way they had come, the pale-blue line of the sea still showed between two hills.

Don Diego Aguilar's eyes flicked restlessly back that way, toward that glimmer of sea. He had seen something there from the last hilltop, and it rankled still in the back of his mind. There had been a sail just beyond the point, just round from the Morro Castle. A pinnace, no more. But the more he thought about it, the surer he became that it had been a sail of no Spanish cut.

"I'll race you to the ceiba tree!" the girl cried suddenly. Without waiting for a response, she touched her horse's flank with her crop and was off down the hill with a shout of glee. In an instant, Aguilar was after her.

Emaciated range cattle moved left and right to make way for them as the two riders came pounding past. The rocky stream at the bottom of the hill exploded in twin geysers as the two horses clattered and splashed across. Then they were driving up the opposite slope. Aguilar's black and Tamar's bay were neck to neck as they plunged into the shadow of the ceiba tree just under the hill's dry crest. They jolted to a laughing halt side by side, less than a lance length from its wide, gnarled trunk.

Aguilar swung down and held up his arms for her.

But Tamar only rested one small gloved hand on his as she sprang lightly to the ground. She had not needed a man to help her dismount a horse since she was six years old.

Sinking down upon the grass, she settled her back against

the tree and looked back down the hillside at the trickling stream and the nervous cows, now munching on the thin grass once more. "Rojas cattle, I suppose," she said, catching her breath. "They are so scrawny."

"The hides are all that matter," said Aguilar shortly. "There will be no market for the beef if the Plate Fleet is not to sail this year." The treasure fleets from Nombre de Dios and Vera Cruz, which rendezvoused and took on supplies at Havana, were the island's best customers.

"It is the corsairs," said the Governor's daughter, shrugging her shoulders. "The French and English especially. My father says they swarm like bees between here and home. His Majesty is surely wise to forbid the sailing of the fleets."

"I wish the corsairs would come here." Don Diego grunted. "I wish they would swarm here, these angry English bees."

"God prevent it!" said Tamar piously. "Besides, they did come once, Don Diego. Ten or twelve years ago, was it not? Drake himself, right off Havana harbor! That should be corsair enough for you!"

Tamar had seen them herself, from an upstairs window of her father's old house on the Plaza de Armas: thirty sail strung out along the horizon, converging on the harbor mouth. They had hovered there for five days, while the town worked frantically to put itself into a posture of defense. Then they had moved off eastward, without once setting foot upon the island. All the church bells in Havana had pealed for hours in thanksgiving.

Tamar had never heard an English voice or seen an English face. But she had seen the English ships—the ships that had already taken Santo Domingo that summer, had ravaged Cartagena and laid St. Augustine waste. She had had the English horrors all through her eighth year, to Marina's gruff dismay and the more voluble consternation of her father. The shudder that coursed through her now, as she sat there in the shade, was real enough.

"Drake!" said Aguilar, the edge in his voice harder still. "They say he is dead. Too bad. I should have liked to have had the honor of dispatching him myself." As he spoke, he turned his eyes upon the girl at his side, to see how she took this fantastic brag.

She looked back at him, and she did not laugh. With anyone else, the laughter that hovered so close to the surface of her life would have come bubbling out. But there was something about Don Diego Aguilar, about the look on his face that moment, that stopped the laughter in her throat.

Instead, she looked away and plucked a ball of the silky, cottonlike substance that filtered down from the ceiba tree. Kneading the false cotton between her fingers, still not looking at him, she said only, "You are a strange man, Don Diego."

A strange man indeed, she thought, if even half the rumors one heard about him were true.

Don Diego Aguilar was known to possess large landholdings and several *encomiendas* of Indians in the Oriente, the mountainous, jungle-ridden eastern end of the island. His grandfather had gotten these lands from Cortez himself, on his return from Mexico, and the family had lived in seclusion there for three generations. Precisely in what way they differed from the other early settlers in Cuba, no one could exactly say. Only that the Aguilars came seldom to Havana, and always returned quickly to the mountains and rain forests of the Oriente.

Then, five years ago, Don Diego had appeared in the city, apparently for good.

He had been rough, uncouth, given to violent explosions of temper. Gradually, he had acquired a veneer of manners and some modicum of acceptance in the provincial society of Havana. Even more slowly, some portion of his story had come out.

He had buried his father that year, it seemed. He had forthwith abandoned the wild ancestral holdings to the Indians and the jungle and had set out, like the first comers seventy or eighty years before, to make his own way in the world. Just what his way was soon became all too vividly apparent.

He had done some hide-hunting on the central plains and in the lush valleys around Havana before he came into the city. He had taken skins in plenty from the wild cattle that were to be found everywhere in the island, and had made a handsome profit from them. With his new veneer of gentility and his acquaintance in the capital, however, he proceeded to change his occupation. He became a hunter of men.

He had hunted runaway slaves first. Then it was rebellious Indians and marauding cimaroons in the jungle fastness which still covered much of the island. After that, he had taken to harrying smugglers along the coasts, especially in the south, around Bayamo. This was less popular, since some of the oldest families in Cuba indulged in a little illegal trade with foreign vessels from time to time. But it was a stepping-stone to what became Don Diego Aguilar's real business in life: the hunting of the corsairs and privateers who cruised the islands in search of unwary prizes. Aguilar had finally won the Governor's consent to organize his own company of coast guards and to build three light, fast pinnaces to patrol the waters around the island.

In all of these ventures, he had been notably successful. So successful that, when the Commander of the Fuerza, the old fort on the Plaza de Armas, had stumbled drunk out of a whore's house along the Xanja Canal, fallen into the ditch, and drowned, Don Diego had had to expend surprisingly little money to win the vacated appointment for himself.

And yet, for all his energy and success, he remained somehow distinctly less than respectable in the eyes of the old families of Havana. Certainly not proper company, Tamar knew, for the Governor's daughter on a Sunday afternoon.

There were too many horrifying rumors about the bloody thoroughness with which he did his work. Stories of brandings and hangings and pirate vessels scuttled with their crews still in them. Exaggerated tales, efforts of his enemies to discredit him, Tamar was sure. He had always been so gentle, so respectful around her.

But one did not have to accept horror stories to consign Don Diego Aguilar to the farthest fringes of respectable society.

Most obviously, he was only marginally a gentleman. He was a caballero only as every man of Spanish blood in the colony was—well above the *mestizos*, the Indians, and the blacks, but several cuts below Spaniards of genuine peninsular Spanish birth, such as Governor de la Barca and his daughter. He was not wealthy, and he had not inherited what wealth he had. His way of life was said to be dissolute, unchanged since his days as a hide-hunter and tracker of runaway slaves. He was invited to official functions when his modest military post warranted it, but he had never dined in any of the fine two-story homes around the Plaza de Armas. And he never would.

Tamar wondered what her father would say when he found out that she had ignored his prohibition once again and gone riding—*alone*—with this terrible man.

"My father will be very angry, you know," she said aloud, "if he learns that I have come so far with you. Especially without a single servant to protect my honor from slanderous tongues."

"If anyone speaks a word against you—"

"What, my noble knight?" The dark-haired girl beside him laughed. "Would you fight for my good name?" She touched his arm lightly, calmingly she hoped. "It would do no good at all, you know."

"What do you mean?"

"I am sure I have no good name left," she answered candidly, "on this silly little island."

"I have never heard a breath—" he began once more. And once again she cut him off with a bantering laugh.

"It is no question of my virtue, sir," she said tartly. "It is—oh, so many things. It is running through the streets like

a ragamuffin when I was a girl. It is laughing too much and
dancing too much and saying what I please. It is—riding out
of a Sunday afternoon with a man alone! It is being *myself*
that makes the Bishop writhe and the Alcalde look uncom-
fortable and the entire Rojas clan sniff in unison!"

She paused for breath.

Aguilar shrugged. But he raised his eyes rather thoughtfully to the green valley spread out before them, to the Rojas
cattle and the Rojas cane, the hacienda and the native shacks.

"My father," Tamar concluded cheerfully, "thinks I am
growing up to be a perfect savage." She glanced at him.
"Like you," she said.

She gave a little gasp then, and shrank involuntarily away.
For her bold sally, intended to draw him into exciting tales
of hunting smugglers in the jungles and pirates on the sea,
brought a more violent reaction than she would have
dreamed. Don Diego rounded upon her with a quick, catlike
motion, his jaw tensing, his face taut with anger. For one
unbelievable moment she thought he might actually be
about to strike her!

Then it was gone. His eyes hooded their inner fires once
again. He rose abruptly to his feet, glanced at the westering
sun, and strode off without a word to fetch their horses,
grazing a few yards away down the sunny slope.

She watched him walk away with the oddest tingling in
her belly. It was a feeling halfway between terror and desire,
partaking deliciously of both. It was, though she scarcely
realized it, an echo of her dream of the night before, of the
passion generated by her imaginings of what it would be like
to feel a man's arms around her, a man's mouth on hers. And
it remained tremblingly alive in her all through the silent
ride back to town.

Don Diego might be a terrible man, the girl thought as
they trotted up a rutty lane toward the city, even a bit of
a savage. But at least he was not dull!

THE CANTINA ON THE XANJA CANAL WAS QUIET THAT NIGHT. Four darkly bearded hide-hunters diced for drinks at the far end of the room. A pair of prostitutes in turbans and dirty petticoats—one black, one Indian—lounged in the doorway, exchanging gibes with passing soldiers. Three Lascars and a Portuguese from the carrack sprawled against a flaking adobe wall, drunk on the black wine of the island. The hot night air was thick with the stench of tobacco and cooking oil, the reek of the canal outside.

The hide-hunters were listlessly rolling their dice at one end of the cantina's single long table. At the other end, Don Diego Aguilar sat drinking with Ensign Barba. Barba, a squat, ugly Basque, had been Aguilar's lieutenant since his first man-hunting expeditions years before.

They had been talking about the sail Aguilar had glimpsed east of the Morro during his ride in the hills with Doña Tamar that afternoon.

A pinnace presented no threat to the fortified city of Havana, of course. It might easily have been a foreign smuggler, sailing in under the guns of the outer harbor to arrange a rendezvous with the greedy great ones of the capital. God knew such illicit trade was common enough. But it rankled with Don Diego nonetheless. In the old days, when he had scoured the jungles and patrolled the coasts with his *guarda-costas*, he would have been after them in a minute.

"Those were good days, my captain," the jowly Basque across from him was saying. "You didn't have to deal with those fine hypocrites on the Plaza de Armas then. Or that soft capon of a Governor and his proud daughter." Barba's voice was blurred with wine.

"You will not talk about Tamar—about Doña Ísabel de la

Barca," said Don Diego flatly. "You will not refer to her again."

Barba shrugged his shoulders. "Still," he said, "it was better before you became Captain of the Fuerza."

"The Fuerza." Aguilar spat on the hard-packed earthen floor of the cantina. "That was all they would give me. I asked for the Morro, the fine new castle on the rock. But that will be saved for some great captain from Europe. Some Spanish hidalgo with a letter from the King." He angled back his head, tilted the leather wine bottle over his open mouth.

"It is not fair, Captain," said Barba. "You are the best soldier in Cuba."

The best soldier in the Indies, thought Don Diego Aguilar. *But my manners are not elegant enough, my family—* He cut off that line of thought at once. Even drunk, he would not follow his brooding thoughts that way.

"But I will have it, Barba," he said aloud. "I will have the Morro—and the Governor's daughter too. Yes, and that soon. Soon."

Barba grunted approbation as he tilted the wine bottle in his turn.

"This Governor will not be governor forever." Aguilar leaned on the table, his face close to his lieutenant's. "This is the last year of his appointment, Barba. And he has enemies, this famous Governor of ours. Enemies—and I am the friend of those enemies. Now do you begin to understand?"

The Basque nodded heavily.

"It will not be long before this Governor is gone. And not as he thinks, not returned in triumph to Spain, but pulled down in disgrace. Brought down by men who will be much beholden to me, Barba, for my help in the destruction of the tyrant!"

"It is your duty," his ensign agreed thickly, "to help bring down the tyrant."

"I shall do my duty. And I shall have my reward."

The command of the Morro, the ear of the new Governor, and the old Governor's beautiful daughter too! Aguilar's eyes gleamed at the splendor of his vision. Then he would dine nightly in the great houses on the plaza. Then he would have such a great house of his own, and have Guzmans and Ynestrosas and Rojases in to dine with them.

All but one Rojas, of course—the one who would no longer live on the plaza, but in the governor's house on the hill.

Above all, he would have Tamar de la Barca for his own. Her wide dark eyes would lower before his at last, her lips would murmur his name submissively. She would come to him in his fine bed, all hung with velvet, and open her embraces to him, to her *lord husband*—

Even as he thought it, even as he visualized it all with an intensity that made his throat ache, he knew it would never happen.

The Morro, yes—he might have that for his help with Don Geronimo Rojas's intrigue. But he would never dine with the families of the first comers. Never own a house beside theirs on the Plaza de Armas. Never in this world have the Governor's daughter of Cuba to be his wife. Some things might be granted him, but never the society of his betters. And never, never the woman of even a defeated member of that island aristocracy.

He tipped the leather bottle and let the thin stream arc into his mouth till his ears sang and he could swallow no more.

Hunter of wild pigs and cattle, he thought. Hunter of red men and black men, smugglers, pirates. Hide-hunter, man-hunter.

What was it she had called him?

Savage.

My father thinks I am becoming a perfect savage. Her face turned toward him, there beneath the ceiba tree. *Like you.* And then the shocked look on her face as she saw the naked murder in his eyes.

Mota, he thought abruptly. Perhaps she had heard about Captain Mota?

"But they were brave times we had then, my captain," Barba was maundering on. "You and I and Robles. And Madrecito." The ensign was drunk and getting maudlin now. It was tiresome when he got that way. Aguilar felt the choleric humor stir within him.

"Madrecito," said Barba slowly. "Poor Madrecito."

Mota had killed him. Madrecito and half a dozen others had been cut down when the French corsair and his crew burned Santiago. They had burned churches, houses, everything, till nothing but smoldering rubbish was left where the town of Santiago had been. And they had killed all of Aguilar's coast guards they had found among the defenders of the town.

But Captain Ricarte, Captain Mota as everyone called him, was a smuggler as well as a pirate. He gave good prices for hides and red meat on the other side of the island. In Bayamo, in the south, Mota was a popular man, drinking and wenching in all the wineshops, doing business like an honest merchant in the houses of the rich. They said he bought the Bishop's hides, and the Alcalde's too. A heretic and a corsair—and there was scarce a man in Bayamo that would not pay for his wine, or a girl that would not spread her legs for him and his Huguenot crew.

Aguilar had hanged him in Bayamo.

Left him dangling in the plaza at dawn, with the ten of his crew that had survived Don Diego's jungle ambuscade. Left him hanging for the people to see when the sun poked through the mountains and the old women opened the shutters and threw out the slops.

No tribunal, no documents, no judges for Captain Mota. Just the rope. They said it was savage, the good people of Bayamo.

"Do you remember Madrecito?" Barba would be tearful soon. "There was a soldier, my captain! There was a man!"

They said it was the ears especially. Eleven men hanging in a row, all with the left ear carefully sliced away. That was what made the deed so barbarous.

Aguilar tilted the limp leather bladder one last time above his mouth. Had they never seen a man's ear cropped before —or an Indian's anyway? Never seen a nose slit, a hand cut off? Such punishments were prescribed in the very lawbooks of Castile, so he had been told. Why then was he the savage? Because he took his ears without benefit of a magistrate?

It was not the martyrdom of the pirate Mota that outraged the people of Bayamo, thought Aguilar. It was the good prices he had given for meat and hides.

But *she*—she thought he was a savage too. No better than an Indian, a drunken cimaroon. *A savage like you.*

"An Indian, I tell you," said a voice. "Not a tame Indian either. A real animal—a savage!"

It was one of the leather-clad hide-hunters at the other end of the table. A big man, black as coal, with white eyes and a red mouth, grinning. The grin vanished in a roar of rage when Aguilar sent the long table crashing over, spilling Barba and half the hiders with it, going around the end with his dagger out, hungry for the big man's blood.

"Gaffed him like a shark, he did!" chortled Barba later, whispering to his mates in the dripping darkness of the Fuerza barracks. "Picked him right up on the dagger blade and threw him half across the room. The big black freedman they call Huevos it was, the hide-hunter, a mad devil when he's in his wine cups. But he went out that door tonight bent over like an old father, holding himself together with both his hands."

"A rare sight," rumbled another voice in the darkness, Basque like Barba's. "And what did Huevos do to rouse the captain to a cutting humor?"

Barba took a final pull at his wineskin, passed it groggily to the nearest hand in the darkness. "Called him *Indio*," he grunted, wiping whiskers. "You know how the captain hates that name."

"*El Indio*," said someone. "But everyone calls him that. All the companions that were with him in the old days."

"But nobody to his face." Barba grunted. "I would not call him that to his face myself, and I have been with him longer than anyone."

"Nobody but that mad devil Huevos would do it."

"And not Huevos anymore. I'll be bound for that. Not Huevos anymore."

THE GOVERNOR BADE HIS GUESTS GOODNIGHT IN THE RECENTLY completed hall of weapons of his fine new house on the hill. There was much bowing and curtseying as the grey-haired gentlemen and ladies in black velvets and satins took their ceremonious departure.

"With God, gentlemen!" Don Gabriel urged effusively, spreading his arms like a magnifico. "All go with God!" Behind his sweating cheeks and nervous moustaches, he was genuinely quite pleased with the success of the occasion.

The room itself was the perfect setting. The carved marble fireplace, the Moorish carpets, the gleaming mahogany furniture provided a fitting background for the ceremonies of leave-taking. The vast display of weaponry bracketed up the walls—spears, halberds, swords and daggers, muskets and arquebuses—added a martial air of authority. An excellent place for official functions, Don Gabriel decided. He would use it for all such henceforth. It would lend a dignity to the office of Governor of Cuba which sometimes seemed unhappily lacking.

"A fine piece of workmanship, Don Gabriel!" wheezed Don Geronimo Rojas, hefting a silver bowl standing on a table by the door.

"Indeed, indeed," Don Gabriel responded airily. "Italian work, I think. Alas," he added, with an appealing glance at Lord Admiral Mendoza, "so long away from home, one forgets such things!"

"Of course." Rojas's eyes twinkled in his round, puffy face. "It is so long since you came to us, Don Gabriel, that we almost forget that Spain's loss has been our gain." He managed a rather graceful bow for so corpulent a man, and passed out through the high carved doors.

He was the last of them. His elegant nephew Don Ricardo

de Olid awaited him in the courtyard, poised to follow him into the only other carriage on the island besides the Governor's. The rest of his Excellency's guests were already mounting horses or settling into sedan chairs in the glow of the huge olive-oil lamps at Don Gabriel's gate.

Liveried footmen closed the double doors. The Governor, his face still creased in a formal smile, turned back to his guest of honor.

"The finest families on the island, Don Fernando. Not one of them—save only Don Geronimo's fop of a nephew—has ever seen Madrid."

"You have a fine house, Don Gabriel," the Admiral replied judiciously. "I congratulate you."

"It has been almost twenty years abuilding," said the Governor. "And in less than a year, I shall be leaving it to my successor. To whomever his gracious Majesty shall see fit to appoint in my place."

"And a lovely daughter," said his guest, declining the subject of Don Gabriel's successor with the firmness of an experienced courtier. "She will grace the palaces of Castile as she has the great houses of New Spain."

"Not for long," replied the Governor. The formal smile was gone now, and he looked rather tired. "I may tell you in confidence that I have Doña Isabel's marriage all but arranged. To an ancient Cádiz house, well connected in Madrid. Her portion, once the alliance is final, will be munificent."

"Again, Don Gabriel, my congratulations."

The Governor looked at the lean, granite-faced old man standing beside the fireplace. "My friend," he said, "will you come with me to my chamber? I have some excellent Malaga, a dozen years aged in the caves of this Godforsaken island."

The lord admiral bowed without a word, and followed his host.

"Who would have thought, Don Fernando, when we wrestled like beggar's brats in the streets of Cádiz, that we would come to this!" The two men sat in low-backed chairs in front of the fireplace in the Governor's private chamber. Some of his Excellency's ebullience seemed to have returned with the wine, which stood between them on a low round table.

The Admiral nodded, his pale cheeks relaxing as he remembered. "Your father's bailiff had me caned outside your front gate!"

The Governor filled their goblets. "Much has happened in our lifetimes." He slid one of the crystal cups toward his guest. "Our flags bear all before them in Christendom, so we hear. Is it true that the heretics are all but beaten in the Low Countries? And they say the Huguenot King of France converted to the true faith! Glorious deeds, Don Fernando! And you—you have been part of it all!" Don Gabriel raised his goblet in a salute. "While I have rusticated here at the ends of the earth for twenty years." He sighed. "It is a strange life, my friend."

"Glorious deeds in the chronicles, perhaps," said the lord admiral, savoring his wine. "Not so glorious in the living of them."

"Don Fernando! Hero of Lepanto, Admiral of the Indian Seas! Not glorious? Come, come, sir!"

"Aye, I was at Lepanto, where we broke the sea power of the Turks forever—so the chroniclers will say." The eyes of a hunting bird hardened under the white brows. "And I sailed with his Majesty's Invincible Armada to break the English heretics in their little island too. There," he added dryly, "Fortune did not look so favorably upon our banners."

The Governor spread his pudgy hands. "The will of God," he said. "But you," he said, brightening, "you have only grown richer in honors and renown. Count of Olmedo, Knight of the Golden Fleece—"

"Indeed. For I spent the years between battles in the Escorial, where King Philip dispenses the titles and the honors." He put down the wine, as though it had turned sour under his tongue. "Honor and renown are won at the court of Madrid, Don Gabriel, not in the Turkish seas or the English Channel."

"I know that well enough," grunted the host, abruptly putting his goblet too down upon the table. He rose and paced the shadowy chamber, his hands clasped behind his back. His brow was damp once more with worry, his plump lips pursed.

"Did you see Rojas fingering that silver bowl tonight?" he asked almost plaintively. "And did you hear the news? That his nephew Don Ricardo is to return to Spain—to the Escorial—as soon as may be arranged?"

"He has asked for passage on my own vessel," said the Admiral. "I have told him that if he can be aboard before the tide turns tomorrow morning—and if he wants to risk the perils of the Atlantic seaways without an escorting fleet—"

"He will run the risks, my friend. His uncle will see to that. He carries with him all the evidence, as they call it. All the complaints of the malcontents, all the bribed testimony the Rojas faction needs to demand an official inquisition into my trusteeship of this island!"

The Governor paced back into the light of the single candle. He really looked rather ludicrous, Don Fernando thought, with his bulging velvet doublet and fat legs. Ludicrous and pitiful, his old friend. But the lord admiral would do what he could to help.

"This popinjay Olid will talk to his friends," said Don Gabriel, "and his friends will talk to the King. And the King will debate and deliberate as he always does. He will consider and reconsider. But by this time next year, he will have dispatched an order to the Audencia at Santo Domingo to conduct a secret investigation of possible malfeasance in my conduct of this office. And every judge of that commission will be of the kindred and connection of Don Geronimo Rojas!"

"His Majesty," said Don Fernando, "would require some proof of such malfeasance. After so many years of good service—"

"I have done nothing that every governor in these islands has not done! I have not hanged every smuggler in Cuba—because every notable on the island smuggles. I have appointed some to official positions at higher salaries than they deserved—and half of them, I assure you, on the urgent recommendation of the good Don Geronimo." He paced off once more, shaking his head at the ingratitude of men. "I have supplemented my own meager emoluments by purchasing half-shares in an occasional merchant ship trading among the colonies. It is in violation of a royal edict. What would you? A man must live in a style befitting the dignity of his office. And I have no vast haciendas, no trading houses to draw upon, as these grandsons of the first comers do, that stripped the island clean."

All true, thought the Admiral sadly, remembering the papers Rojas and Olid had showed him in strictest confidence that very afternoon. Nor have you failed to take your share of those exorbitant salaries, or to fill your own cellars with the foreign luxuries of the smugglers. Including, unless my palate fails me utterly, this fine red wine, which tastes rather of the south of France than of the south of Spain.

"That is why I have asked you to do this thing for me, Don Fernando."

And that is why I shall do it for you, thought the Admiral. For you are right in the end, of course. A man must live in a style befitting the place that God has given him in this world.

"It will be a bold stroke," the Governor hurried nervously on. "I am not a soldier like you, Don Fernando. But I know how to strike a bold stroke for God and my King. His Majesty will appreciate such daring, even if it does cut close to the letter of a temporary edict."

Don Fernando de Mendoza thought of King Philip the Prudent hunched over his endless piles of dispatches, reports, official documents and royal *cédulas* in his monkish cell in the Escorial—and had his doubts. But he looked into his old friend's eyes, and once more he said nothing.

"How could his Majesty," Don Gabriel was demanding now, "pay any attention to the enemies of a man who has replenished the royal coffers with the gold of the Indies so cunningly as I propose to do?" He spread his-short arms in his habitual gesture of confidence. But the desperate look was still in his eyes.

"How indeed," said the Admiral without expression. He was a soldier, he reminded himself, not a politician. He would do his friend a service, as honor bound him to. God would decide the outcome.

It was a daring scheme, certainly. Far too daring for the timid Governor of Cuba to have conceived under any less perilous circumstances.

The gold of the Indies was actually mostly silver. It was dug from the mines of Mexico and Peru by slave labor and shipped home each year in heavily guarded treasure convoys.

The King of Spain depended on the American treasure fleet, the *flota*, even more than he did on the silks and spices of the East to maintain his awesome predominance in Christendom. The deferral of even a single year's shipments could mean armies unpaid, allies unsubsidized, massive reverses anywhere on the chessboard of European power politics.

But there was an even worse possibility than the postponement of the annual shipment of American treasure. That was the loss of it altogether to the hordes of freebooters that made the Atlantic their hunting ground. More than once, when reports from his ambassadors in the capitals of Europe had indicated an excessive number of such expeditions fitting out for sea, King Philip had prudently sent word that the *flota* should not sail. So it was in that year of God's grace 1597.

For another twelvemonth, then, the harvest of the mines was to be stored in the best-defended Spanish stronghold in the West Indies—in the new customs house in Havana, under the protecting guns of the Fuerza and the Morro Castle.

The treasure lay there at that moment. Solid ingots of pure silver, bars and chains of gold. Dark aboriginal hands had dug it from the earth under the vigilant supervision of men in morions and breastplates. Heavily guarded mule trains had transported it by jungle track across the Isthmus of Panama to seaports on the Caribbean. Sleek new treasure ships had carried it to the rendezvous point in Cuba, unloading it at the quayside in Havana. It lay in the storage vaults beneath the customs house now, waiting for the treasure fleets that would not gather that year, the *flota* that would not sail.

Before the sun rose the next morning, the treasure of the West Indies would have joined the wealth of the East in the holds of the *Madre de Dios*.

"It is so simple, my friend," Don Gabriel expostulated with growing enthusiasm. "And yet so sensible, so logical. Perhaps I should have been a man of the sword myself, eh, instead of a magistrate."

He warmed to his theme, moving back and forth with his short-legged stride, rubbing his hands together.

"The pirates will never think that a single vessel might carry so much. The large privateering expeditions will be looking for the treasure fleet, for a whole convoy. You will slip through like a wraith. And if you should encounter a freebooter or two, so great a ship as yours will shake them off with no difficulty. Like a bear shaking off a dog, eh? Truly, I should almost like to be there to see it."

Simple indeed, and ingenious in its way, thought Don Fernando. The royal *cédula* had commanded that no ship of the West Indian fleet should sail with treasure from America. It had made no mention of an East Indian carrack. The lord admiral let a sigh pass between his lips. Simple and ingenious—but a game. A game played with words and logic. King Philip would have more than one question to ask about a governor that played games with the wording of a royal edict.

Or would he? With a year's revenues from New Spain locked away in the House of Trade at Seville, King Philip might be lenient after all.

Ever since the personal union of Spain and Portugal some two decades before, the once rival empires of the East and West Indies had been ruled in tandem from Madrid. This caused some confusion for King Philip's imperial viceroys. By and large, the rule was simple: the two colonial domains were to be administered separately, in complete isolation one from the other. Normally, this was easily enough accomplished, since the two overseas empires lay on opposite sides of the globe. But there were exceptions to every rule.

A Portuguese East Indiaman had put in at a Mexican port on the Pacific only a few years before, and had been reluctantly received by the Spanish Alcalde. All concerned had been reprimanded in the King's own hand.

Now it had happened again. But the Governor of Cuba was clearly willing to risk more than a reprimand to save himself from ruin at the hands of his enemies. And with luck, with a bit of good fortune—

Enough! thought the lord admiral. He would sail the ship. He would fight the pirates. He would deliver his two precious cargoes, one to Lisbon and one to Seville. What happened after that was in the hands of God.

Don Fernando de Mendoza settled back to sip red wine and drink in the mingled scents of tropic flowers drifting through the window. He remembered the fragrance of his own orchards in Asturias. Perhaps after this voyage he would petition his Majesty for permission to leave the royal service and retire to his estates at last.

At sixty-five, surely he had earned the peace of his own orange trees.

6

"TAMAR," GASPED DON RICARDO DE OLID. "STAR OF MY LIFE—goddess of my soul!" He put his hands on her slender waist and bent to kiss her mouth.

Tamar submitted to his lips. Her heart was pounding no less violently for all her awareness of his courtierlike superficiality.

All around them the night was loud with crickets and tree frogs, intoxicating with the odors of tamarind and mango, rosewood and saffron. Lush flowers and tropical ferns swayed about them in the darkness. The Governor had taken infinite pains to make his garden a slice of that ancient Eden which Columbus had described a century before. Among the nodding blossoms at the foot of a royal palm stood the Governor's beautiful daughter and the handsomest young sprig of the Rojas clan, kissing in the fragrant tropic night.

"Oh, Tamar," whispered Don Ricardo as they drew apart after that first, almost experimental kiss. "I can still scarce believe that it is true—that you have really come—" She had rejected his importunities so frequently before.

"Don Ricardo," she murmured—rather too lightly, he thought—"how could I refuse when I learned that you will be gone from the island tomorrow? Surely it is the part of a friend to say good-bye?"

Don Ricardo swore silently in the darkness. For the innocent wench she was, she was the most talented natural coquette he had ever encountered. And Olid had encountered his share of tempting eyes and laughing lips among the aristocracy of Madrid.

"I am deeply honored," he responded easily, "that my lady feels our friendship to be worthy of such a farewell."

"A kiss," the girl answered as easily, disengaging herself from his hands and swaying back against the royal palm behind her. "What is that between two whose souls have met and embraced so frequently as our two have?" Again, she was half smiling at him. And once more, he did not know how to take her words, how to deal with this infuriating creature.

God knew they had sat often enough in quiet alcoves murmuring poetic nonsense, he thought. He had even sung to her, love songs from Andalucía, as though he were some minstrel from the long-dead age of chivalry. Tamar had smiled and sighed, but she had never even come close to committing herself. Now she seemed to be doing it at last—on his last night in Cuba!

Beneath his court polish and Petrarchan conceits, Ricardo de Olid was a man of no great depth. He regarded all attractive women as his legitimate prey—and as little more than that. One day his mother in Madrid, or his uncles here in Cuba, would arrange a suitably prosperous marriage for him. Until then, he enjoyed one courtly conquest as much as the one that went before and felt a vague sense of injustice when any woman put him off for long.

This one, he thought, had withheld her favors overlong already.

"Lady of my heart," he said in the roughened voice that had brought more than one yielding body into his arms, "no two souls could be closer than yours and mine. Feel my soul rise to my lips—and enter yours." And he bent to kiss her once again.

He felt some resistance this time. But he pressed her ardently to him, whispering broken words of love, before his lips settled once more upon hers.

Tamar felt herself growing giddy at the passion of his kisses. This was in fact the first time any man had ever kissed her in this way—on the mouth, and obviously wanting more. She knew she should be frightened, should draw away from his embrace. But the physical presence of him blended with the moonlight and the odor of the flowers to conjure up half-forgotten memories of the morning's dream. She surrendered to the intoxication of it completely now. With the quick passion of youth, she began to kiss him back.

One of his arms was around her, pressing her against his strong, velvet-clad body. His other hand touched her throat, her half-bared shoulder. Then his fingers slid down to caress the rich satin over her breasts.

"My doves," he said against her ear. "My two white doves. Let me uncover their beauty to my lips."

Perhaps it was the unoriginality of the poetical conceit—Tamar really did have a good ear for poetry. Perhaps it was the rigid training of a girl's young lifetime, asserting itself at last. For whatever reason, she felt a sudden chill. Almost a bolt of fear at her position, alone in this far corner of the garden, locked in a man's arms for the first time.

"Don Ricardo—no!" she said, her voice muffled by his shoulder, trying to draw away.

"Alas, my lady, I am but a moth to the candle of your beauty." His fingers stroked her gently, insidiously. "Do not deny me now."

"Please," she whispered, her own voice sounding strange and faraway to her ears. "Please—you must not—we must not—" Even through the stiff satin bodice, her breasts clung to his caresses, strained after his moving hands.

"Be merciful, Tamar," he said thickly against her ear. "You know that I—you cannot believe that I—" He was actually babbling, lost now in a delirium of his own.

Tamar felt her whole body responding to him now, throbbing with sensations she had never known before. Her efforts to escape his arms only intensified the tingles and the tremors that ran through her. Above the rustling palm fronds overhead, the moon swam dizzily across the sky, and the earth seemed unsteady beneath her feet.

With a sudden wrench, she broke free of him at last.

"Don Ricardo!" she said, taking a quick step backward, breathing quickly.

"My lady." He sucked in his breath, choked back the

passion that all but overwhelmed him. "Of course, if—my lady wills it—"

"I came to say good-bye," she said. "We have, I think"—and she could not forbear a shaky laugh—"more than done so."

"Indeed," he replied, "I shall never forget you, Tamar. Or your farewell this night." *And that, God knows, is true,* he thought.

"It is late," said the girl, firmly in command once more. "The moon is almost down. I must go in."

"If I may escort my lady to the house?"

She curtseyed almost coquettishly, but she did not take his arm as they moved off side by side between the pillars of the palm-tree trunks. They did not touch again, even at the vine-shrouded stone doorway where she left him. But before she pulled the heavy door to, she whispered one last time to him.

"I shall be in Madrid myself soon. Within the year, my father says. Perhaps we may see each other again then, Don Ricardo." She smiled up at him, her dark eyes glowing faintly in the moonlight. Then the door swung shut, and he was alone in the garden.

Don Ricardo de Olid turned on his heel and strode away, swearing softly to himself. His servant, Manuel, would be waiting in the lane with the horses, eager to hear—by innuendo at least—of the night's amours. Don Ricardo intensely disliked having to make up lies for his own valet.

Tamar scurried up the stairs and down a dim passageway to her own chamber. She closed the door behind her, leaned against it for a moment, and then darted across the room in a flurry of skirts to peer out the window after her departing lover.

She watched him go down the path, striking aside any bloom or branch that fell across his way with a fury that was all too evident even at that distance. Her eyes sparkled to see it, and she could not resist a gurgling laugh.

He loved her—he wanted her—the handsomest young hidalgo she had ever known! His foolish poetical conceits were all forgotten now. For if this gallant courtier who had known the ladies of Cádiz and Madrid could want her so, what could she not expect of the voyage that was coming, too many months away? Of the future that awaited her in the fairyland that was Castile in her bright imaginings?

Sitting there in the window, her face all but touching the iron grillwork, she did not feel the new coolness against her cheek. It was only when the first drops spattered upon her hand that she realized the wind had changed at last, and the rains were come.

She sat there for a long time, letting the shower wet her hair and face, her shoulders and breast and arms. But the rain could not cool the new fevers that burned now within her. Nothing, she felt, could do that anymore.

CHAPTER

7

Admiral Mendoza stood at the highest point of the poop deck, a shadow against the paling stars. He had given his orders. On the quarterdeck just below, the sailing master, Señor Salazar, was translating Don Fernando's will into the specific commands that would work this monarch of the deep down the estuary and out to the open sea.

A dozen backs were already bent to the capstan, the anchor chain was already rising, dripping with water and weed, when they heard the hail of a boat putting out from shore.

Sailing Master Salazar turned a grizzled countenance toward his commander. The Admiral nodded. The sailing master turned to the men in the waist below him, toiling by lantern light, and shouted. A mate echoed his order. The bent backs of the men relaxed, the rattle of the anchor chain ceased.

So close, meditated Don Fernando. Half an hour longer, and the Rojas faction would have had to find another ship. But then, he thought, they would certainly have found one. He gauged the distance of the approaching small boat and began a slow descent of the sloping aftercastle. Courtesy required that he greet his passenger at the rail—however much of a fop and a fool the young man might be.

In the approaching boat, Don Ricardo stood up in a knee-deep tangle of trunks and bags, watching without enthusiasm as the carrack loomed closer.

His three-month sojourn in the New World, he thought wryly, had been an unmitigated failure from every point of view. He had found no golden empires to conquer—his mother would be duly disappointed. His famous Cuban uncles had been unable—"for the time being," as they said —to offer him any preferment at all. Even the Governor's passionate, reckless daughter had had nothing for him but a kiss and a smile. And he had nothing to look forward to now but weeks of this superannuated admiral's company, replete no doubt with all the traveler's tales and naval exploits of a misspent lifetime.

It was all extremely tiresome, he thought as the small boat scraped alongside and his servant, Manuel, scrabbled to catch the ladder.

He did not even think of the precious box of papers his uncle Geronimo had entrusted to him. He knew what they were and what he was to do with them. He simply did not care. His uncles might become governors of Cuba or of all New Spain, with satrapies by the score to apportion out to deserving relatives; but horses and oxen would not draw Don Ricardo de Olid to these barbarous provinces again.

"Don Ricardo," said Lord Admiral Mendoza, greeting him gravely at the ladder's head. "My ship is honored, señor."

"The honor is entirely mine, Don Fernando," the younger man assured him, bending one knee, extending one leg, and bowing with a flourish. "And, so I dare hope, will be the pleasure of your company." And he bowed again.

Half an hour later, Don Ricardo was ensconced with his servant and his baggage in his small but elegant cabin. Admiral Mendoza stood once more under the great lantern at the highest elevation of the poop. The anchor was up now; the great ship floated free.

The sailing master called another order, heard it echoed by the mate in the waist, the boatswain in the fore-chains. On the dark waters a cable's length ahead, a hundred men in half a dozen longboats bent to their oars. Under the lord admiral's feet, the *Madre de Dios* began to move.

He stood for a long time still, listening to the man in the fore-chains casting the lead, calling out the fathoms as they moved ponderously down the estuary toward the harbor's mouth. He watched the hills take shape on either side, and heard the first cocks crow. He remembered Governor de la Barca's fine house on the hill, with its tropical garden around it, and sighed. He really did tend to get most wretchedly seasick in foul weather.

He stayed where he was until they rounded the Morro Castle, white and new on its rocky headland, into the chop of the open sea. He stayed till the cables fell away and the longboats turned back. He watched the mariners swarm up the ratlines to shake out the canvas, stained and crusted still with the salt winds of the Indian Ocean, opening now to the breezes of the Caribbean, the gales of the Atlantic.

The land smells of fish and rotting fruit were gone, vanished with the dusty little white-walled town and the fine new house on the hill. The Admiral's nostrils filled now with the sharper tang of the salt wind and the brine. Beyond the railing, blue-green water shimmered in full daylight. Off to starboard, the island was a dark strip of jungle now, a purple ridgeline, and the blue of distant mountains.

The lord admiral nodded to Master Salazar and went below to sleep.

Fishermen in smacks and dories, bobbing out between the Punta and the Morro, watched the carrack heel slowly and heavily as the wind bellied her vast sails. They watched with awe as she slid past, deck after looming deck, row on row of gunports, closed now against the spray. They saw the laughing teeth of the Lascars, the gleam of sunlight on a plumed helmet. Then there was only boiling white water and the receding stern—carved and painted and gigantic—of the biggest ship in the world.

A full day's sail to the east, an English pinnace scudded south-southeast before the wind. She was a small, single-masted vessel with a dozen men for her crew. All sails were bellied full, and she heeled so far over that white water creamed repeatedly over the lee bulwarks. Surf broke at her bows, and the men who manned her moved in a haze of spray.

They moved efficiently about their work, these Englishmen so far from home, though they had more the look of smugglers or shipwreckers about them than of honest seamen. They were a hard-faced, sun-browned set of men, and they spoke the English of Devon and Cornwall, whose rocky coasts had bred great sailors and savage pirates since Englishmen first took to the seas.

A grey-haired barrel of a man prowled the stern, keeping his sea legs with difficulty as the pinnace rose and fell on the surge. Matthew Morgan was a soldier, and he had a soldier's distrust of the sea.

"How much farther to the straits, then, master mariner?" he demanded of a swarthy little man in a red-and-white seaman's smock. "How much longer before we can swing south for Cartagena?"

"Another day, if the wind holds," the smaller man replied. "And two days more should bring us to the fleet, if they be cruising still where we left 'em."

"They'll be there." Matthew Morgan grunted, his blue eyes gleaming through the salt sea spray. "They'll be where Sir John said they'd be. God knows but he'll be glad to hear our news!"

The wind strummed in the cordage, the canvas ruffled and cracked in the wind, and the little vessel plunged on, east along the coast of Cuba toward Hispaniola, then south for Cartagena—and the biggest English fleet that had sailed these waters since the days of Francis Drake.

BOOK II

---◆---

THIS SCOURGE
WILL COME

Now crouch, ye kings of greatest Asia,
And tremble when ye hear this Scourge
  will come
That whips down cities and controlleth
  crowns,
Adding their wealth and treasure to
  my store.

> —CHRISTOPHER MARLOWE,
> *The Bloody Conquests*
> *of Mighty Tamburlaine,*
> *Part II*

CHAPTER

8

AT MIDNIGHT ON SATURDAY NIGHT, THE LOOKOUT ON THE foremast of the *Roebuck* glimpsed the first firefly glow of the beacon on the Morro Castle.

"It is Havana, right enough," said Matthew Morgan, squinting across the moonlit water at the dark line of coast. "Ye'll see how the land rises there, falls yonder into the jungle. The light will be the dons' new fortress at the entrance to the outer harbor."

Sir John Burrow, standing at his lieutenant's side high on the poop deck, nodded silently. His eyes too played over the low silhouette of shoreline in the moonlight, trying to see in it the configurations of the rude map in his cabin below. That map and what their own eyes could tell them were their only guides to this, the richest prize—and the most massively defended city—in the Spanish Indies.

"The fortress is well enough," said Burrow presently, bracing his tall, wide-shouldered frame against the roll of the ship. "But the Vera Cruz galleons, Matthew—they will not be waiting for us in the harbor?" He spoke in a slow countryman's voice that somehow sorted ill with the gleaming steel breastplate, the rapier at his hip.

"They were not there when I slipped across the point," said Morgan, "and that was no more than ten days since." The grey-haired soldier's voice had a lilt and a chuckle in it. It was a Welshman's voice, full of the music of his native hills.

"Then by God we'll have her!" said Burrow softly. "We'll have it all!" He rested his heavy hands on the railing and looked down at the seamen and soldiers clustered on the deck below. His gaze rose to the dozen other English warships trailing away to port and starboard across the moon-gilded sea.

"If the captain general pleases," murmured a thin-lipped, flinty-eyed man in black standing at Sir John's elbow, "it would be well to order all lights to be extinguished, and silence in the waist. It would be ill fortune indeed if some late-wandering savage or some early fisherman should carry warning of our coming to the dons."

"True and to the point as ever, Master Adam," Burrow answered, smiling for the first time since the lookout's cry had brought them all tumbling out on deck. "See that it be done at once. And set out the flags to summon all captains of troops and vessels aboard the *Roebuck* for council."

"All captains aboard for council," the somber man in black repeated crisply. Master Adam, sailing master of Captain General Sir John Burrow's flagship, was a precise and narrow Puritan who took his duties seriously and ran his vessel with an exacting hand. "And the voluntary gentlemen, sir? Will you have the chiefest of them aboard as well?"

The smile that had creased Burrow's long, lean cheeks faded into a grimace, but he nodded his assent. "Aye. Westmorland and the rest of them, and Catesby too. They must be told at least, if not consulted."

"Is that needful, Captain?" said Matthew Morgan. "You have full powers here, a free and full commission to sail when and where you will on her Majesty's business. Why have Westmorland and Catesby up, to carp and cavil at every—"

"His grace the most noble Earl of Westmorland," said Captain Burrow wryly, "stands very high in the favor of Her Majesty the Queen. Next only to Essex and Raleigh among the gaudier cavaliers, so I've heard. And Master Catesby is her Majesty's own Paymaster of the Forces, as every man belowdecks can tell ye. So they must both be tolerated, Matthew, by such as we be, poor soldiers of the Queen."

But the captain general's look showed clearly that he shared his lieutenant's opinion of the gentleman volunteers and the meddling officials who had cumbered every expedition since the Spanish wars began a dozen years before.

"Issue pikes and hauberks now, Master Adam," he continued, turning back to the sailing master, "and helmets for such as need 'em. Arquebuses, powder and shot in the morning."

Master Adam nodded, turned on his heel, and vanished down the companionway toward the lower decks.

"The lads will be glad enough of a broil," said Matthew, "after so many weeks at sea." The tone was still melodious and cheerful, but there was a glint in his bright-blue eyes that showed that he too was eager for what lay ahead.

Sir John looked down once more at the men clustered along the portside railing, or moving restlessly in moonlight and in shadow among the cannons and culverins, the longboat, the capstan and the coiled anchor chain that crowded the ship's narrow waist. Many of the soldiers had served with him before in Queen Elizabeth's wars in the Netherlands, in France and Ireland, and even on raids into Portugal and Spain itself. These men he knew, and knew he could trust. The mariners who manned the fleet were another matter, for Sir John Burrow had never commanded on the sea before. But he had faith in Master Adam's calm and total competence. And there was a grizzled toughness to these Devon seamen that he felt he could depend on too.

Essentially they were much of a piece, he realized, looking down at the sun-darkened faces and unkempt beards of these men in leather jerkins and seamen's smocks. Their bodies were lean and scarred like his own by these endless wars. Their bodies and their souls too, he thought ruefully. As his own soul was.

There were Puritan moralists, Sir John Burrow knew, who would damn the lot of them for what they were: the dregs of the camps and the ports, men more likely to loot than fight, and perhaps more likely to desert than either. Brawlers, drunkards, church burners, nun rapers. Men that might share a crust with a comrade while he lived, but would surely pry the gold out of his teeth when he was dead.

The flower of English chivalry they were not, Burrow

grinned sourly to himself. The flower of English chivalry were dead long since. Dead with Sir Philip Sidney and Sir Francis Drake and so many others, back down the years. Only pirates and marauders were left now. These were the survivors—and God help any Spaniard that fell between their hands!

"Broach a keg and issue ale for all hands in the morning, Matthew," said Burrow. "The best that's left us, for this day."

Morgan nodded. "They'll earn it well enough." The blood was still up in him, and his eyes glowed with the lust for battle and sudden death that kept him following the wars long after most men with his grey hairs had retired to their firesides at home.

Matthew Morgan had tried more than once to turn away from the wars himself. Three times he had returned to his Welsh farmstead, hung up his sword, and roasted his feet by the fire. Once it had lasted as long as five years. But he was not the man for a straight furrow and a jack of brown ale in the evening. The months would pass, and he would soon be quarreling with his neighbors and cuffing his sons and kicking his dogs for nothing but sleeping in his way. And soon or late rumors of wars and soldier's pay to be earned would reach him even in his forgotten purple hills. Then he would be up and away again, to seek out some good commander and have another stroke at the dons.

So it had always been with Matthew Morgan, John Burrow knew. So it would always be.

Every man of them would earn his soldier's pay tomorrow, the captain general thought. They would all earn it in smoke and blood and fear, in hard blows given and taken. Those that were whole men still at sunset would have Spanish wine for their reward, no doubt, and Spanish strumpets and Spanish gold too, if Fortune willed it. But the wine and the strumpets would soon be gone, and they would gamble away the gold. They would be off in a day, two days or three, with the pox or the fevers of the island to comfort them on the long voyage home.

I have been too long at the wars, thought John Burrow wryly.

"Come, Matthew," he said aloud, his long face tightening in a smile, "let's get below ourselves and make ready for the captains—*and* the voluntary gentlemen."

Matthew answered his commander's grin, and the two of them descended the companionway into darkness.

9

IN THE CAPTAIN GENERAL'S CABIN, BURROW LAID THE LARGE, roughly drawn chart of the city of Havana across a wide table. Master Adam rolled it out at one end, Matthew Morgan at the other.

The low-raftered cabin was crowded. There were a dozen captains, solid, practical men for the most part, dressed in plain broadcloth, rapiers heavy in their hangers. There were almost as many of the gentleman volunteers, younger men, much more gaudily clad in velvet doublets and satin sleeves, with gold and silver garters at their knees. The room was full of the subdued excitement that even the most experienced captain felt during those last hours before battle.

"Gentlemen, if you please," said Burrow quietly. Silence came quickly, and every face turned toward the tall figure behind the table, his hands spread wide upon the map before him.

Sir John Burrow had never been a handsome man. His roughhewn, darkly weathered features and big-boned limbs were out of fashion for his day. Nor had a dozen years of almost continual fighting done anything to improve his appearance. His body was laced with white scars beneath the worn white doublet. A long pale gash ran down one side of his face, across the cheekbone and into his short, ill-cropped black beard. His great height—he stood six feet and several inches in his leather boots—and the iron-hilted Toledo rapier at his side made him a formidable figure, but not a dashing one.

He cast a hard, half-humorous glance around him now at the varied countenances of his commanders, at the delicately handsome features of young Westmorland, the frankly venal face of jowly, white-bearded Captain Thynne. He himself had been as young and tense as Westmorland once, he thought, as avid for hot strokes and high adventure. And he was as hungry now for booty as any Captain Thynne.

"You will see, gentlemen," he began crisply then, "that the city is on the inner harbor, connected to the sea by a narrow channel."

The officers and gentlemen clustered round. Those closest in—the senior commanders—bent over the long table. Their eyes glistened in the light of the hanging lamp that swung slowly to and fro just above their heads.

"At the outer entrance to this channel, or outer harbor," Burrow continued, "stand two fortresses, the Punta and the Morro. There is an older fort, the Fuerza, on the main square of the town, facing the inner harbor."

"The Morro," said the venerable, portly Captain Thynne, the senior captain present, "was Texeda's work, I think. His Majesty of Spain ordered it built not ten years since, after Drake coasted these parts and put the fear of God and the English into 'em." He shook his white head. "John Hawkins used to say that once the Morro was done, no ship of war would ever sail into Havana harbor again."

"The Morro will fall tonight," said Sir John crisply. "And the Punta. The Fuerza we may leave to the bombardment of the fleet, once we have penetrated the inner harbor. That will be by dawn tomorrow."

Quietly, grimly, he laid out his plans.

Captain Cross, one of his most dashing and aggressive younger commanders, would land east of the entrance to the outer harbor and move on the Morro Castle from the landward side. Another small force would be put ashore west of the channel and overwhelm the smaller fortification on the Punta. A third company under Matthew Morgan would land still farther to the west, here, at Guillén's Inlet, and sweep inland, up the creeks. . . .

If Fortune smiled upon them, they would be in Havana by the next day at noon.

If Fortune smiled. It was an ill-chosen phrase, and more than one pair of eyes flicked over at Sir John when he said it. For John Burrow's ill fortune was notorious among these men. Sir John was in fact the most unlucky of all Queen Elizabeth's fighting captains, and everyone in that room knew it.

It was no small matter to be Fortune's fool, as Sir John had learned ever since his first command in the Low Countries thirteen years before.

He knew as well as any how to feed and shelter and fight his men in a foreign land. How to pull them out of a Spanish ambuscade, or drive them on to victory when there was no powder left and scarce the strength to wield a sword. But all that was to no purpose if Fortune would not smile. And she had smiled rarely indeed on Captain John Burrow.

In the past five years, Burrow's notorious luck had cost him two commands, the Queen's Majesty's favor, and a cut across the face with an axeheaded halberd that had come near finishing him altogether. On this single voyage, Fortune had first refused to let him start at all, penning him up in Plymouth harbor for weeks for want of the favorable wind without which no fleet could sail. His ill fortune had continued once they were at sea. Between England and the Caribbees, they had taken no more than a single grain ship off Cape Finisterre, two Portuguese fishermen in the Azores, and a cog laden with hides and ironware off Cartagena—a pitiful tale of prizes for a summer's cruise.

But now they had reached Havana, and the powerful Vera Cruz galleons, which normally patrolled that part of the Spanish Indies, were not there. The city lay sleeping before them in the night, and Burrow's luck had surely turned at last.

So Sir John ignored the pointed silence among his officers and went on talking, calmly, confidently, his hands moving here and there about the chart. He pointed out the Plaza de Armas and the cathedral behind it, its twin towers an easy landmark. He indicated the Fuerza down close to the seawall, the old fort whose battlements and cannon would be their last obstacle once they had penetrated the inner harbor.

And he planted one square-tipped finger upon the new customs house—the focus of all their hopes, the object of this whole great expedition.

For the grain ships off Finisterre, the cog off Cartagena had all been feints and ruses. The lure that had brought a dozen ships and a thousand men across the broad Atlantic was the customs house at Havana and the treasure of the Indies that was—that must be—lying there.

Captain Burrow had heard it first from a haggard galley slave, newly rescued from the Spaniards, half drunk on English ale in a Southwark ordinary. The King of Spain, so the fellow swore, had sent forth a royal decree to say that the great Plate Fleet was not to sail that year. That the whole year's revenues in gold and silver, fresh from the mines of New Spain and New Granada, were to remain where they had been gathered for the voyage—in the customs house at Havana.

With this wild tale, and with a wilder dream, Burrow had gone before their lordships of the Queen's Majesty's Council. Before Lord Treasurer Burghley and Lord Admiral Howard, tight old hands on the Queen's purse strings. Before Raleigh and Essex, swashbucklers themselves, and jealous of any other man's chances for military glory. Before all those timid civilians and courtly intriguers who had always made a soldier's lot so much harder at home than in the field.

And there, against all odds and probabilities, he had made his case and won. Her gracious Majesty, Lord Burghley had informed him heavily, fixing him with watery eyes beneath white brows, would provide a fleet and a dozen companies. She would issue a full commission empowering her well-beloved subject Sir John Burrow "by sea and by land to invade and destroy the powers, forces, preparations and provisions whatsoever of the King of Spain. . . ."

Now he was here, and the time was come. And he would seize that time.

Grey-haired Matthew Morgan bent close above the chart,

his blue eyes glowing like a boy's at the prospect of battle and sudden death. Captain Cross tugged tensely at one ear with his long white fingers, his eyes fixed on the tiny caricature of a castle scrawled at the entrance to the outer harbor and the cryptic phrase: *El Morro*. At thirty, Cross was the youngest commander there, and avid for honor.

All around the captain general, eyes glittered and fingers touched the hilts of swords and daggers. Havana would be theirs, they swore. In God's name and the Queen's! They separated to their ships, talking excitedly in whispers, though they were still miles out to sea.

"What a pestilent hole you've brought me to, Catesby," muttered the young Earl of Westmorland, settling into the longboat that bore them back to the Queen's ship *Garland*, heaving slowly toward them across the swell. "Better confront the greediest tradesmen and moneylenders in London than face these fevers and agues." He drew his cloak closer about him, though the night was warm.

The Earl of Westmorland was a youth in his early twenties, slender and fine-boned, resplendent in a peascod doublet and knee-length padded breeches of the sort known as Venetians. The fluted ruff about his neck, the lace at his wrists were dazzlingly white. There were emerald buttons on his doublet, and a whiff of perfume rose from his fawn-colored gloves.

Westmorland had been pampered, admired, deferred to all his life, from the family estates to Oxford to the royal court —ill preparation indeed for such a venture as this. But his father had been a famous soldier, had in fact died young fighting heroically in the Irish wars. So when the earl his son found funds and credit exhausted by his extravagant life in London, he had impulsively announced his determination to follow in his father's footsteps.

The pale young courtier had regretted it from the first squall over the Bay of Biscay to his most recent brush with tropical fevers off Cartagena.

"A wretched climate, truly, my lord," sighed his companion, the paymaster Nicholas Catesby. "But if my lord will buckle on his sword to seek honor even in the cannon's mouth—" He spread his hands as if to say, What would you? and fell silent.

"And the company, Catesby!" His lordship, it seemed, was not through complaining. "Scum of the port towns, cripples of the counties pressed into her Majesty's service. Mad for Spanish gold, with no thought of honor or glory, or the service of the Queen."

"Freebooters certainly, my lord, and no better than they should be," said Catesby, his small, close-set eyes flickering nervously over the stolid backs of the seamen leaning easily into their oars. The royal paymaster, who had risen from the London slums himself, was not happy with this line of conversation.

"And this famous Sir John Burrow? This captain general that is set over us all—what sort of a gentleman is he, after all?"

"His scutcheon is no match for my lord of Westmorland's, of course," the other answered judiciously. "But he is the son of a baron, after all, and twice knighted on the field of battle. Indeed, at one time he was a special favorite of her Majesty's, I understand, before ill fortune—"

"The *second* son, Catesby," his lordship cut in, "of an out-at-elbows northern baron. Knighted by Essex and Navarre, both notable prodigals in the distribution of honors." The young gentleman sniffed irritably and fanned himself with his wide plumed hat.

For all his cavalier airs, the earl had not distinguished himself in the skirmishes the expedition had fought thus far. And his best suggestions and advice in council had invariably been politely acknowledged and totally ignored. When to this was added the fact that even the most optimistic calculation of his share of the profits indicated that he had not garnered a tithe of the moneys he owed in London, his discontent was thoroughly understandable.

"A proud man, this captain general of ours," he concluded darkly as the longboat drew in under the gunports of the *Garland*. "And his pride will bring him down—you'll see."

The boat scraped alongside, and Catesby was spared the difficulty of constructing a diplomatic answer. Nicholas Catesby had his own reasons for discontent with the Captain General of the Fleet. But this was not the time or the place to air them with his lordship of Westmorland.

From the rail of the *Roebuck*'s quarterdeck, Sir John Burrow watched the last of his captains depart. He had done well this night, he thought. Each commander knew his part. It would go tomorrow as God and Fortune willed—but he at least had done his best.

His eyes shifted once more to the dim outlines of the Cuban coast, hazier still by starlight now that the moon was down. He breathed in the rich smells of the tropics, odors of flowers and lushly moldering vegetation. Paradise, the great conquistador Columbus had called these islands a hundred years ago.

It would not be paradise tomorrow, thought Sir John, when the freebooters hit Havana.

10

Tamar de la Barca was doing the most dangerous thing she had ever done in her life.

She hurried through the darkened streets at Marina's side, head down, face shrouded in a coarse black shawl. Her body was swathed in a homespun gown, little different from Marina's own—which in fact it was. Scurrying through the unlit streets of the Cerro at her servant's side, she was indistinguishable from any poor woman of that dirty, raucous, reeking section of the city.

"If my lady pleases," said the Indian woman, "it would be best to move more slowly. The people of the Cerro, they have nowhere to go in such a hurry." Marina's voice was wooden with disapproval of the entire venture.

"Yes—of course," the girl replied, slackening her pace so abruptly that a drunken strumpet coming on behind her nearly stumbled over her in the dark. "It is only that I am so excited!"

Marina's only answer was a massive silence.

The muddy lane wound its way among adobe huts, thatched with palm leaves. It had rained earlier in the evening, and the streets were gummy with mud. There were no lights but an occasional candle in a window, or the glow of an open eating-house door. Black washerwomen and turbaned prostitutes, soldiers and sailors, Indian women with loads on their heads brushed shoulders in the gloom. There was talk and laughter, shouted greetings, singing and the oaths of gamblers from noisy wineshops as they passed.

It might have been broad daylight, thought Tamar, who had never set foot in the Cerro after sunset before.

She was here now in answer to one of those strange, impulsive bursts of recklessness that had beset her all that summer. That it was folly she had readily admitted when Marina charged her with it. That it might even be sinful, she was willing to consider. But renounce this particular piece of madness she could not. The compulsions that drove her sprang from the same mysterious source that made her weep at the sunset or laugh at a velvety blossom hanging over a garden wall. She was following now the same sort of foolish impulse that had made her offer her lips to Don Ricardo de Olid on his last night in Cuba.

She was on her way to a supper of chicken and rice and the dark wine of the island in Don Diego Aguilar's private apartments.

"A rude meal cooked by a soldier's rude hands, Tamar," he had told her as they stood outside church on the Plaza de Armas after mass the preceding Sunday. "I am sure you would not find it to your taste. In any case," he had added, with a note of laconic challenge in his voice, "it would not be possible for you to visit my poor quarters so late in the evening."

"Not possible, Don Diego?" She had taken up the challenge at once. "Surely there is no safer place in all Havana than the Fuerza, by day or by night?"

"I was not referring to the Fuerza, my lady. The quarters your father provides there are too formal for a simple soldier. I keep a house in the Cerro, where I am more comfortable." His lashless eyes had fixed her as he spoke. "I am certain your distinguished father would never permit you to go there—especially by night."

"I go where I please!" she had answered at once, her eyes flashing. "I have been through the Cerro many times."

"By daylight and on horseback," he had said, "riding through. But never, I'll wager, after dark. And certainly never to visit a gentleman in his own quarters!"

The dare was too overt to go unanswered.

"I shall dine with you six nights from this," she had promptly declared, "on Saturday night at midnight, in your quarters in the Cerro. And the rice had best not be boiled too much, or cooled too long!"

She had curtseyed grandly to him then, with an arched eyebrow that seemed to say, So much for *you*, Don Diego Aguilar, the terrible hunter of men! She had swept away across the plaza to re-join her father at his coach in front of the cathedral.

Aguilar had watched her go with a mixture of disbelief and calculation. She would never come, of course. But if she did? His heart began to beat heavily in his chest.

It was the sort of ragamuffin defiance that had made Tamar run with the Indian children in the street, or ride in the hills alone with a man. She had made Marina provide a suitable gown and shawl, and had dragged her duenna with her to guide her through the midnight streets. It was just like a scene in a stage play, she told herself, where the heroine goes to meet her lover disguised as a page or a shepherd boy! And it certainly served to break the boredom of the endless Cuban summer.

Not, of course, that Don Diego was her lover, or ever likely to be. That high honor she had firmly reserved for some dashing young nobleman whom she would meet at the Palace of the Escorial in Madrid. But this was an adventure, and fun, and Tamar loved it.

"It is here, my lady," said Marina in a low voice. "He lets out the lower floor to the two Indians who cook and wash for him. His own rooms are up the stair."

Tamar could dimly make out a cracked adobe housefront and the dark maw of an open door. A fire seemed to be burning in the back somewhere, and by its occasional orange glimmers she glimpsed a rickety stair—little more than a ladder, really—just inside the doorway.

"There doesn't seem to be anyone here," she said doubtfully. "There isn't even a candle."

"The Indians are probably in the back," said Marina, "cooking the meal. Or perhaps at some eating house in the neighborhood, buying it."

"Don Diego said he would prepare everything himself."

Marina made no answer to this. Again, her silence was eloquent enough.

There, in the darkness, Tamar's chin went up once more.

"We will go up," she announced, "and see if His Excellency the Commander of the Fuerza is gentleman enough to keep his appointments!" She stepped through the doorway and felt her way over the earthen floor toward the stairs.

Don Diego Aguilar sat on the roof of his house, sipping wine and glowering out over Havana. Behind him stood the little penthouse—little more than an adobe shack—where he lived. In front of him the city stretched away like a vast dark rubbish heap, lit here and there by flickers of orange flame.

Aguilar had learned that day that in matters of political intrigue, he was playing his masters' game—a game in which he had no chance at all of winning. Don Diego did not like the feeling.

He had repaired to Don Geronimo Rojas's ornate mansion on the plaza that morning, carrying his first painfully inscribed account of the administration of Governor Don Gabriel de la Barca. He had gone to the house of Rojas with his head high and pride in his step, prepared to lay down his terms. Nor would his collaboration in the coming investigation of the Governor's conduct in office come cheap. He would have the command of the Morro, certainly. He would hint that a solid pension would not come amiss to a poor but honest soldier. And then, he would declare, looking Don Geronimo straight in the eye, there was his suit for the hand of the Governor's lovely daughter.

Today, he had thought, as he slammed the knocker heavily against the teakwood door, he would dare anything!

Rojas had all but laughed in his face.

The corpulent head of the Rojas clan had flicked condescendingly through the grubby sheaf of papers. He had handed them casually to a secretary to be transcribed. And he had informed Don Diego that he should return the following day to sign his statement. A statement, he added, which would certainly help to buttress the meticulous case which he and Señor Ynestrosa and certain other good citizens had already prepared.

Señor Ynestrosa, thin and white-haired, standing at Rojas's elbow, had nodded judiciously. So had Don Geronimo's brother, the grey-bearded royal treasurer, browsing over a large book in the corner.

Help to buttress it? Don Diego had thought wildly. His testimony, with that of De la Barca's totally corrupted secretary, *was* their case! Who but they could bear witness from inside the Governor's own administration to the sales of offices, the wasted moneys, the smuggling, the exploitation of convict labor, the— Aguilar had gone white to the lips. He had begun to stammer about his reward.

Rojas had smiled. He had fetched out a velvet purse that clinked heavily as he laid it on the table. Would five hundred ducats suffice to reward Don Diego for his public spirit?

But the Morro! Had not Don Geronimo said—the Morro? Aguilar, who would fight any man with any weapon, had felt suddenly helpless and desperate, here in this twilight world of veiled words, secret smiles, ambiguous promises. This was not his world, nor these the sort of adversaries who could be defeated with rapier or dagger.

Don Geronimo had raised his eyebrows in astonishment. The command of the new fortress at El Morro? But of course Don Diego must realize that if Rojas's petition for the governorship were successful, all posts in the new administration would be awarded on pure merit. Rojas's secretary, squaring papers at a smaller table, had crooked his lips in a silent grin, and old Don Ernesto Ynestrosa gave him a disapproving look. Abruptly Aguilar had remembered that Don Ernesto himself had a son who was rumored to covet the command of the Morro Castle.

Don Geronimo Rojas had pushed the velvet purse across the table, touching it only with the tips of his fingers. He had indicated that the interview was over. If Don Diego would be so good as to return in the morning to sign?

Don Diego had snatched up the money and fled from the house. Behind him, the rich chuckle of the future Governor of Cuba had echoed in his ears.

Trembling with rage, Aguilar had flung onto his horse and ridden up to Governor de la Barca's house above the town.

Don Gabriel had received him in an even more elegant chamber than his rival in the city below. Captain Aguilar had poured out the whole story of the intrigues of the Rojas faction. He had offered to stand by the Governor before the judges, to testify openly to the nefarious tactics of the Governor's accusers. De la Barca would return in triumph to Spain, to enjoy his richly deserved retirement in peace and honor. He could even name his own successor, Don Diego had no doubt. And if in so doing he would put in a strong word for Don Diego—perhaps even urging that the Morro—

Don Gabriel de la Barca, sweating and smiling by turns, fiddling with his small, meticulous moustaches, had thanked Don Diego for his public-spiritedness. He, the Governor, was as it happened already aware of the schemes set in motion against him, and had taken his own measures to circumvent them. If, however, there should be any investigation, any ridiculous charges of malfeasance, Don Gabriel would certainly see that Aguilar was called upon to give his evidence. For now, he would take care that Don Geronimo was made aware of Aguilar's willingness to testify against him and his faction. Yes, Don Gabriel had nodded energetically, that would be a very wise thing to do. Forewarned of his witness's defection to the Governor's party, the Rojases might even withdraw their petition for an official inquisition after all.

Too late, Aguilar had realized how he had boxed himself in.

But the Morro? he had all but pleaded. If the Governor would only include a word—

Don Gabriel had smiled faintly and shaken his head. Don

Diego, he had said sadly, had no notion how little power a former governor would have to influence the course of events after his departure. Out of office, out of mind, that was the way of his superiors in Madrid. He much appreciated Don Diego's candor in coming forward, but—

Jesus and Mary! candor and public spirit—my God! Had candor and public spirit built the fine new house in which they stood—or the Rojas mansion in the square below? It was enough to make a plain man with his own fortune still to win feel like puking on the Moorish carpet!

Aguilar had bowed coldly, turned on his heel, and left the Governor's house. He had lashed his horse back down the rain-drenched hill road to the town below, through the jabbering streets to his own adobe hovel in the Cerro. There, on the open roof of his house, he had been sitting alone, drinking wine and brooding over his wrongs all day long.

He had entirely forgotten his bantering exchange with Tamar the previous Sunday morning after church.

"Don Diego!"

He heard his name, spoken in her uncertain voice, when she said it the third time. He turned, rose unsteadily to his feet, and started toward the two dark figures standing at the top of the stair.

"Don Diego—if it is inconvenient—" Tamar began. And then, seeing his weaving gait, feeling Marina's hand on her sleeve, she went on more firmly: "But I see it is an ill-timed visit, sir. Another time, when you are better prepared—" She turned an almost haughty shoulder to him. He saw the defiant tilt of her chin, the disgust in her averted eyes.

He took the Indian duenna by one sinewy arm and flung her down the stairs. Before the Governor's astonished daughter could move an inch, he had seized her in his arms.

11

HE CRUSHED THE GIRL'S SMALL BODY AGAINST HIS OWN WITH such force that she cried out. Or tried to—for his mouth, reeking of wine, came over hers and muffled the cry in her throat.

Don Diego Aguilar could scarcely believe the beauty of the woman he held in his arms. The fragrance, the softness, the supple strength of her inflamed his drunken heart. Her gasping efforts to escape him only intensified the desire that blazed through him. With a single fierce gesture, he tore open her gown and buried his face between her small, firm breasts.

"O God—stop—"

Her nails tore at his cheek.

The pain of it seared through the folds of drunkenness, jolted him like a hot iron on living flesh. And then Don Diego Aguilar went sheerly mad. He yanked the girl's head back by her thick black hair and struck her across the mouth.

Tamar saw the flat of his hand go slanting back, and then the blow exploded across her face.

The little room pinwheeled around her. Her shoulder blades and the back of her head slammed violently against an adobe wall. He struck her again, with the back of his hand this time, and she fell sprawling across a straw-stuffed pallet on the floor.

She tried to rise. Praying to God and His Holy Mother for strength, she drew herself to a kneeling posture. By the flickering light of a candle on the low table, she saw Don Diego looming over her. His chest was heaving under the open shirt, and the whites of his eyes gleamed strangely in the gloom.

"Don Diego," she began in a shaking voice, "please—"

"Don Diego, please!" he mimicked her savagely, his hands balling into fists now. "Is there no end to your hypocrisies? You did not come to my house at midnight for chicken with rice and the wine of the island, my lady. You came for me!"

"Oh, please, Don Diego, I didn't know—"

"You came for a little adventure, eh? For the strangeness of it, for clever talk and a kiss on the hand before you leave, to hurry back to your own white bed in his Excellency's house on the hill! Well, now, by God, you'll get what you deserve for once, and not what your elegant ladyship would have!"

His tongue was unsteady and he swayed on his feet. Tamar knew suddenly, sickeningly, that no word of hers, nothing she said or did, was going to stop him now.

"Now, your ladyship," he said thickly, "take off that gown."

She had dreamed of love, of passion and possession and surrender. But she had never imagined such cold brutality, such mindless aggression as she saw in the dark face and shining eyes of the man who stood over her now. There was no love there, no passion even. There was only a terrible lust to humiliate her, to break her to his will.

She had been so sure of herself, so free and bold, so contemptuous of fainthearts who feared adventures. She had ridden so confidently through the streets of this city, where her father spoke with the voice of the King himself, where she had received the smiles and greetings of the people as serenely as a queen all her young life. She had joked and danced and flirted elegantly with young men of her own class as long as she could remember. She had never dreamed that such terrible fires lay banked behind their laughter and their smiles.

She had never dreamed that it could come to this. To a young and very helpless girl, crouching in this dirty room, clutching a torn bodice across her trembling breasts and staring up at the cold-voiced stranger who dared to say such words as those:

"Now, your ladyship, take off that gown."

She did not do it. She fought him. She fought him with all the strength in her young body. And she never once lost consciousness.

Another blow knocked her off her knees, tumbled her across the pallet once again. She felt his hands on her naked thighs, pushing up her skirts and the linen shift beneath. Then his weight came down upon her, his panting breath was on her face, and the agony began.

The sudden pain of it was like a knife blade driven into her womb. But the shock, the sense of violation was more terrible still. It stunned her, stopped her heart for one eternal moment of disbelief and terror. This could not be happening to her, she told herself over and over as she writhed and wept beneath his plunging body, beneath the fury of his thrusts. Not to her, a good girl, a Christian girl, the daughter of his Excellency, the daughter of his Honor, the daughter of the Governor of—

Don Diego raped the Governor of Cuba's daughter with a crudeness and a brutality he had seldom shown even to blacks and Indian women in the isolated jungle villages of his slave-hunting, Indian-hunting days. He swore at her as he had never sworn at the dirtiest whore in the Cerro. He degraded her with his strength, punishing her white thighs and delicate breasts with a savage exultation beyond anything he had ever known. It was more than a release for him. It was revenge and vindication.

Revenge for that day's litany of humiliations at the hands of the satin-and-velvet grandees into whose genteel intrigues he 'had dared to intrude. Revenge for half a lifetime of condescension and contempt from those families of island aristocrats, with their green haciendas in the hills and their tall town houses around the plaza. Revenge—and vindication. A triumphant vindication of his own way of life, of his brutal soldier's code, of the very blood in his veins, which would never beat thin and tremulous and blue as theirs.

He took no joy in her body, or in his crime. But when it was over, he knew in the depths of his intoxicated soul that somehow, someway, he must have her always. He must have her with him forever, so that he might savor again and again that fierce revenge, that tremendous vindication.

LYING HALF UNDER THE MAN'S HEAVY BODY, SMELLING THE sweat of him and feeling the hardness of his limbs across her own, Tamar felt nothing at first but a terrible revulsion. Revulsion at the man, at the humiliation, the degradation inflicted upon herself, at a world which could permit such unspeakable things to happen to Tamar de la Barca.

The revulsion passed with the last of her spasmodic tears. It was replaced by an even more intense sensation—a desperate desire to escape. To tear her shrinking flesh from his. To flee from this room, from this sinkhole at the far, foul edges of the city. To put half the world if need be between herself and this savage man, who in those few unreal minutes had destroyed her life.

Then, lying there beside her in the darkness, Don Diego Aguilar began to talk. He talked as he had never talked before, drunkenly, disjointedly, while an hour went by and then another. And she lay where she was, trapped between his heavy body and the hard adobe wall, listening for Marina's returning footsteps, with the heavier steps of booted feet behind her, and wondering why they never came.

Aguilar told her about the mountains and the jungles where he had grown up, alone in the great rain forest with his strange family and their *encomienda* of Indian servants and plantation hands. He talked about his father's brutality to him and to his uncomplaining mother, an illiterate indentured servant whose freedom he had purchased in Havana. About his father's cruelty above all to the Indians who cut the ebony and the mahogany they sold, who harvested the yucca and the sago, the sweet and bitter cassava on which they lived.

Then his talk veered in a direction that seemed very strange to the frightened girl. He talked about his grandparents, the first comers to the isolated hacienda in the jungles of the Oriente.

He described his grandmother's grave beneath the purple piñon tree, and the strange fascination it had held for him as a child. The illegible letters, buried in moss, had seemed to him somehow a message intended for him alone, if he could only decipher its meaning.

Again and again, he came back to his grandfather, the founder of that strange reclusive family in the eastern jungles. He saw the emaciated ivory-yellow face of the old man so clearly still in his own mind. He tried to tell her about it.

Then suddenly, almost in spite of herself, Tamar began to understand.

"The scars were still there, below his lower lip. The Caribs all do that, you know—punch holes in the ears and below the lip, and insert heavy green stones. For a jewel, I think. They did it in Mexico, at least, the ones that captured him in his youth. They did it to *him* when he joined their tribe."

Mexico was where Cortez had found him—rescued him, taken him away, whatever he had done.

When the Castilian conqueror of the Aztec Empire had landed in Mexico with his little army, it seemed, he had heard rumors of white men held prisoner in the interior. He had sent out word that all Christian prisoners were to be released at once, and allowed to join him on the coast. Some of them at least had chosen not to come. One Spaniard, who had become a great war chief among the savages, had stayed with them, refusing the call of his own countrymen. But the grandfather of Don Diego Aguilar had come.

He had left the village and the people who had adopted him so many years before, and come down to the coast. He had come bringing his Indian wife, both of them dressed in the simple clothing of her people. He had wept when he had seen the Spanish ships and heard Spanish voices for the first time in so long. He had rushed out onto the beach and thrown himself on his knees before the heavyset man they had pointed out to him as Hernando Cortez.

He had looked up at his savior with tears on his cheeks. Tears that glistened on the purple tattoo marks of his village, on the bright green stone set into his lower lip. His sun-darkened shoulders shook as he raised his hands in gratitude —and found he could scarcely speak the language of his birth anymore.

Cortez had looked down at him, and at the Indian woman kneeling at his side, and had said, with a trace of impatience to a steel-shirted soldier standing by:

"Where is the Spaniard?"

Where is the Spaniard?

"But then," Aguilar explained, "when he understood that my grandfather was in fact a Spaniard and a Christian, of course he took him with him. Or sent him back to Cuba, rather, and settled him at the far end of the island. He settled the old man far from Havana and the other first comers because of his strange ways, and his wife. And his sons."

Two of the *mestizo* sons had died in childhood. Only Don Diego's father had survived to sire a son in his turn.

"But there are no scars on my lips and ears, you see." Don Diego laughed. "No tattoos on my cheeks. Such things are not passed on with the blood. It is well-known." And he looked at her as though for confirmation.

"No," Tamar said quickly, her voice steady now, the tears long dried upon her cheeks. "No, of course they are not." But the sins of the fathers? she thought. Are they not visited upon the sons? And the fathers of this man had cut out the hearts of living men on the altars of their gods!

"You are afraid of me," he said, turning toward her abruptly.

"No," she answered, her voice rising slightly. "No, Don Diego. Please—no!"

His hands were moving again, fondling her breasts with

callused fingers. She could feel his thigh move against her with a renewed sense of purpose.

"You do not need to be afraid of me," he said, his hand sliding down inside the tattered gown.

No! Her own protest echoed in her brain. *No—it will not happen again!*

Blind with mingled fear and rage, Tamar rolled suddenly toward the man beside her, striking at his face with her small closed fists. Her first blow caught him in the eye. He covered his face with one hand and groped for her, cursing, with the other. Then, as she struggled to rise, one flailing knee struck him in the soft part of the groin. With a surge of hope, she saw him shrink together like a wounded worm, clutching at his private parts, shouting with pain.

An instant later, Tamar was on her feet and running toward the open stairwell. She half leaped, half fell down the rickety ladder into the dark room below. With a gasp of joy and disbelief, she darted out through the door and pelted away down the deserted lane.

Tamar was young and strong, and she ran very fast through the early-morning darkness. There was a throbbing ache in her own loins now, but she set her teeth and never slackened her headlong pace. More than once she slipped and fell in the muck of the lanes and alleyways through which she fled. But she rose at once, plucked up her muddy skirts, and ran on.

Nothing must stand in the way of her desperate desire to put a universe of space and time between herself and the man in that rooftop room behind her.

Twice she lost herself in the unfamiliar warren of the Cerro. The second time she came upon the Xanja Canal and resolved to follow it down to the harbor. Once there, she could find her way to the Plaza de Armas easily enough, and from there up the hill to her father's house. It seemed unbelievably lovely and faraway to her now, her father's fine new house among the green parks and flowering gardens. But she would be there by sunup. She would be back in her own dim, lavender-smelling bed, with Marina bending over her. And then everything would be all right.

Tamar was walking wearily up the Street of Trades in the first yellow light of Sunday morning when she heard the thunder of a cannon shot from the harbor.

13

THE FIRST BROADSIDE CRASHED OUT AT DAWN, WITH THE *Roebuck* not more than two hundred yards off the Plaza de Armas and more than half the fleet already into the inner harbor in her wake.

A drowsy sentinel on the parapet of the Fuerza had seen them first, emerging like ghosts out of the morning mists that hung over the channel. He straightened up in astonishment at sight of the first sail, his halberd almost slipping from his fingers. He blinked, muttering darkly about the quality of the wine Ensign Barba had brought round the night before. But it was real—a white mountain of canvas moving majestically in across the·bay.

He opened his mouth to hail the ship, to warn her off till later, till officials could be summoned to receive her papers. She was much too.close in, he thought.

Then the first yellow finger of sun broke through the mists to reveal another ship, and another behind that. Sail beyond sail, ruffling in a smart crosswind. And even as the man on the ramparts stared with sudden terror, the lead vessel came slowly round, broadside on to the town. The sentinel had barely time to dive for cover behind the low parapet before flame spurted from the ship's dark flanks and the world exploded around him in flying earth, falling masonry, and cataracts of sound.

Ensign Barba himself came awake with a grunt, a wineskin clutched tenaciously in his left hand. His first groggy notion was that it must be an earthquake. He had been through one once, in Portugal, and he had never forgotten it.

He sat up, staggered to his feet. He had been sleeping in the antechamber of the Commander's quarters on the top floor of the Fuerza. Don Diego always left his lieutenant in command when he himself felt the need of a retreat to the Cerro for the night. Barba had been up late the night before himself, carousing with his comrades, and his mind was far from clear.

Then the second broadside hit the fortress, and this time the crash of the guns was unmistakable. There were shouts outside, and running feet. Barba dropped the wineskin and reached for his sword and breeches.

Fists pounded on the door.

"What is it, in God's name?" the squat Basque shouted, stuffing his shirt into the top of his padded slops.

"It's Drake!" a voice cried, unrecognizable with fear.

"Drake's dead," Barba answered, spitting the taste of last night's wine out upon the floor.

"It's Drake's ghost then!" wailed the man outside.

Barba was sliding back the bolt when the third shock hit.

The acrid smoke of the *Roebuck*'s guns eddied and thinned. As it cleared away from the towering aftercastle, Sir John Burrow strained his eyes to see more clearly.

In the first flat rays of the morning sun, he saw the squat silhouette of the Fuerza, dust and smoke already rising from its walls. Beyond, he could make out the twin towers of a cathedral church across the plaza, and an assortment of two-storied houses ringing the open space of the square. A substantial quay extended out into the bay under the guns of the fort, and there were several large stone buildings spreading away to left and right on either side of the plaza. Beyond these, the nondescript waterfront of the city stretched away, a panorama of white-walled warehouses and stone wharfs, with fishing smacks, lighters, and lesser craft moored close inshore. Not much different from Plymouth or the Deptford docks, really, save for the clusters of palms, the splashes of brightly colored flowers.

Impatiently, Burrow's eyes turned back to the more promising vistas of the Plaza de Armas.

"Would that be it, think you?" he asked Master Adam,

pointing. "Or that, the red-roofed building next to it?"

Burrow had spent many hours with the sailing master, going over their makeshift charts till he knew every lane and alleyway on the Havana waterfront. Or as many as were indicated with any degree of certainty. But there was the town itself before them now. Which of those white-walled, tile-roofed structures rising blankly from the seawall was in fact the Mecca of their dreams—the customs house at Havana?

Master Adam lowered his eyes from the rigging, where seamen were shortening sail as they prepared to bring the ship about. Squinting through the acrid powder smoke, he said simply, "The long red-tiled house in the shadow of the fort, I think, Captain. They would build it there, under the guns."

"Aye," said Sir John, nodding, "they would." He moved to the after rail under the big ship's lantern, staring back at the receding plaza. Part of his tactical mind noted with approval the broadside of the *Garland*, next in line, pounding the stone-walled fort. But most of his attention was given over to making mental corrections in their map, and to roughing out the inevitable assault.

He had hoped to avoid the bloody business of assaulting the city. But clearly, that must come now.

On the other side of Havana, Matthew Morgan and his men waded chest-deep through the moat, their pikes and arquebuses held well above their heads. They scrambled without much difficulty over the grassy terreplein, shored up here and there with timbers, that served in lieu of a wall. As they poured over the embankment, they saw a lone figure in a gleaming morion standing some distance down the long earthwork. The sentry was staring out over the roofs of the town toward the bay, the boom of the guns and the eddying drift of smoke. A guard from the nearest gate, thought Matthew. He gave him a cheerful wave.

The man in the shining helmet shouted a challenge, raising his heavy musket. But half a dozen of Morgan's men had already leveled their own arquebuses. The bang of the shots merged into one in the morning air, and the Spaniard tumbled over backward out of sight.

Morgan took a quick line of sight upon a nearby church tower as they dropped down the inside of the terreplein, the town's only fortification on the landward side. Then they were down into a labyrinth of narrow lanes, striding along between rows of palm-thatched, mud-walled shacks. Expressionless Indian women, black children, toothless old men squatting in doorways watched them as they passed.

And a glorious spectacle we must be too, thought Matthew with a gleam of Celtic humor.

Muddy to the eyes from many hours in the creeks and swamps west of the city, faces puffed with insect bites, the English privateers were an unprepossessing lot as they hurried through the broadening city streets. As the roads hardened from mud into pavement and the houses grew more impressive, dark-eyed girls came out on wrought-iron balconies to look down at them. One or two even pointed and laughed.

Matthew Morgan grinned back at them and hastened on his way toward the harbor, toward the distant sound of guns and shouting.

"My God," wheezed Don Gabriel de la Barca; "what is happening?" He flung himself off his lathered horse and almost fell into Barba's arms.

Around them, the Plaza de Armas swarmed with people. Smoke funneled up from the Fuerza, and men were running with buckets. On the sunlit waters of the bay a dozen ships, from pinnaces to mighty war galleons, were coming slowly about.

"They are English corsairs, your Excellency," answered Barba. "They have been bombarding the Fuerza for the better part of an hour." The ensign tried to keep the edge of contempt out of his voice. It was a fifteen-minute ride down from the Governor's house to the plaza. The rest of the preceding hour his Excellency must have spent dressing for the occasion in black velvets, shining boots, a snowy ruff.

"But the Morro!" the stricken Governor gasped. "Texeda swore not a ship would ever pass that veiled not her flag to the Morro Castle! And I heard not so much as a challenge gun!"

"They slit every throat in the castle," said Barba disgustedly. "Slipped up in the dark and did for every man. A slave boy only, that slept under a shed outside the fortress, got away and brought us word." He shifted the twelve-foot pike on which he leaned from one hand to the other, and spat on the paving stones. "Would God Texeda and that cursed Italian engineer had been in the Morro too last night, to be stabbed to death in their shirts!"

"My God," said Don Gabriel again. And then, with a helpless glance out toward the bay: "But what will they do now?"

Ensign Barba shrugged. "Come back on the opposite tack, probably," he said, "and lay their larboard broadsides on the Fuerza. Then they'll cast off their ships' boats and come for us."

The Governor drew a deep breath, straightened his shoulders, and looked around him at the swarming plaza. "What steps have been taken to repel them?" he demanded in a firmer voice.

"Señor Rojas, Señor Ynestrosa, and some of the other gentlemen whose houses front on the plaza have set men to work building barricades. They are using timbers left over from the new customs house, and paving stones pried up from the square. Many citizens have come with swords or fowling pieces." Barba gestured toward the mob milling noisily around them. "They await only your Excellency's orders," he added, without irony.

"Of course," said the Governor. "Of course."

"The Fuerza we can hold for a time, I think," Barba went on. "The parapets are too low to protect our cannon, and they have all been smashed off their carriages. But the walls are thick enough, and there is plenty of ball and powder. I have ordered preparations to withstand an assault by push of pike."

"*You* have ordered?" said Don Gabriel sharply. "Where is Don Diego, then? Where is Captain Aguilar, the Commander of the Fuerza?" He couldn't even remember the name of this lieutenant, this menial he was talking to. Where was the famous man-hunter, now that they needed him so desperately?

"Captain Aguilar, your Excellency?" Barba licked his lips. "Captain Aguilar is surveying the seawall and the harbor front. Preparing a counterthrust if the English should manage a foothold on the shore."

"Ah, yes. Quite right, no doubt," said Don Gabriel. "Though I wish he had arranged matters here first," he added petulantly, "before he went riding off to survey the harbor front."

Nevertheless, the Governor thought, things did not look so hopeless after all. There were hundreds of men in the plaza already, most of them armed. Rojas and his neighbors had every servant and slave they could find sweating over their makeshift barricades, and the rough beams were waist-high along the bay already. The Fuerza itself and the new customs house near it looked remarkably sturdy and defensible in the bright morning sun.

Out in the harbor, the leading galleons of the English squadron had come about and were standing in toward shore once again, the opposite broadside presented toward the town.

"How many men do you think they will send ashore?" Don Gabriel asked.

Barba squinted out over the sundazzle on the bay. "Three hundred, perhaps," he said. "They do not have the boats for more, in the first wave anyway. And many, of course, must stay aboard to handle the ships."

"Three hundred!" The Governor's enthusiasm suddenly soared. "Why, we'll have a thousand men in the plaza before they reach shore! We'll cut them to pieces at the tide line! And I personally," he announced with a sudden burst of inspiration, "will direct the defense of the Fuerza in Captain Aguilar's absence!"

Barba nodded dubiously. "Still," he said, "it would be better if they had not smashed our cannon, so that we might sink their boats before they came ashore."

"Lieutenant," said Don Gabriel de la Barca, his moustaches quivering slightly, "you will please hold my horse. I will mount and speak to the crowd. The citizens shall hear their orders from their Governor's own lips!"

Murrain Pikestaff, the English master gunner, scarcely believed it when he peered through a gunport and saw the mob swarming to the loosely built barricades of stone and timber that faced the bay. A fat hidalgo on a horse seemed to be waving them on with magnificent flourishes of his sword.

The English flagship stood not a hundred yards off the plaza. Pikestaff's larboard gun crews bent to their pieces, glowing matches hovering over their touchholes. With the cannons on the Fuerza silenced, Master Adam was bringing the whole fleet in to point-blank range. Ship after ship they came on, up along the crowded waterfront, every gunport open, every cannon and culverin double-charged.

And there the fools were, parading out like trainbands on a holiday, to take their places behind their ramshackle barricades!

The long-jawed master gunner's eyes narrowed. "Ready to fire on the roll, mates," he crooned to the smoke-darkened faces down the long, low-raftered gundeck. "Never mind the fort—fire low for the little wall they've thrown up there, where all the sticks and swords are waving." A barricade no more than waist-high—and not a man of them was crouching

down behind it. Murrain Pikestaff shook his head in disbelief. Then the ship tilted slowly on the next long roll, and
he gave the word to fire.

Sir John Burrow felt the deck shudder beneath him as the
guns bellowed and the Plaza de Armas disappeared once
more in gritty clouds of cannon smoke. Before the deck had
steadied under him, he was moving.

He shouted an order, wheeled, and raced down the rake
of the quarterdeck. With astonishing ease for so big a man,
he vaulted the pinrail into the crowded waist below. Moments later, he was over the side and into the longboat that
waited under the starboard guns, out of sight of the town.
The longboat was bristling with men and weapons.

"Cast off!" he called brusquely. They floated free, rocking
in the wake of the great warship, already moving away from
them. Oars reached out, and then they were driving through
a thinning fog of gunsmoke toward the shore.

Burrow shifted the steel corselet on his chest and leaned
forward to see. The smoke dissolved; the silent fort swam
into view. He saw the barricades, jagged holes already blown
through them, men staggering away. And just to the left of
the Fuerza, there was the windowless white-plastered building with the red roof that they had come so far to find.

Sir John slid his four-foot rapier from its sheath and laid
it across his knees.

"Pull for the red tiles on yonder roof, men," he called.
"Yonder where the sun strikes, and turns it all to gold!"

The freebooters gave a scattered cheer and leaned to their
oars. Behind them, a second broadside roared out as the
next English ship pulled abreast of the plaza. Shot whispered over their heads, and Burrow saw more holes open up
in the enemy's defenses, and heard more shouts and screams.

The point-blank broadsides smashed the makeshift barricades into kindling wood. Some of the last vessels to pass

charged their guns with chain shot and canister, which whistled across the open square like a high wind, strewing the plaza with broken men. Each vessel dropped its ship's boat as it made its pass, so that new landing parties emerged almost from the rising smoke of each broadside, before any counterattack could be organized by the demoralized defenders.

Within minutes, the freebooters were spilling over the docks and the seawall, charging through the shattered barricades into the Plaza de Armas.

Even so, Ensign Barba might have made a fight of it. He rallied hundreds of retreating citizens in the streets around the cathedral, just across from the Fuerza. Newcomers, who had not felt the English artillery, swelled their numbers and bolstered their courage. Barba led them back into the plaza, charging in their turn down upon the corsairs, three pikes to one, with the holy names of half the saints in the Calendar on their lips.

But the freebooters absorbed the shock, recoiled only a pace or two, and held.

Sir John's tall figure towered in the van, legs wide-planted, wielding a halberd snatched from a fallen Spaniard. His eyes were steady, his voice calm as he shouted encouragement to the men around him. Off to his right, he glimpsed the young Earl of Westmorland, his left arm running scarlet, thrusting wildly with his sword and dedicating every stroke to God and Her Majesty the Queen. On his left, a scarred old soldier hissed a steady stream of blasphemies as he parried with his pike. Burrow grinned, glad to have the pikeman on his weaker side.

Nevertheless, Barba might have held them.

Then Matthew Morgan and his company came hurtling out of a side street at the corner of the square and fell upon the backs of the defenders. Matthew's ruddy old cheeks flamed, his eyes were beacons of blue fire as he charged, roaring the battle cry of "Burrow! A Burrow! God and Saint

George!" He would have shouted for Satan's very self, thought John Burrow, if the hosts of Hell were good enough fighting men, and the Archangel on his metal that day!

In fifteen minutes, the heart of Havana was in English hands.

"NOT HERE!" SAID MATTHEW MORGAN, STEPPING OUT THROUGH the broken doors of the customs house. "Hides and dye-woods, tobacco leaves and sugarcane in bales, all stamped with the royal treasurer's seal, ready for shipping. But not a bar of silver. Not a maravedi's worth of gold!"

Others of the freebooters clumped down from the second story, shouting that there were living quarters up there, but no sign of treasure.

Sir John Burrow stood in the sunshine, his rapier in his hand, his face rigid as though carved from marble, and felt the world come apart around him.

"It's a fat town, Captain," said Morgan, resting a hand on his shoulder. "Fat and ripe for picking. The men are into the big houses around the square already. And those fine gentlemen yonder"—he nodded toward a hesitant little group of paunchy, silver-haired hidalgos under a catawba tree nearby—"those gentlemen will be the alderman and magistrates, I'll warrant. Come to offer a sweet ransom to save their town from pillaging."

No doubt they would promise one, thought Burrow. But they could not have it ready in an hour. And they would soon begin to realize that he could not stay a week—not safely stay a day—to receive it. Word of the raid would be spreading through the island at that moment, as fast as an Indian could run or a Spaniard ride. The privateers must take what they could find and be gone, before they had half Cuba down upon their backs.

He had wagered everything upon a quick, clean stroke. And he had lost.

He could hear the whispers already, echoing in his head: *Burrow's luck again! He's a star-crossed man—Fortune's fool. Fortune's fool, and no mistake.*

"Captain," said a voice at Burrow's elbow, "this will be the royal treasurer, one Rojas by name." It was Master Adam, holding a grey-bearded hidalgo by the arm. "He's the fat one yonder's brother," the sailing master continued, nodding curtly at a corpulent gentleman who was evidently the leader of the little group of provincial grandees clustered under guard in the shade of the tree nearby.

"Is it so, then, Master Adam?" said Burrow. He managed a rueful smile. "But we've little need of his treasurership now, I think. We've already paid his customs house a visit without his by-your-leave."

"Aye, sir," said Adam quietly. "And yet I think it would be well to speak a word or two with this gentleman about his customs house and what is stored there."

"And why would that be, Master Adam?"

"Why, Captain, I was standing near him when Master Morgan came out a moment since. And while I speak the language only passably, yet I would swear that these Rojas brothers were more astonished than I was when Matthew Morgan came out without a chest full of gold on his back."

For perhaps a dozen heartbeats, Burrow said nothing at all. He stood looking at the nervous Spanish greybeard, only half hearing the shouted orders, the groans and lamentations from the plaza around him. Then he spoke, slowly and deliberately.

"Master Adam," he said quietly, "will ye ask the royal treasurer if those be his quarters above the customs house here?"

The sailing master posed the question. The Spaniard stared at him, then understood and answered with a stiff affirmative.

"He says they are, Sir John."

"Why, take him up to his own quarters, then, Master Adam," said Burrow, "and I'll follow. Master Morgan, you bring along the other Señor Rojas—the wheezing bladder under the tree, I understand." The captain general laid a hand on the shoulder of a passing English mariner. "You, lad! Fetch me Captain Thynne, and Captain Cross if he's back from the Morro. And quickly, if you please."

There was hope for them yet, by God!

Tamar found that day a more terrible nightmare than the night before.

Her first reaction to the crash of the cannon at dawn was an immediate, childish impulse to go and see what it was. She actually plucked up her muddied skirts and hurried toward the Plaza de Armas, away from her father's house. The second deafening roar, however, slowed her steps appreciably. This did not sound like military exercise on a Sunday afternoon.

Then a ragged mendicant, whose normal post was in front of the cathedral in the plaza, came lurching awkwardly up the street toward her. The girl stopped where she was, staring at him. The beggar went skittering past her, hopping and skipping on a crippled leg which, she had always been given to understand, was totally unusable.

"What is it?" she called after him. "Why are they firing the guns at the Fuerza?"

"It is not the Fuerza," the ragged old man called back in a high, hysterical voice. "It is the corsairs!" He reeled into a narrow side street and was gone.

The corsairs.

The terrors of Tamar's childhood flashed through her mind. She remembered with a rush all the tales she had ever heard about the corsairs. Bloodthirsty robbers, depraved heretics all of them, French, Dutch, or English. Ravishers of women, burners of churches. And now they were here, here in Havana! The girl stood rooted to the spot, watching an eddy of smoke rising from behind the whitewashed building on the corner.

And yet, beneath the childish horrors, another thrill shot through her. It was sheer, perverse exhilaration, a surge of excitement that for that moment wiped away all her weariness and misery.

Until this past night, this present morning, Tamar de la Barca had never known a moment of real danger. There was a part of her now that simply could not believe that the thunder and the smoke at the other end of the street could actually snuff out her life in an instant. A part of her that thrilled to the sheer excitement of it, as oblivious of consequences as she had been the night before when she followed Marina through the narrow, raucous streets of the Cerro. She was the Governor of Cuba's daughter, after all. Nothing could really happen to her.

It was only when she put the thought into words that she recognized it for what it was—the same delusion that had led her to her ruin not twelve hours before.

Then, perhaps ten yards ahead of her, an old adobe wall exploded into the street.

Fragments of clay brick flew past her, stinging her cheek. In an instant, the narrow street was half clogged with debris, the air thick with swirling dust. Tamar stood staring at a ball of iron no bigger than an orange lying half buried in the rubble. The sound buffeted her ears.

So small a thing, she thought, so unimpressive. Yet that lump of flying metal had pulverized a wall that had withstood the hurricanes of half a century. She approached it, reached out and touched it. She jerked her hand away. It was still hot.

The street was filling with people now, screaming, running. Tamar was choking on smoke as well as dust. She looked dazedly around her.

Faces she had known all her life swept past her, distorted with fear or anger. She was jostled, thrust to the wall. A man ran past her in his nightshirt, dragging an ancient pike. A woman rushed by with a squalling child under one arm and a loaf of bread under the other. Then the next ear-numbing crash of artillery blotted out all other sounds. Tiles rained silently into the street.

Tamar herself was running now, back up the lane, away from the plaza, away from the guns. She ran desperately, blindly, fleeing once more toward the safety of her father's house.

In the ornately furnished quarters of the royal treasurer above the customs house, the interrogation was short and to the point.

"Tell them both," said Burrow to Master Adam, "that they will answer all questions precisely and without caviling. Tell them that if their answers are not satisfactory, Master Morgan will begin with the oil and proceed to the knife."

"Ustedes deben responder . . ."

Don Geronimo Rojas paled when he understood. But he answered pithily, in short, sharp phrases, his plump cheeks puckering at every explosive syllable.

"He says, Captain, that they are Castilian gentlemen, and not to be treated like galley slaves or convicts."

"Tell him," said Burrow, "that Master Morgan will now proceed to heat the oil."

"What shall we do?" the royal treasurer asked his brother, tugging at his salt-and-pepper beard, speaking in rapid, nervous Spanish.

Don Geronimo looked at the hard, foreign faces of the English. Through the grilled window at his back came the sounds of weeping women, the odor of wounds thick in the noonday sun. The blood was up in the English faces around them still, he knew. The lust for violence that was so foreign to his own calculating soul.

The head of the house of Rojas shrugged and answered his brother's question without a tremor: "We shall tell them what they want to know."

Sir John Burrow, whose Spanish was in fact at least as adequate as Master Adam's, heard and understood, though he betrayed his understanding by not so much as a quiver of an eyebrow. He asked his first question through his translator, and the Rojases answered.

The caravels that regularly brought the bullion shipments from Porto Bello and Vera Cruz had done so as usual this year, they told him. Treasurer Rojas himself had received every peso's worth in the King's name. All had been stored away in the customs house belowstairs to await the coming of the war galleons that would carry the treasure across the Atlantic. But the galleons had never come. Instead, there was a *cédula* from Spain, a royal order that the fleet was not to sail. The gold, the silver, the pearls from the Panama pearl fisheries and the rest of it had therefore remained where they were, in the locked and bolted storerooms down those very stairs, to await next year's sailing in the spring.

But now it was all gone, Burrow pointed out, his face expressionless.

But now it was gone. Treasurer Rojas was as nonplussed as the English were. He paused a moment to confer with Don Geronimo. There was only one person, he continued carefully then, who could possibly know any more about it.

"And that is?" said Burrow, speaking suddenly in Spanish.

"That is His Excellency the Governor of Cuba," replied the royal treasurer precisely.

"Where shall we find his Excellency?"

"I—we did not see. There was so much confusion when the plaza was overrun—"

"Your answer, Master Treasurer," said Burrow coldly, "is not acceptable."

The Rojas brothers consulted once more, whispering now. Then Don Geronimo himself shrugged slightly once again, moistened his lips, and spoke.

"I believe, sir, that His Excellency the Governor sought refuge in the Fuerza when the Plaza de Armas itself was overrun. Since your men have been in occupation of the plaza ever since, I must assume that his Excellency is in the Fuerza still."

CHAPTER

15

TAMAR STOOD STRICKEN IN THE ORANGE LIGHT THAT FLOODED through the tall open windows of her chamber.

"My father," she said in amazement and disbelief, "is down there—in *that*?" She gestured toward the window and the town below, the caldron of violence from which she had just pulled herself to safety.

"He went down this morning," said Marina woodenly, settling a fresh shift over her mistress's clean white shoulders. "He has not yet come back."

So the nightmare is not ended after all, thought Tamar. It goes on and on. She swayed slightly and crossed herself, praying for strength.

It had been a day as terrifying as the night before, and as punishing to her weary body. The crowds, blind first with outrage, then with fear, had swept her helplessly up one familiar lane and down another. Unrecognized in her coarse servant's gown, she had been shoved and cursed through streets where she had ridden like a princess only the day before. Once she had almost blundered into a roving band of the corsairs themselves, terrible sun-browned men with long pikes and leather jerkins whose laughter had followed her as she fled up the nearest alleyway. It was late afternoon before, wading through the back gardens of native shacks and clambering over the low wall of the Governor's private park, she had stumbled at last through her own garden gate —to find Marina waiting, and her father gone.

But she had not known that her father was gone until this· moment.

Marina had had a weary, brutal time of it herself. Stunned and bruised by the fall down Don Diego's rickety staircase, she had yet risen and tried to climb back up to help her mistress. She had not had the strength. With a silent groan, she had hobbled out the door and set off in search of aid.

She had expected no help in the Cerro, none in fact closer than the Governor's house, where she would be recognized and her wild story believed. But her injuries had included a badly twisted ankle, so that she had proceeded with agonizing slowness through the labyrinth of palm-board and adobe shacks, then among solider houses of rubble or stone across Havana. The sky had begun to pale in the east by the time she left the city behind and began the climb to the Governor's mansion on the hill. She had heard the first boom of the corsairs' guns as she laid a gnarled brown hand on the garden gate.

She tried desperately to get to see the Governor during that next hour. But the whole house was in an uproar; Don Gabriel himself had been far too busy to see his daughter's duenna on any pretext whatever. She had finally slipped secretly into his Excellency's privy chamber—only to be informed by an indignant valet that the Governor was at that moment mounting his horse at the front gate to ride down and take personal command of the defense of the city.

There had been nothing for Marina to do but wait. This she had done. Now her mistress had been restored to her, brutalized, terrified, but alive. Alive in a city where many now were dead. Marina had given thanks to the gods and spirits of her people, and to the God of the Christians too, and set to work to wash and bind up the slender, restless young body that had been the center of her life for almost twenty years. Only now had she seen fit to tell her mistress that her father was not there.

"But where is he?" Tamar blurted out. "What can he do down there? The—the soldiers should do that! The men from the Morro and the Fuerza—not the Governor!"

Marina hesitated a moment, then spoke. "They say, my lady, that he is in the Fuerza."

"In the Fuerza?"

"Yes, my lady. Most of the soldiers were driven out of the city by the corsairs this morning. Some stayed in the fort

and held it against the English. They are still there, with
your father in command. So the men say, at least, that have
been down in the town." Fastening the petticoats about her
mistress's slim waist, she noticed that the girl was trembling
once more.

"He can't stay there," Tamar faltered. "They have cannon." She remembered vividly the exploding wall, and the
round lump of iron lying in the ruins. "They will blow the
Fuerza to pieces."

"His Excellency knows what is best," said Marina quietly,
reaching for the gown lying spread out across the brocaded
bed. "It is not for us to question."

"No!" said Tamar sharply. "Not that gown. The new black
satin—quickly, please."

The wiry Indian woman straightened slowly, looking at
her.

Tamar de la Barca drew a deep breath, summoning all the
reserves of energy and courage left in her young body. "I
must go down to my father," she said simply. "And I must
be worthy of him when I go."

Don Gabriel de la Barca had reached the height of his
peroration when the first crash of the English guns brought
his horse down screaming under him. In moments, the
cheering crowd of his fellow townsmen had turned into a
terrified mob. Lost amid flying fragments of the barricade,
running men, and the horrifying whir of grapeshot, the
Governor had fled with the rest of them, as desperate now
for shelter as any bewildered Indian or slave.

Chance had swept him under the walls of the Fuerza. Blind
fear had driven him through its gates.

The soldiers, stunned by the renewed thunder of the
English cannon, were just swinging the heavy portals shut
when his Excellency stumbled out of swirling brick dust and
flying splinters through the door. They scarcely recognized
him as he burst through, his plumed hat gone, his thin hair
wild, dust and a smear of blood across one plump cheek.

His moustaches trembled as he shouted some unintelligible order and blundered off up the narrow stair to the quarters reserved for the captain of the fortress.

Once safely ensconced in the Commander's empty rooms, however, Don Gabriel felt his furiously beating heart slow to a more regular rhythm, his mind begin to clear. He even experienced a first tremulous return of confidence, despite the continuing roar of the artillery outside.

The walls of the Fuerza were old but stout, and he knew it was well provisioned. They could easily hold out here for days. And long before that, all the soldiers in the island would be buzzing about these ragged freebooters. The pirates would flee, the fortress would be delivered, and His Excellency the Governor, who had held against all odds, would be the hero of the hour! Let Rojas and the rest of them try to pull him down then!

He was so busy meditating on the political possibilities that he scarcely heard the shouting of the English as they charged across the plaza. He witnessed no part of the fighting, and did not deign to look out through a narrow window slit as the corsairs established themselves as masters of the heart of his city. This military catastrophe, he was more and more convinced, could yet be his own political deliverance.

He was smoothing down his tiny moustaches and just beginning to feel almost sanguine about it when there came a knock at the bolted door.

"Yes?" the Governor called, his usual note of ebullient confidence vibrating once more in his voice.

"Your Excellency, the English wish to speak with you."

"To speak with me?" His tone was lofty with contempt. "And what have I to say to those scourings of the sea?" A good phrase, he thought. He must remember it when he was asked about the affair later, when it was all over.

"They say, your Excellency, that they wish to discuss the honorable surrender of the fort."

Don Gabriel swung open the door into the narrow corridor and glared at the men outside—a corporal in a dented breastplate, and two soldiers with pikes. From somewhere belowstairs in that dripping limestone pile, there came the shriek of a wounded man as his injury was dressed.

"Surrender?" The Governor's voice rose, as though he were addressing a far more sizable audience. "Surrender to the English pirates? Tell the corsairs that the Governor of Cuba does not propose to hand over his sword to a ragtag band of freebooters. Tell them—the Fuerza stands!"

"Yes, your Excellency," said the corporal without emotion.

The Fuerza stands! By God, thought Don Gabriel, he would see to it that the King himself heard that phrase!

The shadows were long in the Plaza de Armas by the time they got the stubby thirty-two-pounder set up, leveled point-blank at the heavy wooden gates of the Fuerza. Burrow stepped out of the customs house into the orange light of evening and walked around the fringe of the square toward the cannon and the crowd of townspeople that had gathered near it, in front of the cathedral. The storming party was grouped in the vestibule of the church, joking and passing leather wineskins around. At the potgun's breech stood Murrain Pikestaff, the master gunner from the *Roebuck,* with an unlit match in one hand and a wineskin in the other.

"Is your weapon charged and primed, Master Pikestaff?" said Sir John, with the easy informality of a commander who knew his men.

"Charged and primed and ready to fire, Captain," the gunner answered. His long, stubbly chin was wet with wine, and his eyes had a dark glitter in them. He was a man who had lost two brothers in the wars and had a score to settle with the dons.

"And you, lads?" he called to the storming party, who now came crowding out of the arched portal into the square. "Are ye ready to clean out the last kennelful of dons in Havana?"

There was a muted rumble of acquiescence. The morning's fighting fever still churned in their bellies, Burrow knew. They would do their jobs.

He gave them a wave and turned to his sailing master, looking oddly out of place among the pikemen in his carefully brushed doublet and hose of black broadcloth. "Master Adam," he said briskly, "we'll give yon fortress a final hail now, if you please. Tell them they may march out with their swords at their sides and banners uncased," he added with a grin. Nothing mattered more to the dons, he knew, than such tickle points of honor.

The two of them walked out into the Plaza de Armas. The wounded and the dead of the morning had all been dragged or carried off, and the plaza was empty but for dark smears here and there, an empty boot, a crumpled hat. Burrow stopped, a magnificent target from boots to battered breastplate to the plume that swayed on his own bright steel morion. "Tell them," he said.

"*Señores!*" Adam called toward the grey stone pile of fortress, the vertical slits of windows with their invisible watching eyes, their weapons charged and primed. "*El capitán Burrow dice—*"

No one showed himself on the ramparts of the fort. But the answer came: "*Su excelencia el gobernador declara que la Fuerza no se renda.*" The shouted words echoed flat and without emotion across the plaza, the words of a soldier obeying orders, passing no judgments on even the most foolish commands of his superiors.

Burrow did not require a translation this time. "Tell them," he said, "that if they will not surrender the fortress, we will have the honor of taking it."

In the deepening shadows of the church front, Murrain Pikestaff's long match was glowing now.

"Remember, mates," said Matthew Morgan, above the rattle of weapons, the whisper of swords sliding from their scabbards, "His Excellency the Governor must be taken alive for the captain's questioning." There was a grin and a guffaw here and there among the dirty beards, the greasy leather hauberks. But they knew he meant it. They would bring the Governor at least alive out of the crumbling ancient pile of stone before them.

Sir John Burrow squinted up at the sky, sunset orange now over the rooftops of the town, and then strode back to the waiting cannon. He had just raised his hand to give the signal to Murrain Pikestaff when one of the townspeople grouped around them cried out and pointed. Burrow swung back toward the Fuerza.

He did not believe what he saw.

16

TAMAR SAT VERY STRAIGHT, SIDESADDLE ON HER SLEEK BAY mare. She was dressed in her newest black satin gown, touched with a froth of lace at wrist and throat. There was a gleam of pearl in her high-piled hair. Her cheeks were pale, but her lips were firmly compressed, her chin high. Just behind her and to her left rode Marina, a gaunt figure on a grey mule.

They had entered the plaza from one side and had ridden out almost to the center of that no-man's-land between the cathedral and the Fuerza before anyone had even noticed them. Now the two women had turned their mounts. They were riding at a dignified pace straight toward the curious, half-drunken crowd, the assault force assembled before the church. Riding, quite literally, straight into the cannon's mouth.

"*Dios!*" gasped a Spanish onlooker, and an Englishman muttered a more explicit oath.

Tamar rode straight onward, toward the snout of the leveled potgun and the glittering eyes of the gunner behind the glowing match. She rode as in a dream toward the forest of pikes and the gleaming swords of the freebooters, the terrible invaders from the sea.

The tallest of them moved suddenly, issued a command. She understood no word of it, but it was clearly an order. He stretched out one long arm toward the artilleryman with the glowing splint in his hand. The gunner, his hollow eyes fixed upon the girl, did not answer his commander. The match still hovered, flickering red-orange in the shadows, over the touchhole of the gun.

Tamar had no clear idea why she was doing it. She only knew that they were about to fire upon her father, that she must stop it somehow. And that whatever she did, she must do it with a dignity worthy of her father's rank and station in their little island world.

But she could not take her eyes off the glowing match.

Then the tall man stepped round behind the cannon, took the match from the gunner's hand, and thrust it into a bucket of water standing near the pile of shot. A moment later, a running crowd of her own people closed around her, calling her name.

Some were shouting warnings, some were laughing drunkenly. Tamar saw one old woman weeping and crossing herself. An instant later, she felt a thrill of panic and jerked her foot away as someone fumbled with her jeweled slipper. Behind her, she heard Marina hiss *"Borracho!"* and then a yelp of pain.

Then the tall captain of the corsairs came thrusting through the crowd with a wedge of pikemen at his back. His large hand caught her horse's bridle, and he looked up at her.

She saw a long, ugly foreign face, dark as an Indian's with sun and wind, with a pale scar running down one side of it. The features were rude, the beard ill cut. The wide mouth had an arrogant, half-amused look. But the eyes that gazed up into hers were chips of grey granite, inflexible and cold. It was the face of a man who might do anything, she thought. A man to whom no horror was impossible.

Almost at once, he proved her right.

John Burrow had seen beautiful women in his life. Country lasses with the bloom of first youth still on their cheeks. Court ladies whose beauty—Puritan moralists to the contrary—was considerably enhanced by art. But he had never seen so lovely a creature in his life as this Castilian lady riding toward him across the square. He savored her beauty even as he realized that it did not—could not—matter a groatsworth to him at that moment.

For he had heard the shouts of her people and caught the name they shouted. And even as he put his hand upon her bridle, he had a plan to put this unexpected windfall to good use.

"Lady de la Barca, I understand?" he said, fitting his rough northern tongue as carefully as he could to the Spanish words. "Am I correct?"

"I am Doña Isabel de la Barca." Her voice was clear and wintry. She was not giving an inch, he thought with grudging admiration.

"You are the daughter of the *adelantado* of this island?"

"My father is His Excellency Don Gabriel de la Barca, Governor of Cuba." Her back seemed to straighten even further at the rendition of her father's titles, the remembrance of her place.

"You hear, Master Morgan?" said Burrow in English. "Own daughter to the Governor himself." The burly, grey-haired man at his shoulder grinned up at the girl. "I think," Sir John went on, "that his Excellency will be more than interested to know that his daughter is here among us. Would you not say so, Matthew?"

"Aye, I've no doubt." His lieutenant chuckled. "Shall I summon Master Adam?"

"Do so, Matthew, by all means." Then, looking up: "*Con su permiso*, my lady," he said, and led her horse back into the shadow of the church, where the cannon and the company of freebooters still waited.

It was not till she heard Master Adam's voice hailing the fortress that Tamar realized what was happening.

"The captain general's compliments to His Excellency the Governor, and he wishes to inform him—" the sailing master paused, seeking the words, "to inform him that his Excellency's daughter is unharmed in our hands. That his daughter is here, as a hostage for His Honor the Governor's immediate surrender of the fortress and of his own person into the captain general's hands."

Master Adam's Spanish came out terse and oddly clipped,

even harder to follow than the tall commander's. But Tamar had understood.

The English captain general, the man they called Sir-John, had led the girl, still seated sidesaddle on her glossy mount, up the wide steps of the cathedral and had turned her to face the Fuerza. Where she would be in plain sight —she understood that now. Where her father might see her clearly and know that the corsairs spoke the truth. That their crudely implied threat was not an idle one.

She had come to save her father, and the English pirate had made her the instrument of his undoing.

The tall Englishman still stood close beside her horse's head, not a yard away. Tamar twisted in her saddle and swung her short riding crop round in a savage arc. The blow caught him just behind the ear, sent him staggering halfway down the steps, one hand rising to the scarlet welt that rose instantly across the back of his neck and ear.

When he turned upon her, his dark eyes were as hot with murder as the eyes of the man behind the cannon had been.

"How could any cavalier that calls himself a gentleman use a lady of rank in this way? As a token in a wretched pirate's trade?" Her eyes glistened with outrage and help-lessness. For even as she spoke, she could see the great double barred portals of the Fuerza swing slowly open and her father's portly, unprepossessing figure step out into the square.

"What would you prefer, my lady?" the corsair captain answered, his eyes cooling, the tightness in his cheeks relax-ing with a powerful effort of will. "That we blow in the gates and put your father's soldiers to the sword? Or that we barter his daughter for a score of lives? If we had asked you, lady—which would you have chosen?"

Tamar watched her father approaching, grimy and almost pathetic, at the head of his bedraggled troops.

"I should have chosen to see your own blood spilled across these paving stones, English pirate!" she answered in a voice that quivered with emotion. "As I shall see it, God grant, before you leave these shores."

Sir John Burrow shrugged and turned away to receive the Governor's surrender. But he felt the fierceness of her hatred in the burning of the welt across his neck, the echo of her words across the back of his mind.

17

SIR JOHN BURROW SANK INTO A CHAIR BEHIND THE COMMANDER of the Fuerza's own writing table, laid one booted leg across the corner of the table, and turned cold eyes upon his prisoner. Master Adam stood vigilantly on his right. Matthew Morgan lounged somewhat more casually on his other side. Don Gabriel stood hatless before him, with a guard on either side.

The Governor stared into the savage faces around him. The uncombed beards, the dented breastplates, the merciless blue eyes of the Englishmen filled him with dismay. Surrounded by barbarians, he felt the courage he had so carefully built up in this very room not an hour since evaporate completely.

"I have the honor," he began in an unsteady voice, "to be his Majesty's appointed Governor of the Province of Cuba, in the Audencia of San Domingo and the Viceroyalty of New Spain. I demand—I insist—"

"Ask him," said Sir John harshly, "where is the gold and silver that was in the customs house?"

Master Adam translated crisply, listened coldly to the answer, spoken in a halting monotone. "He says," he translated then, "that it is gone from the island. That it was dispatched on a carrack for Seville."

"Tell him that we know very well that his Majesty has forbidden any ship to sail from the Spanish Indies this year."

Again the crisp translation, the broken, toneless reply.

"He says that that is so, but that this carrack—this carrack was not from the Spanish Indies at all, but from the East. From Goa or Calecut, he is not sure. But being from the East, it was not under the ban, and so did sail, carrying all the treasure stored in the customs house to the House of Trade in Seville."

Burrow looked at the white perspiring face of the man before him. The cheeks trembled, the eyes were bruised and helpless, the eyes of a rabbit in a trap. Surely this was a face that could not lie to him now.

"Ask him when the carrack sailed," he said shortly. "And by what route."

"He says—ten days ago, or slightly less. He does not know by what route. He is not a seaman by trade, and does not understand these matters."

Matthew moved restlessly at Sir John's shoulder, fingering the poniard stuck through his belt. "There was a great ship here ten days since," he said doubtfully, "when we spied out the harbor. But for the rest of it—" He shrugged his beefy shoulders.

Burrow tugged at his beard. It was a wild tale. Too wild to be true. Yet too wild also for a man so totally in terror of his life to invent. What was he to believe?

The seconds lengthened into minutes as he sat there, weighing words and possibilities. The Governor swayed slightly on his feet.

Sir John knew he should be outside, securing his defenses, keeping the men from drifting away through the town. Sentries must be set, most of the men returned to the ships for the night. But the treasure, the treasure of the great Plate Fleet was almost within his grasp. He could not let it go now.

"Confine his Excellency to the guardroom below with his daughter," he snapped to Matthew Morgan finally. He rose briskly as he spoke. "Master Adam, you and I must look further into this matter of the carrack from the East. When did it sail, what was its route and destination. And then," he added with a hard look at the Governor, "we shall speak again with His Excellency of Cuba."

Tamar sat on a damp stone bench in a corner of the guardroom with Marina by her side. She sat in almost total darkness. There was a smell of moldy straw in her nostrils, and of human excrement from the privy across the room. Her fine satin gown was wrinkled and damp as the stone wall against her back. Her head sagged repeatedly onto her chest, overwhelmed by a greater weariness than any she had known in all her twenty years of life.

Fires glowed in the plaza outside the barred windows. Shouts of song and drunken laughter pulsed against her ears. Fighting exhaustion, she rose and went over to the nearest window.

"Oh, Marina!" she said, staring out, the ruddy light reflecting on her face.

Havana seemed to have been transformed in a few hours from a dusty colonial capital into a garish gypsy camp. There were cook fires and bonfires in every street. Huge blazes had been kindled in the Plaza de Armas itself, and she could see people dancing wildly around them. The great houses around the square were being stripped and looted, and one at least —the Ynestrosa mansion—was on fire as well.

Tamar watched one of the English corsairs reel past her window, drunk and roaring, one arm around a *mestiza* strumpet, the other about a black washerwoman. A ragged Spaniard danced along behind, offering *"Señor Inglés"* even more delectable entertainment in a wheedling singsong.

Tamar shuddered. "But why do they do it, Marina?" she asked helplessly. "Why do they dance and revel with their conquerors?"

The Indian woman hesitated a moment, then said in her usual expressionless voice, "It is hard for some of the people to tell their conquerors from their governors, my lady." It was not a judgment—simply a statement of fact.

The Spanish girl turned toward her servant, scarcely comprehending. At that moment, keys rattled in the lock.

The door swung open on the torchlit corridor. The burly grey-haired man who was the English commander's chief lieutenant appeared briefly, pushing a hunched figure before him. He thrust the man into the guardroom and slammed the door to. It was a long moment before Tamar even recognized in that dazed, woebegone figure the ebullient, all-powerful father in whose shadow she had lived all her life. Then she rushed to him and took him in her arms.

"Tamar," he said in a cracked, uncertain voice, using the nickname he almost never used. "Tamar, my daughter, I—"

"Don't talk," she answered fiercely, helping him to the bench. "Sit here. Marina and I will take care of everything." It was all wrong, all backward, that she should care for him, that she should be the strong one, and he broken. But it was no more bewildering than everything else on this unreal day.

With what strength remained to her, she began to minister to her father's needs.

Don Diego Aguilar waited at an outlying hacienda, on the coast road out of town, for the arrival of the Santiago garrison. Ensign Barba sat with him in the absent owner's dining hall, sipping his wine, talking little.

They had rallied the survivors of the Havana garrisons in the cane fields east of the city and had brought them here. Armed men from all the neighboring plantations had been gathering there all night. Once the mounted troops from Santiago arrived, they would have a formidable force indeed.

Meantime, Aguilar had sent his hide-hunters in. At that very moment, he knew, they would be slipping up the unlit lanes and cul-de-sacs of the city's edge, slitting the throat of every English straggler they could find.

Aguilar and Barba sat and did not talk, but drank abstemiously and silently, waiting.

Ensign Barba had known better than to say anything about his captain's absence from the Fuerza, from the fight in the plaza. Nor had he deemed it prudent to enquire about the newly scabbed scratches across his face, or the purple swelling about one eye. Some drunken strumpet in the Cerro, he presumed. He almost pitied the girl.

Indeed, he almost pitied the English, deep in their revels by now, oblivious of what was to come. They had fought like men this morning, he thought, but they would be sheep for the slaughter tonight. Looking into Don Diego's lashless, almost reptilian eyes, he saw a murderous fury there, a killing rage that it would take many deaths to slake.

He wondered again about the strumpet that had dared to resist the demands of Don Diego Aguilar.

Two hours after midnight, they heard the sound of hooves, the jingle of horse furniture, and the sound of many voices in the courtyard. They put down their wineglasses and stood up, reaching for the swords and hangers they had slung over the backs of their chairs.

Minutes later, with a clink of weapons and a glimmer of moonlight on helmets and breastplates, they were riding in through the outlying *barrios* of Havana.

"He has no right, Catesby," protested the Earl of Westmorland. "He has no right to treat me thus—a self-made knight so to treat a peer of the realm."

"Quite so, my lord," said Nicholas Catesby.

The two men stood on the steps of the cathedral, looking across the firelit plaza toward the Fuerza, its angular bulk outlined clearly against the moonsheen on the water beyond. They could dimly make out the pale glow of the second-floor windows where the captain general and his chief lieutenants had been closeted with the Governor and other Cuban dignitaries off and on since sunset. Burrow had invited no other of his captains, and not even the most highborn of the gentleman volunteers to attend.

The rest of the officers and gentlemen of the expedition seemed to be too busy securing their share of silks and satins, silverplate and jewelry from the great houses around the square to resent their exclusion from the captain general's inner councils. But to the young earl, it was a matter of honor. And honor meant a vast deal to his lordship of Westmorland.

"My advices have been sought willingly by some of the highest-placed at the Queen's Majesty's court," the young peer fumed. "It is unconscionable that this upstart from a northern dunghill should reject them now."

"Unconscionable, my lord," said Nicholas Catesby, who never disagreed with a peer of the realm.

In point of fact, the sallow little royal paymaster, despite his starched ruff and his doublet and hose of solemn black, had been born much closer to the dunghill than Sir John Burrow. His father had been a Grey Friars alehouse keeper, plying his dubious trade in the most disreputable part of

London. Catesby had pushed and connived his way to the fringes of respectability by sheer unscrupulousness and total dedication to the main chance. In Westmorland's resentment, he saw only one more rung up the ladder to place and power for himself. He had nurtured that resentment all the way across the Atlantic. He was debating now whether to play the final card that might win the impulsive earl over entirely to his schemes for personal advancement.

"And where has his private council got him, after all?" Westmorland's petulant voice went on. "He has committed the fleet and all its men to the taking of this wretched town —and found its treasure-houses full of cowhides and Indian tobacco! Fine prize goods to carry home to the Queen's Majesty."

"The Queen's Council," said Catesby, choosing his words with care, "will certainly be much displeased if no more reward than this comes from this great expedition. Many of them have adventured their own pounds, crowns, and guineas in the outfitting of the fleet. They will be most vexed if Sir John returns with no more than hides and tobacco to repay them for their ventures."

Westmorland nodded moodily, chewing on his lower lip and gazing across once more at the lights of the Fuerza. Catesby decided to lay his last card upon the table.

"By rights, of course," he continued smoothly, "your lordship should have had a chief voice in Council from the beginning. Such was clearly the will of the Queen's Privy Councillors." He paused just long enough to focus his lordship's attention. "A wretched business, that," he concluded, shaking his head.

"What business, Catesby?" said Wesmorland grudgingly. He disliked to admit ignorance of anything connected with the inner politics of the court.

"Why, the second commission," Catesby replied, keeping just the proper mixture of deference and surprise in his voice and manner. His small, narrowly set eyes gleamed in the firelight. "I presumed your lordship was informed of the will of the Council before—but is it possible that your lordship does not know?"

"I have had little contact with the lords of the Council of late," Westmorland answered irritably. "Old Burghley does not approve of my way of life, my debts—" He shrugged his elegant shoulders. "But what is this second commission, Catesby?"

"Why, your lordship, the new commission Lord Burghley himself ordered to be prepared in full Council assembled. The commission that would have given a quarter-share in the command to your lordship—and one quarter-share to my own poor self."

The beauty of it was that it was quite true. Nicholas Catesby had been there himself, a humble suppliant in the high-ceilinged Privy Council chamber at Whitehall, when the decision had been taken to strip Sir John Burrow of his full command and substitute the divided authority that the Queen always favored for her great military ventures.

He could see the snowy ruffs and the florid, well-fed faces of the lords of the Council now, the golden chains across their portly bellies and the rings on their fingers. He could see Lord Treasurer Burghley's white beard and rheumy eye as he gazed down the table. He could hear the dry voice of Sir Robert Cecil, old Burghley's son and heir apparent, as he methodically demolished the reputation of Captain John Burrow.

"There is not a one of us, I believe, who undervalues Sir John's long years of service in these wars," Cecil had begun, holding a sheet of foolscap in one well-manicured hand. Sir Robert was a short man with a slightly twisted spine, known to his enemies as Robert the Devil. "Sir John's heroism in Flanders, in Normandy, in Ireland, on the Cádiz expedition, at the gates of Lisbon, et cetera, have all been duly recognized." He let Burrow's noble record flutter to the tabletop and picked up another sheet of paper.

"I have here, however," he declared firmly, "some account

of the state of the force which Captain Burrow has so diligently assembled at Plymouth. It seems"—he skimmed over the paper—"that a considerable portion of the victuals provided have spoiled in harbor. That six weeks of wages have been paid out to the crews and companies of soldiers before the fleet has even sailed. That the spirit of the men has dangerously declined. And that with all this, nothing at all has been accomplished—the fleet has not even put to sea."

"My lord, it is the wind!" protested Sir Walter Raleigh from his seat much farther down the long table. "There's been a southwest wind against 'em these two months. No fleet can sail in the teeth of the wind. Tis ill fortune only that has hampered Sir John here, and no fault of his." Raleigh knew whereof he spoke. He had had fleets of his own bottled up in harbor more than once in his earlier, more adventurous years.

"Ill fortune or insufficiency in conducting his command," Cecil answered testily, "the result remains the same. The Queen's Majesty is weary of tales of ill fortune, excuses of inclement weather, camp fevers, leaking ships, and all the rest of it."

"Excuses, sir? Do you see no more but excuses in such manifest—"

Raleigh's Devon blood was up. But the voice of Lord Treasurer Burghley had intervened. "I thank you for your opinions in the matter, Sir Walter," the old man had intoned. And then, more briskly: "You may proceed, Sir Robert." And Raleigh had subsided, for he had his way to make in the world too, and Lord Burghley had been the Queen's right hand these forty years and more.

Sir Robert Cecil had come quickly to his conclusion then.

"It is my judgment, my lords," he declared, "that we have lamentably erred in allowing Burrow's own eloquence to persuade us to put the sole command of the venture into his hands alone, considering how poorly he has managed affairs thus far. I therefore urge the lords of the Council to revoke the commission issued to Sir John Burrow, and to send in its stead this document"—he cast an official-looking piece of foolscap into the middle of the table—"vesting final authority not in Sir John alone, but in a council of four. To wit, Sir John as captain general of the troops, Master Robert Adam the chief navigator, the royal paymaster Nicholas Catesby, and His Grace the Earl of Westmorland, who ranks highest of all the voluntary gentlemen embarking on the voyage."

The men of girth and years around the table had nodded heavily.

By midnight, Paymaster Catesby—whose reports had provided most of the substance of Cecil's charges—had been galloping across London Bridge, riding post to Plymouth and the fleet. He must be with the rest when the new commission arrived, to share the universal astonishment at the demotion of their captain general, to accept his own promotion with all due humility.

But for once in his life, Fortune had favored Sir John Burrow. When Catesby rode over Plymouth Hoe and down into that salt-stained seaport town, the wind was blowing east-northeast, and half the fleet was already warping out of the Catte Water, standing past Drake's Island out to sea.

Catesby had barely reached his own berth aboard the *Garland* in time. And all that voyage, he had bitten his lip in silent fury over a commission that had never arrived—a document of whose very existence he could inform nobody else without raising disturbing questions about his own part in its preparation. And no man in his right senses, thought the little paymaster, would raise disturbing questions in Sir John Burrow's mind out here in this wild world of blood and violence so far beyond the line.

But he had chosen the right time to break silence, and the right man to confide in.

"God's blood, Catesby," said Westmorland, clutching him by the shoulder, "but the man is a villain—a most ambitious and conniving villain!"

"A usurper of authority, certainly," said Catesby more judiciously. "Though of course he may claim no knowledge of the second commission. And since no copy was ever actually delivered into his hands—"

"I'll hurl it into his teeth, Catesby! By God, but I'll give him the lie direct for this, and fight him in my shirt!" The young man's face was ruddier than the glow of the fires with excitement.

"That," said Catesby, "I should most assuredly not do, your lordship." The man of the robe and pen had little patience with fulsome oaths or wild talk of swords and daggers in the dawning.

"What then, Catesby? What then, sir? The man must not be allowed to carry it off unchallenged, to ride roughshod over—"

"If I may, your lordship, I should counsel a more patient and more prudent course. Sir John has failed to find the gold of Havana. He will turn his hand now to some even more desperate venture—Cartagena perhaps, or even Vera Cruz—to make up his losses. And he will fail again." He thought but did not say aloud, These swashbucklers always do. "Let us wait and watch and bide our time, your lordship. When the right time comes, we shall know how to seize it."

"We shall," hissed Westmorland emotionally, clutching at the politician's narrow hand. "By God, but we shall."

Across the square, the Ynestrosa mansion collapsed in flames, and the freebooters rushed in, beating out the fire, pawing through the ruins for what booty might remain.

MATTHEW STALKED RESTLESSLY ABOUT THE PLAZA AND UP THE side streets, checking his sentries, kicking men awake and moving them from shadowy corners down to their comrades by the fires. The captain should be here, he thought. Normally it was for the lieutenant to set up the night's camp, true enough. But in such dangerous circumstances, surely the captain general should be concerned. Certainly Sir John Burrow would normally have taken the matter firmly in his own hands.

But not this night. This night in the captured heart of Havana, Sir John could think of nothing but the missing bullion shipments, the silver and gold of the Spanish Indies. He was still up there, in the Commander's quarters of the Fuerza, questioning, probing, evaluating every word and rumor.

Morgan sighed and shook his grey head. Rainbow gold, he thought. Rainbow gold.

The treasure of the Indies was a powerful dream—but no more than that to him. It was a lovely will-o'-the-wisp, something to talk and dream of in the dockside taverns of Plymouth. But it would never be a concrete reality, a massy bar of battered silver to heft in his own two hands.

The city of Havana was rich enough pickings for Matthew Morgan. If they could only manage another two days here before the counterattack came! He strolled over toward the towering Papist church—a garish sight to his simple Protestant eyes, with its lavish carving and its painted saints—to see if by any unlikely chance the altar plate still remained for looting.

He bowed his head only briefly and grudgingly when he passed His Grace the Earl of Westmorland and Paymaster Catesby hurrying down the steps of the cathedral, murmuring together. Birds of ill omen, he thought, that would pick ɩ graveyard clean, let alone a Papist church. He wondered bitterly why Spanish shot and Spanish halberds always managed to cut down the best and leave such silk-and-velvet amateurs as these unscathed.

Burrow tipped his chair back and put one booted leg on the table. "Well, Master Adam?" he asked. "What d'ye think, then?"

There had been a carrack, of that there could be no doubt. It had in fact come from Asia, loaded to the gunnels with the silks and spices of the King of Spain's Eastern possessions. It had been driven to the West Indies by storms, and had spent the better part of a month refitting in the Havana yards. And it had then departed in the night, as mysteriously as it had come. But had it carried more treasure still when it left than when it arrived? Had it found room in its holds for the year's shipment of royal bullion from these Western Indies too?

There were cargo-movers and hangers-on about the docks who told of having been paid handsomely to load heavy chests and boxes of goods from the customs house onto lighters for the carrack, late the very night of her departure. They did not know what was in the chests—they presumed a little contraband on the side for the lord admiral, who was an old friend of their Governor's. But there had been many soldiers on guard, and the chests had been amazingly heavy. . . .

Beyond that, a sea captain had heard rumors, fishermen had heard stories. But no one knew, nothing was certain.

And so, after a long night of it, Burrow tilted back his chair and asked the phlegmatic sailing master, "What d'ye think, then?"

"Perhaps, Sir John, we might have his Excellency back once more," said Master Adam. "Without his daughter," he added. "The girl steels his backbone. He will not speak freely with her here."

She would steel any man's backbone, thought Burrow, that had blood in his veins. He smiled a crooked smile at the thought.

"Let's do it, then," he said abruptly. He turned to call to a freebooter lounging half awake on a low settle by the door.

"He will not come with you alone!" Tamar snapped in rapid Spanish at the red-faced guard who came for her father. "We shall go up together, or not at all. My father is not well—tell your captain general that. As if he did not know it," she added, stroking Don Gabriel's plump, faintly perspiring hand where it lay between her own.

How they have browbeaten and tormented him, she thought. She would tell that great scarred villain of a corsair chief so when she saw him.

The guard, who had not understood a word of her protest, shrugged impatiently and reached out to take the man he had been sent for. "His Honor only, lady," he repeated in a bored voice. "You and the old woman must stay here."

Don Gabriel himself simply stared listlessly from one to another of them. His optimistic spirit shattered by his accumulated misfortunes, he could only sit and wait, letting others more powerful than he decide his fate.

"Dios!" cried Tamar then, springing to her feet. "But I'll tell your captain general myself! Don't worry anymore, Father," she added in a softer tone, "I'll make him understand somehow that you are ill, that you cannot be badgered like this." She touched his damp cheek, a quick caress, then turned and darted past the startled guard, out of the cell.

She was halfway up the dark stone staircase when she heard the first shots, the first wild shouting from the plaza outside.

CHAPTER

20

MATTHEW MORGAN WAS FINGERING BROCADED ALTAR CLOTHS by candlelight when he heard the death cry of the sentinel at the side door of the church. As he groped his way up the main aisle of the cathedral, the sound of Spanish voices shouting and the first crash of musketry reached him through the open portals ahead. He came out into the plaza just in time to see the massacre begin.

The bangs and flashes of arquebuses, the louder reports and brighter muzzle flashes of muskets seemed to come from all around the square. Spanish soldiery were pouring down every converging street into the Plaza de Armas, firing as they came.

Matthew pressed his big body back against the church wall until the first volley ended. Then, as the shadowy attackers streamed out into the plaza, brandishing swords and halberds, Morgan lumbered out in his turn.

His own shouts roaring above the Spanish battle cry of *"Santiago! Santiago!"* he ran from fire to fire, from one huddled form to the next, cuffing and kicking fuddled soldiers to their feet, thrusting weapons into their hands. But the hopelessness of a stand was clear. Shaking the groggy men awake, he shouted again and again: "To the boats, lads! Back to the seawall and the boats!"

The triumphant shouts of the Spaniards, the screams of dying Englishmen told him how few would ever make the seawall and the boats.

Sir John Burrow came pounding out through the ruins of the main gate of the Fuerza into the darkness, the shouting, the powder flashes of the guns. He paused a moment, trying to adjust his eyes from candlelight to starlight, to get some sense of the melee that swirled around him. Somewhere in the middle of the plaza, he could hear Matthew shouting. On all sides, Spaniards were closing around dazed freebooters, cutting them down.

Burrow swore into the tropic night, then filled his lungs and roared out his own rallying cry: "To me! To me, lads! Rally on the fortress, then to the seawall and the ships! The fortress and the ships!"

He would make a stand here in front of the Fuerza, he thought, while as many men as might be tumbled into the boats. Master Adam vanished unbidden off to the right to see that the longboats were manned and ready. Then Sir John began to move forward into the darkness, half a dozen of his freebooters fanning out behind him, shouting still to rally his men.

It was at that moment that Tamar, with Marina close at her heels, slipped in her turn out of the Fuerza.

The Spanish girl's heart had leaped with joy at the first sound of arquebus fire in the plaza. She had stopped on the black stone stair halfway up to the Commander's quarters and peered out through a narrow window slit, straining to distinguish her deliverers from her captors in the darkness.

As she stood there, her small body pressed against the stone, a door had opened above her, and the captain general himself, followed by two or three of his men, had come bounding down the stairs. They had passed her unseeing in the blackness, and then she had seen a glimmer of torchlight as they were joined by other Englishmen, guards from the lower recesses, among them the red-faced man who had been in the guardroom a moment before. Then the lot of them were gone, rushing out into the battle.

With a quick-beating heart, she had followed them.

She and her father were safe now. Even she could tell through the window slit that the corsairs were being overwhelmed. She had hurried to the open gates, eager to welcome her rescuers, to show them where her father was prisoned. She had seen Marina coming up from below, had called to her and hurried on, out into the plaza.

She realized her mistake almost at once.

Blinking helplessly about her at the flash of musketry, the shouts and heavy feet of running men, she knew she should have stayed within the stout walls of the Fuerza. She should go back now, to console her father and await rescue at his side. But she could not bring herself to turn back, to return to that place of captivity and humiliation. She hesitated, then moved forward once again.

She stumbled almost at once into the arms of the very men she had been fleeing. Or more accurately, trod upon their heels: for they were moving slowly away from her when she blundered into them in the darkness.

"Who in God's name turned the wench out into this?" cried the tallest of them, swinging around upon her.

Tamar did not understand the foreign words, but she recognized Sir John Burrow's voice. And she understood the import of the powerful hand that closed about her shoulder, thrusting her back toward her prison.

"No!" she shouted, struggling to free herself. "No—you shall not take me there—not there again—" The words were only half intelligible, an incoherent wail of protest. But the words were Spanish words, and they brought her help at last.

Don Diego Aguilar had led the charge into the Plaza de Armas himself. His voice was the first to shout for Santiago, his rapier the first to run a reeling freebooter through. With Ensign Barba at his side, he ran at the head of his men from one smoldering fire to the next, stabbing at the sleeping and at those who stood to arms, sending his troops with a shout or a gesture in pursuit of those who fled.

It was Ensign Barba who recognized Sir John Burrow's voice, shouting to rally his men.

"*El jéfe inglés,*" he grunted.

Aguilar nodded in the darkness and veered off toward the sound.

They were angling toward the Fuerza, with a score of Spanish halberdiers in their train, when Tamar's cry rang out. Don Diego heard—and he knew that voice. With his heart thudding violently in his chest at the conflicting emotions that voice conjured up, he broke into a dead run across the stone-paved square.

"Get you to shelter, lady!" Burrow was shouting at the struggling girl. And then, his Spanish as terse and uncourteous as his English: *"En la Fuerza, pronto, pronto!"* He thrust her vigorously behind him, then swung back toward the plaza, lungs swelling to shout his rallying cry once more.

His men were gathering now from all directions, pelting past him toward the seawall. For one all but fatal moment, he failed to distinguish the oncoming Spanish cohort from his own fleeing companies. Then someone cried a warning, and Sir John dodged to one side, avoiding the Spanish captain's flashing rapier point by a handsbreadth. An instant later, Burrow was in the center of a furious melee, surrounded by the plumed morions and axe-bladed halberds of the Spanish soldiers, the leather hauberks and clanging swords of his freebooters.

In the darkness off to his left, a fire flared up, illuminating helmets and cuirasses, flashing blades and panting faces. In that red-orange glow, Burrow glimpsed for the first time the strange lashless eyes and flat cheekbones of Don Diego Aguilar. He saw the Spanish captain crouching low, rapier poised to thrust again, a wicked hide-hunter's knife in his other hand.

Behind him, Tamar de la Barca cried out again. Out of the corner of his eye, he saw her shrink behind him, of her own will this time. It was almost, John Burrow thought fleetingly, as if she were seeking protection from her captor against her rescuers!

Then the Spaniard lunged once more, his sword blade driving for the Englishman's throat.

Sir John saw the rapier gleam in the glare of the firelight and batted it aside. A moment later, he felt the hiding knife rip through his doublet.

The English captain general had removed his heavy breastplate earlier in the day, and his doublet was only half laced up. The knife blade, whetted to a razor edge for lifting the hides of tough range cattle, ripped through doublet and shirt. But it only scraped across the skin beneath, and Burrow leaped back and away, escaping with a bubbling surface cut.

Then he thrust savagely in his turn into the flickering darkness, the struggling silhouettes of men. He felt his own point drive through leather and flesh to scrape on living bone.

The nearest fire blazed up fitfully once more. Burrow saw the Spanish captain stagger backward, dropping his sword, clutching one arm tight to his body, trying to hold in the blood that welled from a shattered elbow. The man's face was contorted with rage and pain, and with the unspeakable malignity of one who had never before met a man whose blade was quicker than his own.

For an instant only the two confronted each other, the tall Englishman and the broad-shouldered, powerful Spaniard. Then a Spanish soldier reeled from the fray and fell with a shriek across the flaring fire, half extinguishing it in a shower of sparks. The face of the wounded Spanish captain vanished in the darkness, and Burrow turned to fend off another rush of enemies upon his other side.

With Matthew Morgan now at his right hand, he fought with his usual calm, almost phlegmatic courage to defend the rear of the retreat. The fury of the Spanish Commander and the unaccountable behavior of the Governor's daughter were almost immediately forgotten in the press.

Tamar had all but fallen when Sir John thrust her so violently back toward the Fuerza. She stumbled among the rubble and would certainly have gone down if the sinewy grip of old Marina had not caught and steadied her. "My lady," the old woman hissed in her ear, "we must return." Tamar was about to answer when the nearest fire curled up and she saw, just beyond the tall figure of the corsair captain, the powerful silhouette and flat, Indian features of Don Diego Aguilar.

All the horror of the night before flooded her reeling

mind. Her longing for deliverance was washed away in an instant at the sight of that face, the wide lips parted, the whites of the eyes glowing in the firelight. She could even see the half-scabbed scars her own nails had trenched across his cheek. Involuntarily, unthinking, she shrank back into the shadow of the English pirate.

She saw little of what followed. She heard grunting and the thud of feet, the clang and rasp of sword blades, a gasp of pain. Then the firelight faded, and she was trembling in darkness once again.

Marina plucked urgently at her sleeve. There was a renewed volley of arquebus fire away to her left, and then suddenly the corsairs were rushing past her, their retreat turned into a rout. Isabel heard Marina call her name. A moment later, she was swallowed up in the pandemonium, swept away in the stampede.

She fought against the buffeting flood, strove to get out of it, but the momentum of the retreat carried her along. At the very worst of it, she tripped over her own bedraggled skirts. She fell with a shriek among the churning legs and pounding boots of the men.

She found herself crouching on her hands and knees, not on the wide paving stones of the plaza, but on the wet cobbles of the quay. Somewhere very close at hand, she could hear men tumbling into the longboats that bumped and scraped against the seawall. She clutched at a mossy stone pier and started to pull herself erect once more.

An arquebus crashed deafeningly, almost in her ear. Someone groaned and collapsed heavily against her, catching her off balance, knocking her off her feet once more.

This time she did not roll jarringly on stone. This time, to her horror, she was falling through empty space. The stars flashed over her, and she caught the reek of salt-brackish water somersaulting up. Then her head slammed brutally against wood. The whole world turned slowly over one more time and faded into silence and oblivion.

BOOK III

YET
WHAT IS
LOVE?

Yet what is Love, I pray thee sayn?
It is a sunshine mixed with rain,
It is a toothache or like pain,
It is a game where none hath gain;
The lass saith no, yet would full fain;
And this is love, as I hear sayn.

—Sir Walter Raleigh,
"A Description of Love"

21

HIS EXCELLENCY DON GABRIEL DE LA BARCA RECEIVED DON
Diego Aguilar in his weapon-lined hall of state. Aguilar, his
arm stiff and painful in its sling, was not too exhausted to
notice the honor paid him. Squaring his heavy shoulders
and straightening his back, he bowed with a special flourish
—and set himself to improve his situation still further before
the interview ended.

At first, it did not look propitious.

There were sentinels in shining breastplates at the wide
double doors. The Governor looked stout and impressive
once again, with snowy lace at his wrists and a freshly
starched ruff at his neck. Aguilar, weary and blood-spattered
from a night and a day of hunting the remnants of the
English through the byways of the city, looked slovenly by
comparison.

Don Gabriel's first words were clearly calculated to complete the process of putting the hero of the hour in his
proper place.

"You have not found my daughter," he said sternly.

"I have not, your Excellency. But I have brought you the
ears of the last of the Englishmen." He touched a barbaric
necklace of them strung across his chest. "And I have brought
sure intelligence of the way the rest of them have fled."

"But you have not brought my daughter back," the Governor persisted, averting his eyes from his military commander's grim relics.

"I regret to inform your Excellency that your daughter
is not to be found in Havana," said Aguilar. "She has
clearly been carried off by the corsairs. But I shall bring her
back to you, your Honor—and the head of the English captain too."

"And how will you do that?"

"With the intelligence we have gained from the English captives, my lord. And with those." He nodded brusquely toward the windows on his left, overlooking the bay.

In the calm waters off the Fuerza, the galleons of the Vera Cruz squadron swung gently at their anchors. There were three of them, arrived in Havana just the day before. They were fine new ships, heavy-gunned, fast sailers. They were the King of Spain's very efficient answer to the challenge of the corsairs that had so long roved the Caribbean with impunity. And fate had brought them to Havana harbor just in time to give Don Diego Aguilar the tools he needed. With the Vera Cruz galleons, he would have the revenge he lusted after, the dazzling future that his revenge would bring him.

He caressed the stiff, aching arm inside his sling and waited, looking the Governor straight in the eye.

"And why should I give you these ships?" asked Don Gabriel. "When you have so signally failed to protect this city from these corsairs, why should I give you ships to pursue them over the seas?"

"I drove the English out of Havana, my lord. I harried the English commander into the sea. I do not think that Don Geronimo Rojas, for instance, considers all this a total failure."

"But you have not brought my daughter back to me!"

The plaintive note was there now, no question. To another listener, it might have revealed the depth of this paunchy old trimmer's affection for his only daughter. To Don Diego, it revealed only feebleness, the weakness that left Don Gabriel open to the younger man's assault.

"I shall bring her back, your Excellency," said Aguilar. "I have more experience by sea than anyone else on the island, on the coast guards which I myself built and commanded. And I alone know which way the English have gone—and how they have gone."

"How they have gone?" said the Governor petulantly.

"Very strangely, your Honor. According to those captives

whom we prevailed upon to speak, the English fleet that fought its way past the Morro last night was to rendezvous at the Isle of Pines, off the southern coast."

"The smugglers' island?"

"The same, my lord. I know it well."

"But what hope would you have against so great a fleet as theirs even if you could take them unawares at the Isle of Pines?"

"The men who retook the Morro from the pirates last night," Aguilar explained, "turned her guns upon the fleeing English vessels to good effect, my lord. Two were sunk, two were listing badly as they rounded the Punta. And we have already had word from an Indian runner that one of these was abandoned down the coast."

"Yet the survivors are still more than twice as many as those three galleons in the harbor." Don Gabriel, who knew nothing of military matters, asserted himself with particular passion after his humiliation at the hands of the English.

"Eleven English vessels sailed into Havana, your Excellency," said Aguilar patiently, "and seven have sailed whole away, it is true. But some of these are mere pinnaces and flyboats, no match for our galleons. And there is even more hopeful word from one or two of the prisoners who were put most rigorously to the question."

"What word?"

"Word of disaffection, of a mutinous spirit among some of the officers at least. A spirit which cannot but be even stronger now, after the disastrous defeat which we have inflicted upon them. It is believed that there will soon be open challengers to the authority of the corsair chief, one Captain John Burrow by name." Aguilar's jaw tightened as he said the name. "A divided force, my lord, is a much weakened force."

"Nevertheless—" said the Governor doubtfully.

"And one thing more, by your leave," said Aguilar. "It seems that this Captain Burrow spent many hours asking questions of various officials, his Excellency the royal treasurer among them, about the great carrack from the East that put to sea some ten days since. It seems, from what we have heard, that Burrow may well intend to set off in pursuit of this vessel next."

"The *Mother of God?*" The chill in Don Gabriel's voice caught Aguilar's attention at once.

"Even so, your Honor. Hoping no doubt to save their voyage after all with the rich cargo from Calecut reposing in her holds."

And with the even richer cargo hidden in her strong-room! thought Governor de la Barca, his plump cheeks paling. Treasurer Rojas knew the bullion should have been in the customs house. He or Don Geronimo would have guessed where it has gone. And if they knew, and the English questioned them—then the English knew it too.

"These corsairs must not take the carrack, Don Diego," said the Governor carefully.

"Give me the Vera Cruz squadron," replied Aguilar, "and they will not."

"The *Mother of God* would be a grave loss," the Governor went on. "His Catholic Majesty would not easily forgive those who let one of his great Eastern carracks fall into the hands of the English heretics."

"His Majesty's gratitude," said Don Diego, more boldly now, "to one who rescued his great ship from the corsairs would no doubt be equally great."

"I cannot speak for his Majesty," replied Don Gabriel. "For myself, I can assure you of my own eternal gratitude if you should perform this service for him."

And for yourself as well, thought Aguilar. For there was surely more than loyalty to King Philip in the Governor's sudden passion for the safety of the great ship. Don Diego began to reevaluate the stories of secret cargos loaded by night that he had picked up from the stevedores he had interrogated.

"Depend upon the service, my lord," he said with a crisp bow. "As I shall depend upon your gratitude hereafter."

It almost made him giddy, the thought of all this pyramiding gratitude. The Rojas faction doted upon him now. Old Don Geronimo, it seemed, had a nephew on the *Mother of God* who must on no account be prevented from reaching Spain. And here was Don Gabriel de la Barca, equally desperate for the safety of the great carrack, willing to give almost anything to guarantee its safe crossing.

Don Diego drew a deep breath and made his final and most daring play.

"Your Excellency honors me with his confidence," he said carefully. "May I dare to hope that your Excellency might honor me still further?"

"In what way, sir?" said Don Gabriel nervously.

"With leave to pay formal court to your daughter, Tamar —the Doña Isabel."

It was a wild gamble. But Don Diego was driving ahead, grasping for all his hands could hold.

Don Gabriel blinked once, quickly. He gazed through small, moist eyes at the stocky *mestizo* before him. He took in the skin drawn tight across the cheekbones, the Indian twist at the corners of the lips. He looked into the dark, feral eyes of the man-hunter. And he could not believe it.

That he, Don Gabriel Francisco María de la Barca y Sánchez, whose ancient family had marched to victory with the Catholic kings of old, whose name had been honored in Madrid for two hundred years, should stand here and seriously consider permitting this half-caste mercenary to sue for the hand of his daughter in marriage!

And yet he had no choice, and he knew it. He had taken the only bold action of his life in shipping the year's revenues home to Seville in the lord admiral's great ship. If he were to lose the gold and silver now, it would not be his honor and his career that would be forfeit. It would be his head.

Aguilar was waiting.

Don Gabriel spread his soft, plump hands. "I should not of course stand in the way of my daughter's wishes," he said, with only the faintest of tremors in his voice, "in so important a matter."

Don Diego still waited. It was not enough.

"I would"—Don Gabriel moistened his lips unhappily—"I would further feel it my duty to encourage Doña Isabel to give every consideration—every consideration, sir—to the suit of one who had achieved such signal successes on the field as yourself. Assuming, of course," he added savagely, "that those successes included the final destruction of this pirate Burrow and the safe convoying of the *Mother of God* home to Spain!"

He was breathing heavily, his full cheeks damp with perspiration. His abject surrender was complete.

"I thank your Excellency most humbly," said Don Diego Aguilar. "And I know that so dutiful a daughter as Tamar is would never reject such an admonition from her father." His voice, his face, the tense pose of his body all radiated the joy of his triumph.

"I shall sail with the tide!" he said, and bowed himself with a flourish from the room.

22

TAMAR SCREAMED, BUT NO SOUND CAME. THE MAN GRIPPED her throat in the vise of one hard hand, smothering her cries, pinioning her helpless under him. She felt the rough pallet beneath her writhing body. She smelled the reek of him, heard his heavy breathing in the dimness as he pulled up her skirts, pried her trembling legs apart. Screaming silently, she fought him still, striking and clawing at him, trying to make it not happen, not have happened, not ever have happened at all.

God, God, she wept, *God and Mary the Mother of God—*
She saw his face edged with candlelight, the eyes all white and glowing, and so close above her. Then he came driving into her struggling body, and she screamed aloud at last.

"It is all right," said Marina, bending over her, turning a cool compress on her brow. "It is all right now, child."

The Indian woman's face turned to burnished copper, to a darkly shining copper coin, and spun away into the vortex of nightmare once more.

Tamar was dreaming, she knew. She had been dreaming off and on for a long time now—for days and days, it seemed. Terrifying dreams which seemed to have no end.

Dreams of savage violence. Lurid skies were flaring above her now, forest fires overhead. White adobe walls exploded at her in a shower of dust and debris. Men with swords and pikes and blood-smeared breastplates swept over her, bore her down, trampled her bruised and helpless body into the paving stones.

And then the man was there again, crushing her under him once more, violating her body, savaging her soul.

Mingled with this endlessly uncoiling cycle of dreams were other memories now, memories that might have been real.

There was the crash of great guns over the water—the cannon of her father's fine new Morro Castle, but leveled now at her across the moon-gilded swells! She was peering through mullioned windows across a narrow stretch of sea, and the guns were blasting away at her, raising gouts of water just outside the leaded panes.

She felt dizzy and hot and fearfully confused, and men were shouting overhead. She heard her own voice shouting at the guns, trying to tell them who she was, and that they must not fire at her, at the Governor's own daughter of Cuba. But the water foamed over the mullioned glass, and there was something burning on the waves astern, another ship, and men were screaming now.

And then Marina's sinewy old hands were drawing her away, pressing her gently back into a curtained bed once more.

Winds were blowing now. The moon was gone, and rain lashed across the darkened cabin windows. The bed in which she slept heaved up and then fell sickeningly away. The feverish heat was gone from her body, and the dreams were fading. But she was sick still. Her body felt soiled and full of aches, her stomach churned on the heaving sea. She groaned with misery in the darkness, and heard her old nurse's voice, patient and soothing:

"Rest, my lady. Rest your body and sleep, and you will soon be well."

Soon be well, thought Tamar, stifling another groan, remembering her fever dreams, the guns and the violence—and the man with the glowing lashless eyes coming down upon her. How could she ever be well again?

She opened her eyes and there was sunlight in the cabin—and a man looking at her.

She saw his head and his wide shoulders outlined against the row of mullioned windows across the back of the cabin. The daylight was very strong outside, the face and shoulders little more than a featureless silhouette against the light. For one heart-stopping moment, she thought it was the man of her nightmares once again. She started up in bed, a strangled shriek rising once more in her throat.

"My lady is awake?" the shadowed figure said in ill-accented Spanish. "And recovered somewhat of your indisposition, I hope?"

She gasped as her vision cleared and she saw the captain general of the English corsairs sitting in a low-backed chair, one booted leg flung over a corner of the long polished table in front of him.

His beard was trimmed, his doublet and hose brushed and clean. The lace that showed at his wrists, the small white ruff at his neck were clearly fresh. He looked, Tamar thought in those first dazed moments, altogether more civilized than he had done. The scar across his face was somehow much less fierce than it had been above a steel corselet in the Plaza de Armas.

But fresh linen and a trimmed beard did not make him any the less the pirate, she thought angrily. She was fully awake now, and full of a sense of her place and situation.

"Quite recovered, thank you," she answered coldly.

"And you find your quarters adequate to your needs?"

"Adequate," she replied, not going a step beyond. And then, drawing the covers about her and sitting up against the bolster: "Adequate enough, for a prison."

The lean face of the man opposite her smiled. "I hope, Lady Tamar," he said, "that you find my own humble quarters something more to your taste than a prison cell." His slow gesture took in the heavily carved furniture, the bronze candelabra, the comfortable curtained bed where the girl sat. A trifle snug, perhaps, and no doubt spartan by her ladyship's standards, that gesture seemed to say, but really somewhat better than a prison.

The girl bit her lip, confused, not knowing what to say. How had he learned her nickname, she wondered—and how

dare he use it? And did this corsair who had carried her off
by force really expect her to be grateful for the use of his
wretched cabin?

"I hope," Sir John continued, "that you will consider
yourself a guest aboard this ship. An unexpected visitor—we
found you unconscious in the bottom of a longboat as we
warped out of Havana harbor—but a visitor nonetheless."

Tamar's chin rose a millimeter in defiance. "I am neither
guest nor visitor here, Sir-John Burrow, or whatever your
freebooters call you! I am your prisoner. I shall conduct myself as such until whatever ransom you demand is paid!"

That should not be long, she thought. Outside the windows she could see a high ridge thick with palms. They had
put in somewhere down the coast, she assumed. From there,
they would send to her father. As soon as the customary
ransom was paid, she would be bound for home.

She sat up the straighter, oblivious even to the awkward-
ness of this interview between a Spanish lady in her shift
and an English privateer—conducted in the latter's cabin,
with the lady in his bed!

Then the corsair chief stunned her once more with a single
sentence.

"Alas, my lady," he said, "but I am afraid there can be
no ransom in this case—and no swift return for you at all."

Sir John had had the Governor's daughter carried to his
own cabin as a matter of course when she had been brought
aboard the *Roebuck* battered and feverish three nights before. He was a gentleman born, after all, albeit it from the
rough northern shires, his manners hardened by the wars.
The Indian serving woman, who had apparently clambered
deliberately into one of the boats when she saw her mistress
fall, had had everything the ship could provide for her ladyship's illness.

Beyond such elementary courtesies, he owed her nothing.
Yet here he was, patiently putting up with the sharpness of

her tongue, attempting to make the obvious facts of her situation clear to her. He wondered vaguely why.

He knew why, of course, as he looked at the girl sitting in the curtained bed across from him. Her eyes were dark and strange, her skin more tanned by the tropical sun than was fashionable in Europe. Her hair was certainly not spun gold, like the hair of ladies in courtly poetry, but black and lustrous as the proverbial Egyptian's. Yet she was beyond any doubt, as he had known the first moment he saw her, the loveliest girl he had ever seen.

Burrow was no courtier poet, inditing sonnets to his mistress's eyebrow. He was a blunt man of simple pleasures and uncomplicated desires. So he did not wax lyrical, even to himself, about the loveliness of Tamar de la Barca. He remembered with simple admiration her queenlike courage as she rode across the plaza toward the English cannon. He looked at her slender body beneath the bedclothes—the small, high breasts, the curve of hip and thigh—and felt without surprise the quickening of desire in his loins.

He would do nothing about it, of course. He was a hard man, a man who could be brutal—but he was no ravisher of helpless women. Still, he could look upon her beauty and admire her courage. And he could try to make it as clear as possible to her that she must bear with his company for some time to come.

"We are anchored in Siguanea Bay, my lady," he began carefully, "on the lee shore of the Isle of Pines. We have been here a day and a half already, revictualing the fleet and refitting as much as may be after the ravages of your Morro guns, and after the gale we ran through rounding the western parts of Cuba. But by this time tomorrow, God willing, we shall be gone from here."

"Gone?" she said uncertainly. "Gone tomorrow? But that is scarcely time for a ransom—"

"There is no time at all, my lady. We have other business

to transact that will not wait. Business that will take us halfway home at least, back across the Atlantic Sea."

"But how then—but what will you do with us? With
Marina and—" The girl's eyes were wide. The wild thought
darted through her head that they meant to abandon the
two women on the island, for smugglers or wild Indians or
other corsairs like themselves to find.

"I am afraid there is naught for it," Burrow said with a
sigh, "but ye must come to England with us. We cannot
wait longer about these waters, even for so fine a ransom
as your father would surely pay."

Sir John spoke calmly, like an up-country *encomiendero*
discussing cattle or the sugar crop. But it was Tamar's life
he was speaking of so casually. The girl turned quickly toward the window, that he might not see the mingled fear
and fury in her eyes.

"Am I never to see my own people again?"

The question burst out unbidden. Beyond the wide stern
windows, she could see the wooded slopes of the Isle of
Pines, the low swamps to the west, the clustered palms along
the shore. It was the only home she had ever known, this
vivid tropical world of sea and jungle and graceful palms
against a hot blue sky. Now she was to be torn out of that
beloved landscape and carried off to the cold and barbarous
land of England, somewhere beyond the northern mists.

Burrow hesitated only an instant. She was so young and
helpless, after all, for all her spirit, all her lithe young
strength. And he had long since shrugged off the fading welt
her riding crop had laid across his neck.

"You shall return soon enough, my lady," he told her
firmly. "To Spain, certainly, and to the Indies as soon thereafter as your own people may arrange."

She turned her face back toward him, startled and bewildered.

"But if there is to be no ransom—"

"Leave me to handle that," he answered quite cheerfully
now. "There will be prize money enough to glut the greedi-

est appetite before we're done, I think. And if the lads should insist upon a ransom for your ladyship, why, I shall oblige them myself!"

He rose, bowed, and left her, ducking his head to pass out through the low cabin door.

Tamar was still sitting bolt upright in her bed, staring somewhat dazedly at the dark oak door, when it swung open once again. Her old duenna stepped over the high threshold into the cabin.

"Marina!" the girl exclaimed. "Is it all true—what that corsair says?"

"It is true that you have been very ill these last three days, my lady," said the Indian woman, setting down a brimming bucket just inside the door. "And that you are almost well again now, I think. Well enough at least to converse with the chief of these English in your shift," she added, looking severely at her young mistress.

"Oh, Marina! I wrapped myself quite demurely while he was here," said Tamar. "But is it true that we have been— that we are going—" The words stumbled so rapidly on her tongue that she could scarcely get them out.

"It is true that these English have lost many ships in the storm and in the fighting as they fled Havana. Now they are filling their water casks and other stores from the island cimaroons. They will soon sail for England. And we with them, so that sour-faced master of the ship informs me." Marina had dealt primarily with the thin-faced Master Adam since she had been aboard the *Roebuck*, and neither had taken to the other.

"But England, Marina! And then to Spain! The English pirate has said that he will send us to Castile even if he must ransom us himself. *That* isn't true, surely? For why would any corsair—" Once again she rather gestured than completed her sentence. She was feeling light-headed still, though infinitely better than she had the last time she had awakened, with a head full of dreams and delirium.

"It may be so, my lady. The English captain general has

-made all things available to hasten your recovery. He bears you no ill will, I think." Tamar did not even notice the ironic gleam in her servant's eyes.

"But that's ridiculous. Why would the same man who burned half Havana down and carried us off by force now pay my ransom and send me home? Folly even to think it," she concluded firmly, settling back and drawing the coverlets more closely about her as she spoke.

"I think this Sir John has other business on his mind besides your ladyship's ransom," said Marina quietly. "And then, he is no worse than other men, my lady."

"But how can you say that?" the girl protested, suddenly querulous with hunger and weakness after her three days of almost total collapse. "How can you say that, after what these villains did in Havana?"

"Your pardon, my lady." The Indian woman had poured out water into a basin and was busy washing something in it. But Tamar, irritated and imperious now, was not disposed to let her off so easily.

"Marina," she repeated sharply, "how *can* you be so—so unconcerned about what these English corsairs have done to my father's island?" She remembered Indian strumpets and black washerwomen dancing with the freebooters in the great square at Havana, and all at once she really did want to know why.

"It was my people's island once," the old Indian woman said finally. "Before it was your father's, the whole island belonged to the Taino people. Before the Castilians burned our *bohios* and took our people to labor for them in the mines and fields, to serve you in your houses."

It was a long speech for the wrinkled duenna. The words were uttered without rancor, simply as a statement of fact, an answer to a question. But it had a profound and immediate impact on her mistress.

"Oh, Marina," exclaimed Tamar, as contrite now as she had been imperious before, "you know how sorry I am for —those awful things."

She had in fact heard horror stories of the things the first comers had done to the Indians in the early days—the floggings, the brandings, the dogs. She had been told the story of Marina's own village by a feebleminded Indian stablehand who, like the wrinkled duenna, had been a child at the time. Marina's two sisters had been raped and murdered by the Spaniards, her brothers hunted through the jungle by mastiffs, her father—the *cacique* of her people—flayed alive.

Revolted and shamed, Tamar had wept bitter tears on her nurse's narrow breast over this, pleading for forgiveness. But it had all happened so long ago, sixty or eighty years at least, so long before she or her father had ever set foot in the island. Normally she could feel no guilt for the transgressions of an earlier generation. But she could feel it now.

"Marina," she said almost timidly, "how—how could you serve in my father's house all these years without—" She stopped, not saying the phrase she had intended: *hating us all.*

The older woman shrugged, busy still with her washing. "I think it is the nature of men to fight, my lady," she said finally. "To kill each other and to die upon each other's spears."

"But surely—some can change?"

"The Castilians killed the people of my village and took us into bondage. The English corsairs have killed many Spanish and spoiled Havana. And the time will come for the English to choke on blood in their turn."

Tamar, nestled among her blankets, nevertheless felt a sudden chill. She remembered the thunder of the great guns, the screams of full-grown men in the Plaza de Armas. God knew she did not want to see any more of that.

Yet these corsairs were her enemies, she reminded herself sharply. Her father's enemies and her own. And she must deal with them as such.

She had told Sir John that she was his prisoner, and that was what she would be. She would confine herself to this cabin as to a dungeon cell. She would be icily courteous—for as long as they were, at least. Aloof but proper, that would be her manner from thenceforward. Aloof but proper, for as long as she was in their hands.

Quite convinced that she had formulated a fixed and dignified policy for dealing with her captors, Tamar de la Barca let herself relax beneath the coverlets. She was almost instantly asleep.

24

THE COUNCIL ASSEMBLED IN MASTER ADAM'S CABIN, SOMEWHAT smaller and more cramped than Sir John's own, that same afternoon. The Captain General of the Fleet had never felt more bayed about by enemies than he did as he watched his own commanders troop in that day.

It was to be a consultation only. He made that clear by tone and gesture from the moment they came crowding into the cabin. He had the royal commission beside him on the table where he stood, as a reminder of his own final authority. But he knew too that that authority was not worth a snap of the fingers if he could not speedily reestablish that personal allegiance which was always the essence of command.

For that personal allegiance was clearly frayed to the breaking point in the men gathered here before him.

Sir John Burrow had sailed from Plymouth with thirteen vessels, four of them mere pinnaces. They had lost one ship off the coast of Portugal, and another had turned back after a clumsy caulking job in the Azores. Eleven ships had sailed into Havana harbor. But there were no more than seven vessels anchored in the roadstead at Siguanea Bay.

The *Great Raleigh*, with half the loot of Havana on her decks, had been sunk outright by the guns of the Morro Castle, and one of the pinnaces as well. Two others, damaged in the fight, had been lost two days later in the storm around the western end of Cuba, on the way to the Isle of Pines. With crews depleted by wounds and scurvy and now the fevers of the island—so many of Captain Thynne's men down already—they were less than half the fighting force that had sailed from Plymouth Hoe.

The officers and gentlemen grouped about the cabin were clearly bitter men.

"Gentlemen," began Sir John Burrow slowly, "it has been

a long cruise and a hard one." There were murmurs of assent. "But not, I think, an unsuccessful venture." There was no response at all to this.

"We have singed the beard of the King of Spain in this island of Cuba, gentlemen—a thing which even Sir Francis Drake dared not attempt. The dons will not soon forget us in these waters, nor our countrymen at home. Much honor has been won, glory to add luster to even the noblest name."

The gentleman volunteers who were clustered around the Earl of Westmorland looked up at this. In their faces showed the hungry look of men to whom honor was life itself.

"Nor will any of us go home with empty purses once the booty we have taken in the Queen's name is duly sold and shared out among us according to the articles."

The captains of the remaining vessels of the fleet stared woodenly at him. They knew to a penny what their shares were in the pillage that had been brought aboard ship before the debacle in the Plaza de Armas. And they knew that they could have made more profit cruising the Bay of Biscay than they had so far beyond the line.

Burrow knew what they were thinking. And he knew where their discontent would find a spokesman.

"If I may speak, Sir John?" It was the earl, resplendent as usual in a wide wheel-ruff and sumptuous satin.

"Of course, your lordship," said Burrow. He could feel Matthew Morgan, standing with folded arms upon his left, stiffen at the very sound of the young nobleman's voice. Master Adam, on the captain general's other side, remained unmoved.

"A hard voyage it has been, certainly," the earl began pompously, as though he had been cruising the Spanish Main all his life. "And quite long enough for some of us, I think." His sycophants, a half-dozen other young gallants, laughed appreciatively. "But fortunate? There, I fear, I must beg to differ with you, sir."

Even a grizzled sea captain nodded here and there at this. Westmorland might be a fop and a fool, but he had one thing they lacked: the noble title, the influence at court, the sheer weight in the world to speak the things they all felt.

This the handsome young peer proceeded to do. One by one, as though by rote, he ticked off the misfortunes of the expedition: bad weather, the fleet shrunk to half its size, the Havana raid little short of a disaster. His words dripped with courtesy, commiseration, and a heavy undertone of fashionable irony. He was sure Sir John, whose investment in the venture was greater than anyone else's, understood the general dismay. Yet the facts remained, and would not be gainsaid. He therefore urged—and he felt that he spoke for others there present as well—that the ships replenish their stores and sail at once for home, before any more lives or vessels might be lost in a cruise that seemed doomed to misfortune from the beginning.

He came as near as any man had ever dared to saying it to the commander's face: that Burrow's luck had ruined them all.

Catesby had coached him well, thought Burrow. And he had clothed the paymaster's cavils in the charm of the born courtier, the self-assurance of one whose short, pampered lifetime had been swathed in deference and fawning from the moment of his birth. Altogether a splendid performance, as Westmorland himself well knew. His lordship tossed his long, chestnut-colored hair and looked about him like an actor on the stage waiting for the audience to applaud.

"I thank your lordship," said the captain general aloud. "Are there others who would speak now?"

"If I may, Sir John?"

It was the paymaster Nicholas Catesby, his voice smooth, his close-set eyes impenetrable. Of course, thought Burrow, he would reserve the *sic probo* for himself.

"Speak, Master Catesby," he said. "The views of the Queen's paymaster are always of interest to her humble servants."

There was a ripple of laughter. Burrow had won a small point at least. He had effectively set off the civilian money-man from the men of the sword and the sea who thronged the cabin. But he had no illusions that his case was won.

"I thank the captain general," said Catesby, smiling. We are all good fellows here together, that smile seemed to say, and I can take a jest at my own expense. "But I would speak not of pounds and pence, or of the success or unsuccess of this our mutual venture. I will rather leave all such judgments to the captains here assembled, to whose province such judgments more properly belong."

Very neatly done, thought Burrow. He's won his jury back again.

"I would speak rather of that paper there on the table by your right hand, Sir John."

There were two or three rolled-up charts on the long table, and several other papers. But the royal functionary's object was clear enough. It was the Queen's commission he would discuss.

Burrow shook the sheet of foolscap out and laid it face up, the royal seal prominently displayed.

"Thank you, Sir John," said Catesby affably. "I am generally familiar with the terms of your commission." He turned slightly, so as to address the assembled officers as much as the man behind the table. "Or should I say—the terms of the commission under which we *all* sail, in her Majesty's royal service. I at least would yield to no man in the ardor of my dedication to that service."

There was a polite rumble of agreement. It was like pronouncing oneself as good a Christian as any man: who would be behindhand in insisting that he too was of that company?

"As I understand it, gentlemen," Catesby continued smoothly, "this document provides that Sir John Burrow shall have sole command of this armado, accepting the advice of his captains, and of such noble volunteers as his lordship of Westmorland, only when and as he may think fit. A somewhat unusual commission, I believe." He paused a bare moment, to let the unusualness of it sink in. "Sir John's long experience at the wars evidently justifies her Majesty's gracious judgment. Yet let me say that I am most grateful for captains of such experience and reputation as yourselves to second Sir John in all these matters."

"May I ask, sir," said Burrow, "where this line of reasoning may be leading?"

"Why, just to this, sir," said Catesby. "To a heartfelt petition that in whatever decisions may now be made touching this joint venture, this royal service in which we are all alike enrolled, the frank opinions of all may be heard. And that, on so critical a matter, these advices and opinions may in fact be heeded—whatever the *commission* may say about it. That is all, Sir John," the paymaster concluded blandly. "And I thank you for your hearing."

There was a stillness in the cabin. Outside, the sounds of men at work had fallen silent too. There was only the plash and suck of the sea, the distant call of a gull.

"Are there other voices that would be heard?" said Burrow crisply. There was no answer. "Why, then, I have one more thing myself to say."

The captains and the voluntary gentlemen looked back at him, waiting. Clearly many of them agreed with Catesby and with Westmorland. Silently they stood to hear their captain general's reply.

"You will most of you know," Burrow began slowly, "that we came to Havana for more than to brave the King of Spain, and spoil the houses of his subjects. We came for treasure. We came for the gold and silver of the Indies, which is the sinews of his Majesty's war against us, and the source of all his strength. We came for gold. And we did not find it."

The eyes before him were looking at him with interest now. Such straight talk was not common, even in ship's council.

"But we did bring one thing of value out of the Havana treasure-house," said Burrow. "We brought new intelligence, of greater moment than any we have yet."

Skepticism showed at once on every face. They had heard this sort of thing before.

"News of where that treasure is, that we have come so far to seek. Where we may seek it out, if we be men enough, and have the stomach for it."

There was a ruffling and preening at this challenge to their courage. Did he dare to suggest that there was any venture—most especially a venture involving Spanish gold—that they had not stomach for?

Swiftly, in plain blunt words, Burrow outlined the situation. He told them of the coming of the sea-battered *Madre de Dios* to Havana, already laden with riches beyond calculation from King Philip's Eastern Empire. He told how the great ship had sailed away again, freighted not only with the wealth of the East, but with the precious metals of Mexico and Peru as well.

The value of the carrack's Eastern cargo he did not make bold to guess. But the worth of the Western treasure had been estimated by the Governor himself, in a broken, trembling voice across the Commander's quarters in the Fuerza. "The value of that bullion alone," said Sir John quietly, "would amount to one million five hundred thousand pesos —so sworn to by the Governor himself."

He paused a moment to let the sheer unthinkable immensity of it penetrate the souls of the men gathered across the table from him. Then he raised his voice to repeat it.

"A million and five hundred thousand pesos, in bars of silver and ingots of pure gold!" He looked at Nicholas Catesby. "Will you take due note of the sum, then, Master Catesby? I have no head for figures myself, and will not try to turn it into pounds, shillings, and pence. But I think you will find that so much white and yellow metal brings a tidy enough return on 'Change!"

The captains laughed at the paymaster's discomfiture. Even the voluntary gentlemen stared at Burrow as if mesmerized, thinking of all the unpaid debts, the coaches and clothes and painted strumpets their share of such a sum might buy.

"Which shall it be, then, gentlemen?" Sir John concluded

briskly then. "Home with our tails between our legs, for every man to laugh at behind his hand? Or after this great carrack, and a treasure so rich it will make old Drake's ghost pale with envy?"

"By God, sir," blurted an excited voice, "but I'm with you!"

It was Captain Cross, the youngest captain in the council, commander of the smallest vessel remaining in the little fleet. Cross dressed like a lord, looted like a pirate, and had slaughtered the Morro garrison without a moment of compunction. He was as recklessly gallant, and as cynically venal, as any freebooter who had ever sailed for England. He stepped forward theatrically as he spoke and slammed a long, thin fist down upon the table. "To the death, Sir John! To the death!"

"I too."

"And I."

One by one, the others nodded, grunted, murmured their assent. Their flushed cheeks, their glittering eyes told Sir John more clearly than their words that he had won them back again.

"I thank you, gentlemen," said Burrow, "for your opinions and advices." He barely stressed the last words, and did not even glance at Catesby as he spoke them. "We shall sail with the morning tide."

Of all the men clustered in the cabin, only Matthew Morgan looked closely at his commander's face, and saw that his eyes too gleamed with the same unearthly fire that blazed up in the cheeks and eyes of all his captains. Matthew only saw it, and remembered what he had thought that night in the plaza at Havana, when John Burrow had paid so much attention to the carrack and so little to his men. The same thoughts, the same words pulsed behind his ruddy brow and pale-blue eyes now: *Rainbow gold—rainbow gold.*

"HE'S MAD!" HIS GRACE THE EARL OF WESTMORLAND HISSED in the darkness under the *Garland*'s ornamental poop. "A raving Bedlamite, run lunatic with his dreams of Spanish fairy-gold!" The young man's eyes glowed pale green in a barred filter of moonlight through the ratlines far above.

"Indeed, your Grace," murmured Catesby, standing in deeper shadow beneath the companionway. "Sir John's common sense does seem affected. Whether it be the misfortunes of this voyage, or—"

"He's no way fit to command this expedition further," Westmorland cut off the royal paymaster. The young earl's voice was querulous, his delicate features pale in the moonlight. "If that second commission you told me of had but reached Plymouth ere we sailed, the two of us might challenge him openly." He chewed his lower lip moodily. "But most of the rogues are mad as he is with dreams of Spanish gold." The earl's defeat in council seethed like vitriol in his veins.

"I fear they are, my lord," said Catesby.

"It is our clear duty, then—our very *duty*, sir—to take what ships of the Queen's we may out of his hands, that they may survive to sail again in her Majesty's service."

"As your lordship wishes," murmured the sallow-faced little politician, who had manipulated Westmorland like a marionette ever since they had left England.

On the poop deck above them, the sailing master of the *Garland* rumbled a hoarse command. The mate leaned over the rail above their heads and repeated the order through cupped hands. A hundred feet away across the moon-gilded sea, dripping oars rose and fell for the last time. Then the towing cable sank into the swell as the ship's boat hove to. They had towed her far enough out of Siguanea Bay.

Another low command rapped out, and mariners sprang like monkeys into the rigging. In moments patched and battered sails were rattling down from the yards. Wind filled the canvas, and the vessel heeled, creaking, before the breeze.

Westmorland swung nervously around and gazed back toward the Isle of Pines.

The sea stretched grey and oily under an intermittent moon. The hills that fringed the bay were shadows in the darkness now. There was no sign at all of the rest of the little fleet, sleeping still behind the low peninsula. Close astern, two other vessels rode seaward with the *Garland* beneath the drifting clouds.

By God, the earl swore silently, *but this will teach that dunghill climber of a Burrow what it is to ride roughshod over a peer of the realm!*

Catesby had been right, he told himself as he watched the island fade slowly into the dark. Catesby had been right all along. Burrow had trod most shamefully upon them all —his captains, his gentleman volunteers, even his exalted Grace of Westmorland. By God, but he at least would not put up with it.

Her Majesty would surely be grateful that even three ships were saved from this lunatic's hands. White teeth shining in the fading moonlight, the young nobleman began to muse upon just what concrete form the Queen's gratitude might take. For he had creditors still to pay when he returned to London.

Nicholas Catesby, shivering in the sea breeze, let his mind wander along equally practical lines.

There was, he thought, still hope for him. The impetuous earl's influence might soar at court, at least among the elegant fops with whom he most commonly consorted. But in the antechambers of the Queen's most trusted Councillors, Catesby's own prudent and politic role in the affair would receive its recognition. And it was the approbation of these men of power that mattered in the end at the court of Queen Elizabeth.

The unimpressive little man in black began to work out in intricate detail the politics of six weeks hence, when he would stand respectfully before the Royal Council and explain why it was that three ships only of Sir John Burrow's fleet had returned unbroken from the Spanish Indies. Sir Robert Cecil—Robert the Devil—would be for him, he knew, using him as a pawn in his private war with Essex and Raleigh. Lord Treasurer Burghley would be glad of any testimony which would discourage further costly military expeditions. Admiral Howard would no doubt follow Burghley's lead. . . . Catesby went on down the list, working out the politics of his own salvation.

Neither the calculating paymaster nor the young earl gave a moment's thought to the unlikely possibility that they would ever see Sir John Burrow again.

Matthew Morgan brought the news to Burrow at first light.

"That velvet-pants popinjay! That smiling villain of a paymaster!" the burly lieutenant swore, his square face red to the roots of his iron-grey hair.

"Indeed," said Burrow softly, in an oddly matter-of-fact voice. "I must certainly have a word with his lordship of Westmorland when this voyage is over." His eyes were momentarily bleak at the thought of that reckoning to come.

"They've taken half the ships we had still left us," said Morgan bitterly. "And the fleetest among 'em too. Even if we put to sea at the turn of the tide, there's little chance we'd catch sight of 'em this side o' Plymouth Hoe!"

Burrow nodded absently. He had risen from his bed and strode to the mullioned windows aft to look out upon the bay, half empty under the morning sun. Now he turned back to his lieutenant with a quizzical expression on his face.

"But then, why should we sail after them at all, pray?"

"Why, to hang every mutinous officer on every vessel from his own mainmast yard! And if we cannot do the same by his noble lordship and her Majesty's royal paymaster, we can at least give 'em a voyage home belowdecks that they'll not soon forget."

"And while we were exacting such retribution, Matthew —what of the *Madre de Dios*? What of the great carrack, man?"

"Why—" blinked Morgan, "why—what o' her?"

"Would you let the wealth of both the Indies slip through our hands to exact vengeance from such paltry rogues?" The quizzical smile still played about Burrow's lips. "Would you abandon our own great venture for so feeble a cause?"

"But surely," said Morgan, bewildered, "if seven sail be scarce enough to bring down this monstrous carrack, this Leviathan of the sea, then four vessels, and one o' them the merest flyboat, shall never attempt it!"

Sir John Burrow laughed aloud, his lean cheeks creasing, his forehead ridging in the dawn.

"The fewer of us there be the better, Matthew Morgan!" He clapped the Welshman on the shoulder. "The fewer to attempt this famous ship, the greater the honor in its taking. The fewer to share what lies beneath her hatches, the heavier each man's purse that's there to share it! D'ye not see that, Matthew?"

Morgan shook his head, and then burst out laughing in his turn. He laughed the strange boyish laugh of a fifty-year-old man who had never outgrown a young man's lust for battle and sudden death.

"Aye, John," he said, " 'tis clear enough, when ye lay it out so simply." He huffed and blew and shook his head again. "Simple as folly and straight as the road to perdition, as the old pastor o' Llandock would say. And I'm with ye to the end, man. I'm with ye to the death!" The words that had seemed so theatrical coming from Captain Cross rang absolutely true from so old a comrade-in-arms as Matthew Morgan.

But Sir John Burrow, reaching for his slops and hose, scarcely heard. He was calculating already what guns and soldiers, what captains by sea and land remained to him for the coming venture. For him there was no lust for battle in it, nor the mad passion for rainbow gold that Matthew had read in his eyes the day before. For him, there was only the cold, hard realization that if he could not bring down the *Madre de Dios* and tow her home in glory to Plymouth Hoe, there would be no point in his going home at all.

CHAPTER

26

"COME, THEN, MARINA," TAMAR SAID FIRMLY, SMOOTHING her shawl of black lace over her satin gown, "and let us see what this corsair ship is really like." Bracing herself against the disconcerting roll of the ship, she crossed the cabin to the door and fumbled with the latch.

"If my lady wills it," said her duenna without enthusiasm.

Marina preferred her mistress's firm policy of a few days before, by which they were to consider themselves as prisoners of the English, and to conduct themselves accordingly. The open deck, with the heaving blue-green sea so close all around, made the old Indian woman acutely nervous. But with the return of strength and health, Tamar had begun to feel quite cramped, even in the captain general's relatively spacious cabin. Young limbs must stretch themselves, healthy lungs breathe in the open air. On her third day at sea, the Governor's daughter had abruptly jettisoned her previous policy and determined on its direct opposite: to give herself the run of the ship.

"Oh, come on, Marina!" the young mistress urged. "And please don't growl so." She lifted the latch and stepped buoyantly through the door.

She paused uncertainly for a moment as she stepped out onto the tilting, creaking planks, into the sunglare and the whipping wind. She swayed as the *Roebuck* heeled far over, paused, then swung back, rolling with the surge and roll of the sea. Above her, shrouds and ratlines strummed, the great sails bellied and cracked. She had seldom felt so defenseless somehow as she did then, standing on that bare deck between the sky and the sea. She felt a panicky urge to flee back to the protective closeness of the cabin's oaken walls.

But the protection of the cabin was purely illusory, she knew. It was as much a part of this new world of melting

foam and scudding clouds as the open deck. Tamar raised
her skirts from the green-scummed planking and strode determinedly across the afterdeck to gaze down into the waist
of the British privateer.

It was a far smaller, more cramped space than the decks
of the great carrack had been. The girl stared down in be-
wilderment at the looming iron pump head, the white longboat in its davits, the gleaming brass barrels of the guns,
the massy coil of the anchor chain in the shadow of the
forecastle. The knotted cables underfoot, the network of
tarry ropes overhead all seemed terribly confusing to her.

The sailors in red caps and work-stained smocks went so
purposefully about their mysterious labors, their bowed legs
adapting themselves with the ease of long experience to the
roll of the ship. The sun-browned soldiers, stripped to the
waist, lounging, talking, drowsing in what patches of shade
the clutter of the deck afforded, seemed like beings of another species than her own. Tamar gripped the railing and
looked down, trying to make some sense out of the confusion
of a ship at sea.

"I am glad to see my lady's health so much improved,"
said Sir John Burrow's voice, "and that your ladyship deigns
to take her exercise upon our decks."

Tamar swung round to look at him, tall and lean and
considerably less tidy than at their last encounter, with his
doublet only half laced up and no neck ruff at all. She looked
suspiciously at his grey eyes, at the trenched smile around
the edges of his mouth, to see if he were mocking her. De-
tecting nothing but a certain easy good humor, she relaxed
and gave him half a smile in her turn.

"I am quite well now, thank you, Captain," she answered
his query briskly. "And as for your decks—why, a prisoner
may still explore the confines of her jail, I think!"

His grin broadened at this attempt to salvage her defiant
attitude of three days before. In spite of herself, Tamar
smiled too.

Tamar de la Barca was by no means a frivolous girl, for all

her wildness and her headstrong independent spirit. She had in fact a strong sense of duty and of right and wrong. But she was very young, and much a creature of the passions too. And on a day like this, with the sea wind in her nostrils and the sun touching her cheeks for the first time in more than a week, she simply could not maintain the rigid posture she had labored to adopt. She remembered well enough who she was and to whom she spoke. But the sun was dazzling off the foam-flecked ocean, and the tall man before her seemed somehow to have very little in common with the corsair chief who had seized her bridle halfway across the plaza in Havana.

"Have you always followed the wars, then, Captain?" she demanded suddenly.

"Since I have been a man, I have followed the wars, my lady."

"And before the wars began? What then?"

"Before the wars, I was much in the country."

"The countryside of England," said the girl. "And what is this English country like, then, to which we go?" She was, she realized, genuinely curious. She had heard of the English corsairs all her life, and of their heretic Queen. But she knew almost literally nothing about England itself.

"I am a Yorkshireman," said Burrow, resting his elbows on the railing beside hers. "My father's lands, where I was raised up, are most of them in the Vale of York."

"Is this York-shire—" she stumbled over the alien syllables, "is this country of yours as lovely and warm as my islands are?"

"By no means as warm, Lady Tamar. But lovely enough to me."

"Tell me," said the girl.

To his own astonishment, he did.

Leaning beside her there, with the tropic sun hot upon their backs, he told the Spanish girl about the land of his birth. He told her of the rich fields of oats and barley around his father's ancient manor house. He told her of the sheep-walks on the high wolds and cows grazing in the fat green valleys. He remembered things loved and long forgotten: the tall grey towers of York Minster in the twilight, and dry stone walls along a country lane in spring. He told her of a wild ride along the high chalk cliffs he had taken once as a half-grown lad, from Flamborough down to Spurn Head. And telling her, he felt it all again—the buffeting of the wind, and the horse thundering between his thighs.

Listening, Tamar remembered her own last ride in the hills outside Havana, and the galloping race to the ceiba tree with Don Diego Aguilar. She shuddered at the thought of the man-hunter from the Oriente. But her heart beat up as Burrow's did at the memory of the jolting hooves beneath her, her hair blowing free and the wind in her face.

Burrow told the girl too about the last bit of land remaining to him, out of all the vast estates he had roved across as a boy. His elder brother had had all their father's property along with their father's title, when the old lord had died a decade since. But this one small portion of their mother's dower lands had been made a gift to young John many years before. It had remained his while all the entailed properties of the barony went to Brother Tom.

It was a small patch of rocky ground high on the wolds. Scarce a decent yeoman farmer's hold, really, though his mother had loved it dearly before her own untimely death. And John Burrow had loved it in his turn.

As a boy, he had chased sheep and hunted wild strawberries there. In his youth, he had helped old Wat, the tenant who ran the farm, with planting and with harvesting. Wat was a gnarled and silent man, gruff in his ways, stern even with his young master when it was a question of plowing a straight furrow, or getting the grain in before a storm. But he had made the barren land flourish, there on the high chalk wolds. John Burrow had learned more about farming from him than he ever had from his father's bailiffs in the fat valleys down below.

Tamar listened in amazement as the tall, fierce-looking man talked of beans and barley, his scarred face softening with a countryman's enthusiasm for the turning of the seasons, the ripening of crops. Listening, she felt another memory stir to life within her—the recollection of a tiny kitchen garden Marina had helped her plant herself one spring when she was a little girl. She remembered the black, moist soil between her fingers, the warmth of the sun, the pleasant ache at the back of her legs from bending to the hoe. And Marina's words, harsh and strange in her ears: *You must learn to make food grow from the earth, child. For everything changes in life, but the earth remains. The earth will provide.*

Tamar had laughed at the Indian woman then. She was the Governor of Cuba's daughter. How would she ever have to grow food from the earth?

"But your ladyship cannot care for such follies," said Sir John, checking himself as her eyes filled with her own memories.

"Have we not all of us our follies, Captain?" the girl parried easily, cheerful again. She was actually arch—almost coquettish—with the English corsair!

"Alas, we have indeed, my lady," the captain general sighed. "Like yonder gull, for instance, that labors so hard for so little."

The sea gull, wide-winged and savage-eyed, was just rising over the grey swell, its parted beak dripping sea-foam, but no fish. It was climbing for cruising space once more, and another plunge for prey. The Englishman and the Spanish girl watched it rise laboriously against a brisk southwest wind.

"A foolish bird indeed," said Tamar lightly, "to beat its wings against the wind to such little purpose."

"And yet, my lady," said Burrow, "a gull that flies against the wind may climb high and higher still." This in fact the gull was slowly doing, clambering upward, then sliding away across the wind, only to circle and rise again. "Aye," he said, as though to himself, "till it challenges the sun for glory."

It was a younger John Burrow speaking, the awkward cavalier from the North Country who had once believed in glory. A Burrow that spoke very seldom now from the weathered face of this thirty-four-year-old man.

"Or it may beat its wings in vain," said Tamar, feeling suddenly melancholy, "till it wearies at last and falls into the sea."

"Aye, indeed," said Sir John Burrow with a crooked grin. Then, sobering, his dark face turning once more to the restless sky: "But what is a gull to do but fly, my lady? And if it is its nature, to batter the wind until it falls? What else can the poor gull do, but follow its nature to the end?"

He leaned on the quarterdeck rail, one heavy forearm resting against the knuckle guard of his cup-hilted rapier. His grey eyes, which had looked so cold and hard to Tamar that afternoon in the Plaza de Armas, were grey as the sea now, and somehow infinitely sad.

"A gull can do no more," she answered him tartly. "But a man can perhaps do better!"

After which she plucked up her skirts and turned away, leaving him alone to brood upon the sea gulls and the empty sea.

" 'T IS A NEEDLE IN THE HAY AND NO MISTAKE," SIGHED MAT-
thew Morgan, gazing down at the broad Atlantic unrolled
upon the table before them. "One ship in so many thousand
miles of sea."

Sir John Burrow and his depleted corps of officers stood
around the chart table in Master Adam's cabin. The map laid
out before them pictured all the sea-lanes of the Atlantic,
from Europe to the Spanish Indies. It spilled over the edges
of the table, crinkled against their doublets as they leaned
close.

"The vastness of the Atlantic is precisely our advantage,"
said Master Adam quietly, and the older captains nodded.
"The *Madre de Dios* has four thousand miles to cross between Havana and the coast of Spain, and she is a slow sailer.
Even with two weeks' start, our fleeter vessels should run her
down before she's covered half the distance."

"But her course, Master Adam!" another of the infantry
officers objected. "How shall we know where to seek her in
such a waste of water?"

"There again, the size of this vast ocean is our best help,"
said Adam. "Ye'll notice that there be few islands in the
midparts of this sea, and one small archipelago only where
all sea-lanes converge. One place where all ships must break
their voyages for water and food and refitting after the perils
of half the crossing."

The sailing master planted a clean, short-fingered hand
across a cluster of islets.

"The Azores," said white-haired Captain Thynne, without
looking.

"The Isles of the Azores," said Adam. "Somewhere between Flores and St. Michael's we shall come up with our

great carrack, lying in a roadstead or lumbering ponderously between the islands. But here assuredly she shall be."

"To the Azores, then!" exulted Captain Cross, his eyes glittering. "And how far is that, Sailing Master?"

"Fifteen hundred miles to Flores, the westernmost island of them all, where we must start our search."

"Lay us a course for Flores, then, Master Adam," said Sir John Burrow, "the fastest way ye can."

"There is only one—the route of the treasure fleets of Spain. The route the *Madre de Dios* herself is taking, I've no doubt. The route that we are taking now." Adam's finger traced a line up and to the right across the chart. "North by northeast up the Florida Straits, across the Bahama Banks here, between Andros and Grand Bahama. Then out through the Northeast Providence Channel into the Atlantic. . . ."

Burrow tried to listen, and found to his surprise that he could not. He, whose determined attention to terrain and timing had earned him more than one hard-fought victory, found himself unable to follow such details now. Master Adam's clipped commentary droned on as he traced their route across the chart. But John Burrow's mind drifted inexorably away from the great carrack they pursued to the girl who had become their inadvertent prisoner.

They had spoken to each other quite frequently in recent days, strolling on the quarterdeck or seated in his own cabin, which she had made so comfortably her own. They had admired the working of the ship together, a matter of which he in fact knew little more than she did. They had talked of Europe—a battlefield to him, a fairyland to her, which she had not seen since she was three. But above all, their conversations had turned repeatedly back to their own past lives. As on that first morning on the deck, each had spoken most enthusiastically about the countryside of their own vanished childhood.

John Burrow had no sense of nuance in the Spanish tongue, and she had only a smattering of English as yet. Yet from her eager words, her dark, sparkling eyes, he had constructed a vivid picture of the growing girl.

He smiled in spite of himself, there in the murmurous cabin, his mind wandering far from the council of war. He smiled at the tempestuous little Governor's daughter of Cuba, as she had described herself so often. He saw her clearly in his mind's eye, brown as an Indian, rolling in the dust with the servants' children. He grinned particularly at the image of the outraged pedagogue who had all unknowing given her her name: "Vandal! Tartar! Tamerlane . . ."

Then, suddenly and more somberly, he was remembering his own youth in the far-off countryside of northern England. The world that Isabel in her turn had evoked with her quick questions and quicker smiles.

Abruptly, that world was with him once again. The cabin was gone, and the fleet itself, and it was haying time on his father's lands in Yorkshire. The summer heat was all around him, seeds prickled inside his shirt, and he was swinging a pitchfork on top of a rickety wain. All about him stretched blue sky and golden fields and farm lads with their smocks off, laboring in the sun.

His older brother, Tom, was riding toward him up the lane.

Lord Thomas Burrow—lord by courtesy, since his father was still alive—was impeccably clad as usual, his doublet brushed, his starched ruff spotless. He was looking up at Brother John and shaking his head already at such violation of due decorum—a baron's son out haying with his own cottagers!

"Ye'll burn the skin off your back up there, John," Tom called up to him. But John, who was dark as a blackamoor already, had only laughed.

"You ride up to London for me, Brother Tom," he called down, "and tell her Majesty I am detained by a sun-blistered back from attending her at court! Or whatever excuse comes best, Tom. I'm sure ye'll find the words." Thomas was a natural courtier: he would find the words.

Thomas had shaken his head and ridden on, that summer afternoon fifteen years before. And John Burrow, in the prime of his youth, had stretched up his arms and laughed in the sun. There would be none of the courtier's life for him, he swore. No bowing and scraping, no fawning on the great men up in London who could ruin a man's fondest dreams with the arching of an eyebrow, the whisper of a word.

An old jingle came back to him as he stood, legs wide-planted, high on the hay wagon there:

> *Cog, lie, flatter and face,*
> *Four ways in court to win your place.*
> *If you be thrall to none of these,*
> *Away, good Piers! Home, John Cheese!*

Let Brother Tom dream of glory and power beyond his birthright. John Burrow would be John Cheese indeed, stay home in his father's counties, and die a happy man.

Why had it not worked out that way?

Was it the first command in the Netherlands that had planted the seeds of ambition in his soul? The first victory, the first words of praise from men in fur-trimmed robes, the first compelling smile from the hawk-faced old woman who was England's Queen?

John Burrow did not know.

He knew only that on that vanished summer afternoon, his highest aspiration had been to best Rafe Hatton the blacksmith's son two falls out of three at the festival after sheep-shearing. He no longer remembered who had won that epic contest. But he was clear enough on one thing: the John Burrow who had heaved hay with his cottagers and wrestled the blacksmith's boy was long gone, lost somewhere down the years. In his place stood Sir John Burrow, Captain General of the Fleet, a lean and hungry man of thirty-four with a future still to win. A man whose highest hopes rode with the great ship *Madre de Dios* somewhere far ahead across the broad Atlantic.

* * *

Sir John Burrow shook off his reverie and turned his mind again to business. Damn the girl, he told himself irritably, that brings such foolish memories to mind. And then he smiled ruefully once more. For the fact of the matter was that he looked forward with an almost boyish eagerness to seeing Tamar again that afternoon. To finding surcease from the cares of a climbing man in the voice and smile and in the eyes of this strange Spanish girl.

28

THE MAN WAS COMING TOWARD HER AGAIN, WIDE SHOULDERS slightly hunched, the whites of his eyes glowing in the light of the single flickering candle. Once more, as so many times before, she tried frantically, desperately to scream, and could not do it. Then she felt his weight come down upon her, his hands upon her body.

No, she wept. *Oh, God, no!*

The floor was bucking and heaving under her as she struggled beneath him. The coarse servant's gown was up about her waist, the rough pallet scraping against her naked skin. The man's strength savaged her body, degraded her soul.

She woke up sweating and gasping in her darkened bed. She had not screamed this time, she thought, for Marina was snoring undisturbed in her small bunk across the room. She had not screamed, and that was good. She crossed herself and murmured a prayer of gratitude to Mary the Mother of God.

The bed, she realized as she came fully awake, was moving under her as the pallet had done in her dream, rising and plunging far more violently than the normal pitch and roll of the ship. The bed-curtains—half open, she always slept with them half open now—swayed away and fluttered back as the cabin tilted dangerously one way and then the other. The girl had to clutch at a bedpost to keep from falling out at each heart-stopping roll and heave. Between the swaying curtains, she saw rain pounding on the windows. Lightning crackled jaggedly across the sky behind the mullioned panes.

Another storm, she thought, and a big one. She had seen the hurricano roar in over Cuba, and she knew a big storm when she saw one.

Then suddenly, astonishingly, she was afraid.

Not of the storm, nor even specifically of her dream, still

hovering around the fringes of her consciousness. Suddenly she was afraid of herself.

All that summer, Tamar had tried to face the changes coming over her. The fits of restlessness and wildness that dwarfed all her childish escapades. The unfamiliar waves of sensuality that pulsed through her trembling limbs. She had been a creature of passion and feeling all her young life, but she had never felt emotional upheavals like these.

It was this new sensuality, she realized now with crushing certainty, that had carried her down into her father's garden, into the waiting arms of Don Ricardo de Olid. And it was these same imperious passions that had taken her at last to Don Diego Aguilar's little room in the Cerro.

The bed swayed sickeningly downward, then jolted up once more. Lightning blazed whitely behind the windows, and a clap of thunder seemed to explode just overhead. Something fell with a long tearing sound and a terrific thump across the deck above, and the girl heard muffled shouts and running footsteps over her head.

Tamar paid it all no heed. She was facing the most disturbing thought of all.

After the Cerro, after Don Diego Aguilar—could she ever really let another human being touch her again? Could she ever open herself once more to those wild sweet stirrings she had just begun to feel? Would she ever again dare to feel the wonder of other lips on hers, the closeness of another body against her own, of another living human spirit brushing against hers?

The room in which she lay seemed suddenly to suffocate her. The square silhouette of a chair back, shifting with a creak as the room plunged once more, looked vividly, terrifyingly like the hunched shoulders of a man. With a small, unhappy sound in her throat, Tamar slid out of bed, flung the heavy cape that hung on a peg by the door around her shoulders, and bolted out into the storm.

Sir John Burrow stood with his legs wide apart, one arm

locked through the tarry ratlines, watching the men cut through the last tangle of ropes to free the broken spar that had fallen across the poop deck. Master Adam, adjusting with ease to the roll and plunge of the storm-tossed vessel, stood in the middle of the deck, shouting terse orders into the gale. Off to larboard, Burrow glimpsed the little *Lark*, bright in a glimmer of lightning, making heavy weather of it through mountainous, wind-lashed seas.

"Captain Burrow!" He scarcely heard the voice above the howling of wind and sea. "John—Sir John."

He turned and saw Tamar, pale in the glare of the lightning, looking at him. She stood at the head of the companionway that led to the quarterdeck below, clutching his own court cape about her body.

"God's blood, woman—" he began, and then in Spanish: "Tamar, you must get down at once. Get back to your cabin, before the sea—" He gestured sharply toward the great waves that swelled higher than the poop deck itself on all sides. Even as he spoke, one crashed in a shower of foam over the forecastle head, leaving a dozen seamen rolling in the sluicing water, clinging to ropes and railings for their lives.

The lightning flickered and was gone, but even in the denser darkness that followed, he could see that she was still there, swaying as the ship swayed, at the head of the companionway.

With a hearty oath, Burrow stepped over to her, caught her about the waist, and hurried her back down the ladder to the lower deck. But as he drew her in under the ladder and began to hurry her along the cabin wall toward the door, she suddenly turned back against his arm, resisting his strength with all of hers. Pausing, astonished, he heard a stifled "No!" above the roaring of the wind. "No—I will not go back there!"

He could have dragged her on by main force, flung her through the door to safety, and gotten back to his work. Instead, he heard himself saying, in Spanish made even more awkward by confusion and irritation, "But why not, Tamar?

No man but those that must will be out on the open deck this night. Why then should you—"

"I will not go back into that room!" she flared defiantly at him. Suddenly she was the proud Governor of Cuba's daughter once again, chin up, eyes flashing in a glare of lightning.

She stood with her back against the cabin wall, in the shadow of the ladder. Her gaze flicked past him to the huge combers, the racing seas behind him. Her eyes were wide and dark. She clearly had the sense to be frightened, he thought. Yet she clung to her mad whim to stay upon the open deck in spite of all.

"My lady—Tamar—" he began once more, shouting into her ear. At that moment, the sea fell on them.

Tamar saw the wave coming, a feathery wall of white exploding through the ratlines, over the railing, the companionway ladder, the corner of the poop. She saw it coming and clutched involuntarily at Sir John's tall frame braced between her and what was to come, his back to it, unseeing. She screamed his name as the wall of water struck them.

They were falling together, rolling, tumbling through the whiteness. She saw him slam into the pump handle through the foam, and she herself caromed painfully off a rolling culverin, straining against its ropes. Then the two of them fetched up together, sprawling in a foot of icy water under the lee bulwarks.

They rose together too, drenched and gasping, clinging to each other once more as that side of the ship rose up and the water flooded away to windward across the deck.

Tamar felt herself shaking violently from the cold seawater that seemed to soak her to the very bones. The cape she had wrapped round her was gone, and the linen shift she slept in was plastered to her skin. It was as though she wore no clothes at all in the driving wind and rain. Her head rang with the force of her tumble, yet she could still hear, as though from far away, the sound of her own voice—laughing!

She laughed at her own folly, at the ridiculous figure the Governor's elegant daughter must cut at this moment. Above all, she flung back her head and laughed with sheer relief that the bogies of the night were gone, washed away in a flood of plain, prosaic salt water!

She was still laughing as Burrow flung his own heavy cloak about her shivering body and drew her toward the cabin door once more. She stopped laughing only when he bent abruptly over her and put his mouth on hers.

If John Burrow had been asked on his dying day why he kissed the Governor's daughter of Cuba on the *Roebuck's* foam-swept quarterdeck that night, he could not have answered. And yet there were obvious explanations enough.

Lightning zigzagged across the heavens at that moment, lighting up her laughing face. And the soft cheeks streaked with rain, the shining hair plastered to her neck and shoulders, the shining eyes looking up at him were sheerly beautiful. So he kissed her.

Then too there was the young body trembling close against his own within the circle of the heavy cloak. John Burrow would have had to be more or less than a man not to experience some quickening of passion when he felt that slender waist moving in the angle of his arm, and the pressure of one small breast, all but naked in the soaking shift, coming against his chest. How could any man help but draw her closer still, and press his lips to hers?

There were other reasons too, of course. The vivid presence of this girl had been so much a part of him for many days, the desire maturing beneath the level of his own awareness ever since he saw her for the first time, riding across the square in Havana. And he was a lonely man, that had found little comfort in the hard and desperate life he had led for so many years. There were so many reasons.

But none of them mattered at all when he pulled Tamar in against him under the dripping larboard companionway and clamped his mouth on hers.

John Burrow was no womanizer, but he had had his share of women, his share of kisses in his life. Even the gawkiest country lad, the most reluctant courtier, the most single-minded of captains must have felt the need of women, and have satisfied that need. But he had never held a woman like this before, or felt such lips open beneath his own.

He felt the shock of her surprise. And then he felt her mouth responding, her small arms sliding up around his neck. He pressed her tight against him and felt her pressing tighter still, her breasts flattening against his chest now, her thighs against his own. A tempest of passion blazed up in her —and in himself—that for long minutes dimmed the thunder of the sea, the howling of the storm to a distant echo of their own breathing, their own pounding hearts.

Then, as suddenly as it had begun, it was over. The girl broke from him in the rain-whipped darkness. He heard—he swore he heard—a low, happy laugh, a tinkle of relief and joy. He saw her flit across the deck and vanish through the cabin door.

He stood there in the rain, dazed and baffled, wondering if he had really heard those last whispered words, as she turned back toward him, a vague shadow in the doorway:

"Thank you, Sir John Burrow. Oh, thank you, more than you can know!"

CHAPTER

29

TAMAR FACED HER OWN ODDLY CONTRADICTORY FEELINGS about John Burrow on a twilit evening in her own cabin some days later.

Sir John himself had been with her much of the afternoon, had in fact just left her. Marina, busy elsewhere about the ship on the little chores that made life more comfortable for her young mistress, had not yet returned. Tamar, thus left alone, sat in the captain's chair, her cheek resting on her hand, watching the twilight shimmer beyond the stern windows as she brooded over the strange man who had shouldered his way so violently into her life.

His presence still seemed to hover there in the musty cabin. The leathery smell of his hauberk was still in her nostrils. She could still sense the sheer bigness of him, now gone from the low-backed chair across the table from her, and the bantering but gentle glint in his eyes. She remembered the jest with which he had left her, and the slant of his shoulders as he bent to pass out the low doorway.

She remembered him vividly. But it was herself she thought about as she gazed out at the sea gulls floating past in the lemon light of evening.

She thought of how she had laughed at his quaint, unidiomatic Spanish as much as at his last jest, not arrogantly, but with the easy laughter of a friend. For had they not become friends over these slow weeks at sea? Friends—and was that all? She felt her cheeks color suddenly at the thought.

The kiss under the companionway the night of the great storm she had put firmly—if with some difficulty—in its proper perspective. It was, she told herself, the night, the tempest, their sudden closeness—and above all, her own feverish and melancholy state of mind. She had needed that kiss, and the experience of her own passionate responsiveness, to reassure her that she was still capable of responding to a man's embrace. She had laughed with happy relief at this, and thanked him for it, and prayed heartily to the Virgin Mother that she might be forgiven for it.

Beyond that, Tamar had not dared to let her thoughts wander. Neither of them had mentioned it the following day. They had gone on essentially as before. A bit less formally, perhaps, but with never so much as a touch of the hand that might carry them into a realm of possibilities that was, for her at least, almost literally unthinkable.

For she was a Spanish grandee's daughter, after all, and he was an English pirate.

A friendly conversation was one thing. A flirtation was quite possible—had she not flirted outrageously with Don Ricardo, whose uncles desired nothing more than to ruin her father utterly? Even a single kiss might be forgiven—Mary Mother was infinitely forgiving—considering what it had done to soothe the sickness in her soul. But more than that —the thought of more than that—

She rose and paced the cabin, ticking off to herself once more all the things John Burrow had done to earn her animosity, to merit her disdain. She heard again the sudden ear-stunning crash of the English artillery over Havana. She winced once more at the thought of the pirates' arrogant boots striding the familiar streets of the town that had been hers all her conscious life. She remembered her own fear, her humiliation at the hands of these men, these blue-eyed, sunburned devils from the sea.

His doing, all of it. His will and his alone had brought it all to pass.

And was she to throw herself like some moonstruck Indian girl at the head of such a man?

"He is a pleasant gentleman, your English captain," said Marina, stepping slowly through the door.

"He is not *my* captain, Marina!" Tamar snapped back. "And he is certainly not a pleasant gentleman!" That she

herself had thought precisely that a moment since had completely slipped her mind.

"It is well, my lady," the old woman answered in her toneless, guttural Spanish. "Since all of them will so soon be
dead."

Tamar's heartbeat changed its rhythm. "What do you
mean, Marina?" she asked, struggling to keep her tone casual.

"When the English attack the great ship," the Indian
woman answered flatly, "they will all surely die."

"The great ship?"

"Yes, my lady. The great ship that you went to see yourself
in the harbor before it sailed away. The one called the
Mother of God. They mean to come up with her soon, in the
next day or two. So the boy who serves the captain general's
table says. And when they do this, they will all surely die."

Tamar sat down on the leather-covered bench beneath the
windows.

She and John Burrow had never spoken of the precise nature of the "business" he had to transact on his way home to
England, the crucial appointment that had brought him away
from the Isle of Pines in such haste. By tacit consent, they
had avoided a subject that could do nothing but divide them.
Or remind them how totally they were in fact already sun-
dered by circumstances one from the other.

She sat there, her face as drained of blood as it had been
flushed a short time since, and let the desperate thoughts
wheel and collide within her.

She remembered the great carrack up whose dizzy flanks
she had ascended on a Sunday afternoon. She saw again the
tufted brows and indomitable face of Don Fernando de
Mendoza, Count of Olmedo, Knight of the Golden Fleece,
the great lord admiral who commanded that floating fortress
from the East. She saw the soldiers in their gleaming morions,
lined up rank on rank to receive them. And the ugly snouts
of the guns, tier on tier, waiting even now somewhere ahead
of them to receive the English corsairs when they came.

It would be her salvation, she knew. The *Madre de Dios*

was untakable, unsinkable. When the English laid her alongside, they would be taken instead, and those that survived
would be put to rowing Spanish galleys for the rest of their
lives. If they were not all blown out of the water first by those
endless rows of guns.

Sir John Burrow would bring his ship alongside, even in
the teeth of the terrible guns. Tamar knew that with certainty. And then she would be saved.

Why then was her heart not beating up with joy? Why was
she not thinking about herself at all, for once in her passionately self-concerned life, but only about Sir John Burrow?

And why would foolish old Marina's stupid, *stupid* words
not leave her, not cease echoing over and over in her head,
for all she could do to still them: *When the English attack
the great ship—When the English attack the great ship—
When the English attack the great ship—*

They will all surely die.

CHAPTER

30

Don Diego Aguilar paced the quarterdeck of the *Trinidad* with a short-legged, energetic stride. The wind whined and whistled in the shrouds above him, the grey sea surged below. Both seemed to echo the seething passions within the man himself.

Aguilar had sailed in the small, swift *guardacostas* around Cuba. But he had scarcely ever been out of sight of his native island before. The elemental power of the open sea, the driving fury of the sea winds intoxicated him. It was as if the whole world were opening up to him for the first time. He paced the decks at all hours, reveling in the wind's buffeting, the sting of the salt spray, and dreaming of the future.

He had taken a long gamble to win that future, but he had no doubt at all that it would succeed.

His powerful little flotilla had missed the freebooters at the Isle of Pines by no more than a day. Wild Indians who lived on the island had told him how half the English fleet had parted company and slipped away by stealth in the night. How the rest had followed soon thereafter, but taking a slightly different course, disappearing over the horizon *there*, not straight into the sunrise but that way, north of it.

North to the Bahama Banks, Aguilar's navigators had murmured, and then swing east for the Azores. The route of the *flota* itself when it made sail for Spain. And the route of the great carrack? Aguilar had demanded sharply. The route of the *Madre de Dios*? Indeed, the navigators had assured him, very like.

And so he had gambled on their word, and on his own run of luck. He had ordered the Vera Cruz galleons to be provisioned from the island for a long, deep-sea voyage. In three days, they had sailed.

In so doing, he vastly exceeded his own commission from

the Governor of Cuba, which gave him authority only to seek out the English corsairs at the offshore Isle of Pines. But who would quibble over means and ends, when he brought what was left of the English corsairs home in chains? And that he would surely do.

Don Diego glanced port and starboard at the *Trinidad*'s sister galleons, long and lean and deadly, that plowed the Atlantic on either side of his own. The Vera Cruz galleons were King's ships, designed and built especially to stop the depredations of the corsairs. They could easily match the vaunted speed and maneuverability of the English ships, the deadly weight of the English shot. And their crews were all picked men, young and eager as Aguilar himself to find and fight the English sea dogs.

Soon now they would come up with them, he thought. Three or four battered ships manned by weary freebooters—that was all that was left to Sir John Burrow. Not a vessel, not a man of them would ever see England again.

And the English captain general himself—he would be Aguilar's own most particular business!

Don Diego Aquilar was a bloody-minded man. He had never forgiven a slight, never avoided a challenge—and never lost an affray in his life. Never, until he had met the tall Englishman in that midnight melee in the Plaza de Armas. He had an arm that ached and moved stiffly still to remind him of that meeting. But it would be serviceable enough when he met the English Sir-John once again. He dreamed almost nightly of that coming confrontation with the only man that had ever bested him with weapons in his hands.

And after that—anything and everything!

The *mestizo* from the Cuban jungles dared to dream now as he had never dreamed before. He saw himself lionized at the Escorial as the hero of the Battle of Havana and of the coming fight in the Azores, as the killer of corsairs, the defender of the Spanish Indies. And he could almost smell the scented sheets and damask hangings of the bed where his triumph over Tamar de la Barca—and through her over all the island aristocracy—would be acted out again and again, for as long as he deigned to have her.

Aguilar was exalted as he had never been before with bloodlust, with lust for women and for glory. And between him and all good things stood only a ragged band of English privateers—and the tall, saturnine figure of Sir John Burrow.

The Lord Admiral Don Fernando de Mendoza stood under the lantern at the height of his own poop deck, gazing out across the little inlet at the stark hills of Flores. His craggy face was darker with wind and weather, his hair and beard bleached whiter by the sun than when he had sailed from Cuba. But he was dreaming here, as he had when he sailed out under the guns of Morro Castle, of the peaceful hills and orange groves that awaited him on the other side of the Atlantic.

A longboat bobbed toward him across the choppy bay, bringing the last casks of sweet water. Fruits, vegetables, great sides of beef would be coming on the morrow. The rude Portuguese fishermen who inhabited this westernmost sentinel of the Azores were only too glad to sell their produce. Within two days the *Madre de Dios* would put to sea once more.

For the last time with *him* as her commander, Don Fernando devoutly prayed.

The lord admiral had served King Philip for thirty years. He had been at the Battle of Lepanto, had been shipwrecked on the sands of Juda, had been twice taken prisoner by the Moors. He had had two tall ships sunk under him, and had seen twice that number of enemy vessels founder and expire under the pounding of his guns.

And he had had enough.

The salty reek of the sea air clogged his nostrils. The slightest stirring of the huge ship under him, swinging ponderously on its anchor, stirred nausea in his belly. The old man longed for the dry, lime-scented air of Granada, for the solid earth of his own orange groves beneath his feet. He wanted to die in his bed, he realized with a thin-lipped smile, as a Christian man ought to do. Not with a sword in his hand and blood upon his hands.

The longboat scraped alongside and the loading was begun.

CHAPTER

31

A MOON SWAYED BEHIND THE FOREMAST SHROUDS, LAYING A flickering path across the sea. The *Roebuck* made way steadily under slapping sails, only half filled by a temperamental wind. It was late, and the men were snoring below or curled up in corners on the open deck. A stocking-capped seaman stood to the tiller aft, and there was a watch on the poop, where the great lantern burned. Beyond these, the ship was still.

Sir John Burrow was still abroad, prowling restlessly about the ship. The cluttered, narrow waist, the gun deck below, even the forecastle head with its carved and gilded roe deer vaulting into space—he had been everywhere that day and night. With his own hands and eyes he had checked weapons, lashings, preparations of every sort. Everywhere he had greeted the men with the easy, jesting familiarity of a popular commander on the eve of an engagement.

Now the men slept, and the commander continued his lonely vigil, dodging beneath a boarding net, descending a companion ladder, moving slowly among the culverins and cannon drawn up behind their gunports. Unable to stop, unable to rest until it all began.

He knew that it must come soon, that they were near upon the carrack now. How it would end, he did not speculate. But whether he rode up from the Thames in triumph, with the loot of both the Indies in his train, or whether he bled his life away in the scuppers of the great ship that waited for him beyond the grey horizon, yet he would have done his best. Neither God nor man could ask more than that.

Burrow stepped off the ladder onto the quarterdeck and stopped.

Standing at the railing in the shadow of the poop was a

slender figure in a fluttering gown. Her face was beautiful as a child's in the faint moonglow. But the dark eyes she turned on him were no child's eyes.

"My lady," said Sir John. "Tamar. It is late for your ladyship to be abroad."

"Do I not then have the freedom of the ship?" the girl answered with a lightness that was somehow not convincing. "Surely this is not too far to wander from my cell."

"Of course, my lady," he bowed, responding to her banter. "But I should suggest a warmer cloak perhaps, when next you venture forth so late."

"I have no cloak at all, Sir John," she reminded him. "I lost it overside on a stormy night not too long since. As you may recall."

Burrow grinned and rested his elbows upon the rail beside her. It made him feel good simply to be there with her, elbow to elbow, gazing out over the sea.

Tamar looked at the older man. His dark hair and beard were uncombed and windblown as usual, his worn doublet only half laced up. He dressed with none of the elegance and grace of the gentlemen she had always known. And she had seen what savage violence he was capable of when he had four feet of steel in his hand and a battle cry in his throat.

Six feet and several inches of lean, piratical villainy, she told herself, that was Sir John Burrow! Yet the eyes in that long, large-featured face were the quietest eyes she had ever seen.

"How is it," she asked him finally, "that you came to follow this corsair trade, John Burrow?" There was only the faintest tremor in her voice.

Sir John smiled in the shifting moonlight. "I am no pirate, Tamar," he answered her quite seriously. "I am a privateer. I sail under a royal letter of marque authorizing me to prey at will upon the ships, towns, and possessions whatsoever of his Majesty of Spain. Your sovereign and mine have been at war for a long time, my lady."

She shrugged her shoulders. "Pirate—privateer—it is all the same. Your men killed our soldiers, burned our houses, looted and robbed us. It is not the way a Spanish gentleman would behave." Or the way a man with such quiet eyes should be, she added to herself. A man that loves his country-side, and growing things in the sun.

"It is the way some Spanish gentlemen do behave, Tamar," he answered gently. "I have fought in the Netherlands, and seen what King Philip's Council of Blood has done there to those they call heretics and rebels."

"That is politics," she snapped back impatiently. "I do not understand politics. I asked you about yourself."

It was his turn to shrug. "I am a man with my way to make in the world, my lady. My brother is older by a year than I, as I have told you, and all my father's lands are his. I shall have lands of my own one day, and a great house in the Vale of York as well. But I shall have to earn them with my sword."

"You will earn your house and your lands by burning and spoiling ours?"

He smiled still, but with a touch of bitterness now. "More politics, I am afraid. The road to royal favor, and the fat purses and broad lands that come thereby, lies in good service to my Queen. I serve her Majesty"—he touched his heavy iron sword hilt as he said it—"with this."

The girl shook her head. A stubborn wench, he thought, and yet a shrewd one too. For how *was* he earning his house and his country peace, but by spoiling her of hers?

"Marina says it is the way of the world," said Tamar, controlling her voice with a real effort now. "She says you will all die soon, as others have died at your hands."

"That is quite possible," he agreed. Indeed, he added to himself, it is quite likely. The pale scar burned across his cheek. Another inch, and he would have been bones beneath the peaty soil of Ireland these five years. Another day, and he and all his men might be drained corpses rolling in the wake of this great carrack of Spain they sought so ardently. "But that," he concluded aloud, "as your Marina says, is the way of the world, Tamar."

He straightened from the railing, prepared to leave her. But she held him suddenly with her eyes. "Must it always be your way, John Burrow?" she demanded almost harshly of him now.

He thought of grain and sheep and a country hearth. But as he turned toward her, his bronzed hand brushed once more against the cupped hilt and curving knuckle guard of his long Toledo blade. "I fear, my lady," he answered simply, "that it must."

He bowed and went his way, off across the darkened deck. Tamar stood alone by the rail, one small hand resting on a salt-caked ratline, shivering in the night wind.

BOOK IV

---◆---

THUNDER
WRAPP'D
IN
A BALL OF FIRE

They do not always scape, that's
  some comfort.
Ay, ay, ay; and then time steals on,
And steals, and steals, till violence
  leaps forth
Like thunder wrapp'd in a ball of fire,
And so doth bring confusion to them all.

—THOMAS KYD,
  The Spanish Tragedy

32

LINES CROSSED ON THE MAP. THE WINDS BLEW, FLICKING FOAM off a choppy sea. Across a thousand miles of ocean, the ships converged.

They were battered and weary ships. Their bottoms were caked with weed and shells, their cordage rotten, their sails stained and patched. Main beams in the holds of the *Madre de Dios* were twisted and splintered with the shifting of the bales and casks and chests of precious cargo that filled her from the orlop to the main deck. The *Roebuck* had been taking water for days, a slow, steady leak that was kept down only by daily pumping. Pursuers and pursued alike were feeling the effects of the long Atlantic passage.

But still they bellied onward through the salt grey combers. And on the thirtieth of August, two leagues south of Flores in the westernmost Azores, the arcs of their charted courses crossed at last.

It was the *Lark* that saw her first, at daybreak on the thirtieth. The *Lark* was the smallest vessel in the English fleet, eighty tons and fifty men, Robert Cross, captain. Cross was the most flamboyant of the commanders, the most savage in a fight, the most ardent in pursuit of martial glory.

"*Sail ho!*" The shout from the foremast head cut across the yammer of gulls wheeling against the dawn.

"Where away, lad?" shouted Cross, bursting out of his low cabin aft, uncharacteristically disheveled in his shirt and slops.

"South-southeast, before the wind."

"I see her, Captain," a mariner in the fore-chains shouted over an outflung arm. "Yonder where the mist breaks. South of the headland—yonder."

Flores was a jagged presence to port, hills just pricking

through the shredding fogs. Almost dead ahead, no more than a mile away, the sails of the great carrack stood out black against an orange strip of sun.

Captain Cross looked sharply round him, getting his bearings. The *Foresight* was nearest, a league off to starboard, with the *Susan Bonaventure* beyond. The *Roebuck* was no more than the glimmer of her stern lantern on the grey horizon. The island loomed close to port, mists drifting among its crags. Less than a mile down the wind, the biggest ship in the world floated lazily on the swell.

The eyes of Captain Robert Cross flamed up with sudden joy.

"Fire a gun for the fleet, Master Seall," he called down the length of his deck, "and lay out every inch o' canvas the yards will bear. By God, but we'll be the first to lay a shot across her decks!"

Tamar raised her face dripping from the basin and listened for the sound again. Far off and flat, like the morning gun in the Plaza de Armas, so long ago and far away.

"Marina?" she called, steadying herself against the slow roll of the ship. "Marina? What is that?"

"I do not know, my lady." But the Indian woman's tight lips, the skin drawn taut across the cheekbones showed otherwise.

Footsteps pounded across the deck overhead. Excited voices sounded, and there was a distant masthead shout. Then Tamar knew too.

"The *Mother of God*," she said. "They've found her."

She remembered the *Mother of God* once more as she had seen it towering above Havana harbor as her father's punt drew near. Then suddenly all Havana was there about her with a pungent reality she had not felt for weeks. She heard the church bells of the Franciscans as she had heard them that summer morning, smelled the dust in the streets, and tropic flowers cascading over garden walls. Swaying slightly there by the table in the English captain general's cabin,

Tamar felt a sudden pulse of hope after so many days of confusion and misery. Havana was real, and really there—and she was going home.

"If my lady pleases?"

Sir John Burrow's body blocked the doorway, stooping slightly, as he always did to pass through doors not made for so tall a man. He wore a battered steel corselet and carried a plumed helmet on his left arm. His rapier hilt banged against the doorframe as he entered. His voice was as cold and impersonal as though they had never stood together by the rail in the moonlight, or kissed each other in the rain.

"We are sailing into action, my lady," he said, as matter-of-factly as if he were telling her of a festival in the plaza, or a day's excursion to the works at Morro. "You will be pleased to stay in your cabin till the matter is decided."

Tamar looked at his weathered cheeks and quiet English eyes, and she felt her heart turn over in her breast.

It took Lord Admiral Don Fernando de Mendoza twelve minutes from shirt-and-breeches in his cabin to his quarter-deck, an engraved steel corselet over his black velvet, a plumed helmet on his head. He mounted to the poop with dignity, the morning breeze ruffling his beard. He surveyed the ship once—armed men already lining the rail in the waist, seamen scampering aloft like monkeys. Sailing Master Salazar was in his place, and a dozen senior officers clustered with him at the highest point of the poop deck. Among them, elegant in dark satin, a slim gilt rapier at his side, stood Don Ricardo de Olid.

"Don Ricardo." The lord admiral saluted him almost brusquely. "Your presence here does you honor, sir. Yet I must ask that you withdraw. You are a guest aboard this vessel, and this place is unnecessarily exposed. Neither your distinguished uncles nor your noble kin at court would ever forgive me if—"

"It is precisely for my honor's sake, my lord, that I must stay," Don Ricardo answered with a nervous laugh. His handsome dark eyes blinked rapidly in the wind, and his narrow moustaches were wet. "And then," he added with an uneasy attempt at nonchalance, "I have never seen a battle, and I cannot imagine a better point of vantage. So, with your permission—"

"Of course, Don Ricardo," the lord admiral responded gravely. The first round shot through the rigging, he judged, would send this gallant cavalier scuttling to his cabin.

Putting so minor an irritation out of his mind at once, Admiral Mendoza turned to look aft, past Señor Salazar's grizzled face, past the huge gilded lantern on the stern post, toward the island behind them and the approaching sails.

There were three vessels—no, four of them now. The nearest, and the smallest, was a long culverin shot away, fairly skipping toward him over the sparkling waves.

Admiral Mendoza smiled. It was a public smile, a smile for all his men. But it was a smile of genuine wonder too.

"A flyboat," he said aloud to the sailing master. "A pinnace only, and she leads all the rest. These English must be mad."

Señor Salazar laughed, a sharp, nervous burst of sound. Behind him the clustered officers began to chuckle too. Laughter rolled like a cleansing wave across the quarterdeck and the half deck, down into the milling waist. It rose to the masthead seamen, the musketeers already deploying themselves in the rigging. It flowed down the companionways and across the low, rumbling gun decks below. From keel to foretop, the *Madre de Dios* laughed at her pursuers.

CHAPTER

33

MIDMORNING. THE *Madre de Dios* HAD FLUNG OUT ALL HER sails, and her gigantic mainsail filled like a bladder in the breeze. But even Captain Thynne's slow-sailing *Susan Bonaventure* was no more than two miles astern now, the *Roebuck* and the *Foresight* less than a mile. The *Lark*, still the nearest of the pursuers, was closing fast.

On the quarterdeck of his flagship, Burrow stood with Master Adam and Matthew Morgan, looking at the ship they had come so far to find.

"It is a carrack," said Master Adam quietly. "A *não*, the Portugals call it. I count seven decks, from the main orlop to the poop. Three gun decks, double spar, double forecastle—" He shook his head. "It is the greatest of all the great ships. Ye'll scarce see them outside Pacific waters, or the Indian Ocean. It is the greatest ship in the world."

"What's her size, think you?" asked Matthew Morgan.

"Fifteen hundred tons or thereabout," said Adam. "And all our ships together are not eight hundred tons."

"How many men will she muster?"

"Eight hundred, perhaps a thousand."

"With so many of Captain Thynne's men flat on their backs," said Burrow, "we have not half so many."

"Aye," said Matthew, "and we'll have less than that if Captain Cross does not hold back."

Sir John followed his lieutenant's eyes and sucked in a sharp breath. The *Lark* was close in now. Much too close.

"She'll be a demiculverin's length already," said Master Adam, squinting across the wind. "And still not a shot out of her. 'Tis strange."

"It will be the end of her," said Matthew Morgan positively, "if she does not sheer off soon. My God, she'll be under the transom in a minute."

The little two-masted vessel did in fact seem to be cutting across under the towering transom stern of the *Mother of God*. The English ship was leaning hard over, tacking into the wind.

"He'll be taking the weather gauge of her," said Adam. "Getting to windward, so he can choose the range and time to fight, instead of the Spaniard. He'll be safe enough now, under her stern chasers, too close for the high guns to hit. But when he swings around with the wind again, and runs broadside to her—"

He stopped. Even John Burrow and Matthew Morgan, with little experience at sea, could understand what might happen then. Running flank to flank with the *Madre de Dios*, the *Lark* would be sailing square across the larboard gunports of the lumbering carrack.

"If she pulls out of point-blank range before she turns again," said Master Adam, "she'll have a chance at least to lay her own shot across the Spaniard's decks and pull on ahead with little damage. But if she tacks too soon, God help her and all good men aboard her. They'll blow her into kindling."

Captain Cross had followed the Spaniard too far down the wind, and he knew it. But the rest of the fleet was pressing so close behind him, eager for the honor of drawing first blood. The *Foresight* especially—they had jury-rigged a mizzen abaft the mainmast and were coming on apace. Cross, resplendent now in a silver-threaded doublet and a white-plumed hat, his finest court rapier at his side, tugged at his ear with long white fingers and swore aloud. He was the youngest commander, his the meagerest command in all the fleet. He would have the honor of first shot, or die in the attempt!

But when he looked up at what he had challenged, even he felt a touch of perspiration on his brow.

The great gilded stern of the *Madre de Dios* loomed like a floating castle over him, not two hundred feet away. He could see the glitter of Spanish breastplates lining her stern galleries, helmeted heads peering down at him from her carved poop. Two short rows of guns faced the *Lark* even from the carrack's stern. What they would confront when they swung back on a southeasterly tack, broadside to the Spaniard, Cross did not dare to think.

"Shall we put our iron into her arse now, Captain?" Master Seall called nervously from the main deck. "And then drop off and let her pull ahead a bit?"

The *Lark* mounted half a dozen demicannon on each side, all under the low quarterdeck aft, and several breech-loading little man-killers in slings on the forecastle. But even so meagerly armed, she faced best odds by far at this moment—her three starboard guns facing only eight Spanish stern chasers. There was desperate sense in the master's urging. Fire now, and drop back, praying the answering fire would inflict no fatal injury.

"By God, Master Seall," shouted Cross, loud enough for all the ship to hear, "would ye have us cut and run? We'll sail her length around, God's death, and pepper her fore and aft, like a horsefly round a Dutch mare. Fall back from yon great wallowing hulk? I'll see us all in hell first, and every grinning don on yonder poop gone with us!"

"Aye, sir," the master answered him. He could see the wildness in the captain's eyes. "We'll put the helm alee at half a culverin shot, then, and rake her on the turn."

"Half a culverin, by God! Say rather a musket's length, Master Seall! And swing the forecastle guns to play upon 'em too."

Seall, a stocky Cornishman, watched his captain swab his forehead and cast another quick look at the oncoming *Foresight*.

To challenge the mighty *Mother of God* no more than a musket shot away was sheer and certain suicide. Master Seall looked his commander straight in the eye. *You have your meed of honor to win*, that steady stare seemed to say. *But I have a wife to warm my bed at home, daughters to marry and sons to 'prentice out. Neither I nor any of the lads in yonder forecastle are such roaring boys, to go to our deaths for a point of honor.*

If his captain did not repeat the order, the master might ignore it. He could let the *Lark* get the better part of a culverin shot away before discovering his misjudgment of the distance and bringing the ship about.

But Cross's eyes were hot and bright, his long fingers white and tense about his elegant rapier hilt. He pulled his gaze from Seall's accusing face and shouted in a voice that broke with fury.

"Hard alee, helmsman—now!"

"What's our range, Master Adam?" demanded Burrow, his eyes fixed on the distant carrack and her tiny challenger. "What chance for Murrain Pikestaff to strike her from here?"

"The better part of a mile, Captain. Random firing. It would take a miracle even to straddle her with a broadside at such a distance."

"But he might bring some disarray to her decks at least? Draw her attention till the *Lark* has made her pass?"

"It might be," said Adam dubiously.

"God's death, John," whispered Matthew. "She's turning now! Cross is bringing her about—close enough to swab the Spaniard's guns out for her with a boarding pike!"

No time to bring the *Roebuck* round for a broadside, Burrow knew. Almost no time at all left, now.

"Tell Master Pikestaff," he roared at a hovering mate, "to have a try at her with the bow guns. Tell him to sight and fire himself. Now, man, for your life!"

The mate touched his forelock and was gone, swinging down the ladder into the waist.

"If he can come within fifty feet o' her," grunted Matthew Morgan, "he'll turn the head o' any commander living. For a time at least."

Master Adam said nothing.

* * *

"She comes smartly about, my lord," Señor Salazar observed. "These English ships are so fast and nimble, they can do anything they like with them."

"It is true." Admiral Mendoza nodded, watching the little ship wear about, less than a hundred yards away. His old eyes glittered like a hawk's under tufted white brows.

"Why do we not let the English come up with us, then, my lord?" Don Ricardo de Olid enquired almost pettishly. He had been pacing the poop deck all the morning, striving to look military and portentous. In fact, he was finding his first battle something of a bore.

Don Fernando ignored him. A trumpeter stood ready on the quarterdeck, awaiting the lord admiral's pleasure. Mendoza adjusted the engraved steel corselet across his thin chest and placed the morion with its nodding plume once more upon his head. It was time to begin.

"She'll fire on the turn, my lord," said Salazar. "As soon as the tack's complete."

Don Fernando nodded. Decidedly, he had waited long enough. "Tell Señor Soto to fire when he wishes," he said. "A deck at a time, and allow the smoke to clear." He sighed almost inaudibly as he said it. The gunners never would wait for the smoke to clear.

Murrain Pikestaff laid his long, stubbly jaw almost lovingly alongside the cannon's barrel and sighted his bobbing target, three-quarters of a mile away.

The gun beneath his hands was a culverin, a nine-foot tapered barrel with a six-inch bore set on a wooden carriage, roped through deadeyes to the forecastle wall on either side of the gunport. She would hurl an eighteen-pound ball for seven hundred yards with remarkable accuracy, even from the rolling, pitching platform that was the *Roebuck's* deck. But at such a range as this, it would be a miracle if he came even close.

He watched the grey horizon rise and swing, the white

sails and jutting poop of the distant ship. With a grating whisper, like a lover speaking against the ear of his beloved, he stepped back and lowered the glowing match to the touchhole.

The *Lark* came about. Round and slowly round she came, sails fluttering, yards creaking, till she stood broadside to broadside with her colossal adversary, not fifty yards distant now. Three dozen English seamen and a score of musketeers stared up in stark disbelief at what they had come to fight.

"Fire, gentlemen!" Captain Cross shouted at the mariners manning the sling guns in the bow, the gunners and the arquebusiers crouched behind the starboard bulwark. "Fire, and shout for the Queen! Fire all, and go to God!"

With a sudden whoop of laughter, he whipped off his white-plumed hat and skirled it high and wide across the lathering sea.

Murrain Pikestaff got his miracle. Three-quarters of a mile away, he never knew it.

Don Ricardo stood no more than a yard from his white-haired commander, licking at his thin moustaches with a nervous tongue. Squinting into the morning sun, he saw the brief flash of light from the distant *Roebuck*, and the first tiny billow of dark smoke. For a second he was not at all sure that he had seen it. Then the sharp crack of the report reached his ears.

"I really think—" he began querulously. Then the round shot hit him.

It nearly missed him. The roughly cast, grapefruit-sized ball caught him on the side of the head, taking off most of it and spattering two helmeted officers standing even closer than the Admiral with bits of brain and bone. The corpse was thrown half across the poop deck to fetch up in a shuddering heap under the lee railing.

Don Fernando de Mendoza did not even look around.

An instant later, an avalanche of sound rolled out as the

first tier of artillery below went off with a crash that shook the ship.

"*Sweet Lord Jesus*," whispered Matthew Morgan, his fingers closing about the railing beneath his hands. John Burrow said nothing at all, but only looked.

The first Spanish broadside brought the *Lark*'s mainmast down, raked her decks, left her helpless under the guns. She was drifting slowly around, presenting a three-quarter view to the *Madre de Dios*, when the second tier of artillery boomed out with another belch of powder smoke. Burrow saw the pinnace jolt once more under the shock of the Spanish shot. From the flapping of her canvas, he knew the sails were shredded, the rigging and the sailors aloft all swept away. The third broadside took her at the waterline— seawater gouted under her stern and bow where the Spanish gunners missed. The foremast swayed and settled slowly into the tangle of spars and sailcloth over her decks.

Another broadside crashed out, and another.

The *Mother of God* moved on, smoke fading off to leeward in the breeze, leaving a dead ship settling slowly in her wake.

CHAPTER

34

"My God—my God, Marina, how long can it go on?"

Tamar crouched beside her old nurse in a corner of the littered cabin, while the din crashed and thundered around them. The deck tilted steeply. Shards of broken glass from shattered windows, splinters and fragments of a demolished wardrobe slid across the floor. At each ear-shattering roar of the artillery, Tamar pressed futile arms across the sides of her head and bit her lower lip to keep from screaming.

"Until they have all killed each other," Marina answered her mistress's question. "Does not your Scripture say that he who takes up the sword shall never put it down again until he dies?" The Indian woman's voice was gruff, but her taut cheeks told Isabel that even Marina felt the terror that beat and thundered all around them.

Something slammed terrifically into the wall behind them, shaking the room, sending Tamar sprawling. She sat up slowly, skirts tangled about her knees.

"Oh, Marina," she said, "he must be all right. He must be."

Marina said nothing. There was nothing she could say.

For hours the tall ships had fought it out at musket range with cannons and culverins and massive, short-range potguns. These marvels of the shipwright's art had been methodically pounding each other to pieces. Sometimes Tamar could scarce believe that anyone could be left alive on the decks outside, in that wilderness of smoke and screams and flying wood and metal.

But he must be alive, she thought. Pirate, Protestant, whatever terrible things he was—dear God, let him still be alive.

Then suddenly there came a slackening.

"What—what is it?" she asked, sitting up, resting her

aching back against the side of the narrow four-poster. "What is happening?"

The old duenna rose stiffly and walked to the windy gap in the stern wall where the leaded windows had once been. She looked out through thinning smoke.

"We are coming up alongside the *Madre de Dios,*" she said. "They are going to climb aboard her now, and fight with their spears and their swords."

Tamar covered her face with her hands and began very determinedly to pray.

Sir John Burrow and Matthew Morgan crouched in the shadow of the starboard bulwarks, watching painted shields and shredded ratlines heaving closer as the two ships converged. The long, steel-pointed pike was heavy in Burrow's hands, the plumed helmet shadowed his eyes. Left and right along the poop-deck rail the rest of the boarding party knelt or crouched, three rows of men with swords and pikes and arquebuses, poised for the attack.

"We'll have 'em, John!" said Matthew Morgan, clapping him on the shoulder. Morgan's face was pink as a girl's, his blue eyes bright with eagerness for the coming fight. "We'll have 'em all, and the great ship too, whether Fortune will or no! It's men as win a fight, by God, not Fortune and her wheel!"

Yet we'll need luck now, and no mistake, John Burrow thought, watching the glitter of sunlight on the Spanish morions, on gleaming breastplates and axe-bladed halberds.

"Ready the boarders!" he called to the tense, balanced rows of waiting men. And then, to others with pronged grappling hooks in their hands: "Ready the irons, lads!"

It was too soon, he thought, even as he braced himself for the impact. They should have kept their distance and raked the carrack's decks with artillery fire for hours yet, until the odds were nearer even. But the sun was westering rapidly now, plunging toward the darkening horizon. And Master Adam had warned him that once the sun was gone, the carrack might well vanish too, into the murky night among the islands. So there was nothing for it but to attempt her now.

Burrow had signaled the *Foresight* to close upon her leeward side while the *Roebuck* boarded from windward. Beyond the high, bright-painted forecastle of the *Madre de Dios*, he could see the masts of the English vessel swaying close. From the shouting and the increased volume of Spanish musketry, he judged they must be boarding now.

"Arquebusiers aloft!" he called. "Grappling irons out!" And to the men with swords and pikes around him: "Remember the brave hearts butchered in their sleep in the great square at Havana, lads! And the gold of the Indies, not a pike's length distant now!"

The lowest tier of the carrack's guns boomed suddenly, tremendously, a final broadside that rocked the fast-closing *Roebuck*. Smoke boiled up from between the vessels, obscuring their enemy halfway to the mainsail yard. Then the two came crashing together, and the total chaos of hand-to-hand combat at sea closed over them all.

"Santiago! Santiago!" screamed the Spaniards. "A Burrow! A Burrow! Saint George for England!" the English howled.

For a moment the battle swayed over open water that spread and closed again, crushing more than one falling man between the wooden ships. Then the freebooters came on. They slashed through the Spanish netting and clawed their way over the bulwarks into the waist of the *Mother of God*.

Matthew Morgan drove like a juggernaut into the steel-shirted ranks of his enemies, roaring for England and Saint George. In the screaming momentum of that first charge, it seemed almost as though the freebooters might sweep their foes off their own main deck into the sea. But John Burrow, shouting his own battle cry, had vaulted onto the *Madre de Dios*'s quarterdeck, where he could see more clearly through the thinning smoke. And his heart turned to ice at what he saw.

The decks across which his men were cutting their way—more slowly now, and at what cost in falling comrades only he could clearly see—were packed with Spanish soldiers. They leaped yelling down from the forecastle, poured up from the gun decks below in unending numbers. Most of the *Foresight*'s crew were tumbling in disarray back over the opposite rail, some to their own decks, some into the sea. And now Burrow's own men were beginning to give way, to fall back on the rail and the *Roebuck* beyond.

It had been too soon—too soon.

"Back to the *Roebuck*, lad," called Burrow, dropping once more into the seething waist, where Matthew Morgan still fought mightily in the van. Thank God they had used few grappling hooks, he thought as he re-joined his lieutenant. They could cut free easily enough once they had pulled their boarders back. What was left of them.

"What, back already, and go to thrumming with 'em once again, when we're so close as this?" Morgan's grey hair was wild, his face mottled with mingled joy and fury as he fought. "By God, John, but I'd not do it for any man but you!"

"We've bloodied the dons enough, Matthew. We'll finish 'em when next we come. Now back, and let Murrain Pike-staff have his way with 'em yet awhile." Perhaps the master gunner might bring the fore- or mainmast down, he told himself, and cripple the Spaniard till dawn. But that, he knew, would require more of Fortune's favor than John Burrow had ever yet had.

Back to back, driving and slashing at the faces of stocky Spanish infantrymen, Burrow and Morgan retreated toward the railing. The Welshman's barrel-like body, the Englishman's lean, broad-shouldered one stood out above the press, fair targets for every arquebus and halberd, sword and pike. But the reach of the freebooters was long, and their enemies gave way as they fought their way toward safety.

Once only did Sir John's eyes flick away from the sweating faces of the soldiery that hemmed him in. For one instant, he looked up at the poop of the *Madre de Dios*. There, silhouetted against the great gilded lantern and the swirling banner of Castile, stood a gaunt figure in graven breastplate and fluted tassets, his plumed morion square upon his head, his white beard streaming in the breeze. Burrow knew him at once. It was the famous Spanish admiral Don Fernando de Mendoza, standing stiff and unbending above the carnage on his decks. As the English captain general looked up, the plumed head turned slightly toward him, and a steel-gauntleted hand rose in an ironical salute. *Welcome, Englishman, to my ship. Welcome and farewell.*

Then Burrow felt the splintered rail against him. He turned and saw the *Roebuck* already swinging free, a six-foot leap away over open water. Most of his men were already back aboard, and Master Adam had axemen poised over the last remaining grappling lines, prepared to cut loose entirely as soon as Sir John and Matthew were once more upon the English flagship's decks.

"Now, Matthew, for your life!" cried Burrow, turning back into a thunder of musketry and a final rush of Spanish steel to cover his lieutenant's leap. He heard Morgan grunt, and the creak of broken planking underfoot as the big Welshman sprang into empty space. Then Burrow hurled his pike into a frieze of Castilian faces, pivoted on a booted heel, and flung his own tall body toward the *Roebuck*'s rail.

He landed hard and swung round to see that the last of his men were away. He heard axes chunk, saw the last of the grappling lines fall free. A dozen yards, a score now of boiling water separated the two parting vessels.

"Master Adam," he called, breathing heavily and wiping blood off one cheek, "have Master Pikestaff lay a parting broadside into 'em, that they may not forget us till we come again. Quick, man, before—"

Master Adam was staring at the receding flank of the

great carrack. Burrow's eyes followed the sailing master's, and the order died in his throat.

Swinging head downward across the carrack's gilded poop, one leg tangled tight in a loose-hanging main brace, the body of Matthew Morgan swayed and banged against the ship's timbered sides. His heavy arms hung limp, and his face ran redder even than the flush of battle as his blood spilled over him into the sea.

HE STOOD ON HIS QUARTERDECK, BRUISED AND BATTERED, BLEEDing from three separate wounds, and watched the great carrack roll away from him across the darkening swell. The *Foresight* drifted free to starboard, her demoralized crew taking no care for her sails. The *Susan Bonaventure* laid a ragged broadside into the carrack from a prudent three hundred yards. But the *Mother of God* moved majestically onward, despite riddled sails and a trail of wreckage bobbing in her wake, toward the southeast. And night was settling fast over the Atlantic.

Someone on the carrack's poop had cut the main brace free, and the body of Matthew Morgan had fallen into the slow grey swells.

"Signal the *Bonaventure* and the *Foresight* now, Master Adam," said Burrow in a voice that was flat and cold and emptied of all emotion. "Tell them to draw near for a parley."

Adam nodded and turned away. Neither spoke of what both had seen. But both knew they had suffered a shrewder loss than any yet on that ill-fated voyage. And for John Burrow, it was far more than that.

"No parleys," said a girl's voice peremptorily in Spanish. "You shall do no parleying with your captains now, Sir John Burrow." Tamar de la Barca, pale but determined, strode toward him across his own quarterdeck, her full skirts ruffling in the evening breeze. Marina's dark shape followed, carrying a basin and cloths.

"Take off—that," said the girl in her halting English to the nearest gawking mariner. She pointed to Burrow's bloodsmeared corselet.

"My lady—" Burrow began dully; but she signed him

imperiously to silence. The captain general started to speak, then shrugged and let her have her way.

A fumbling seaman's hands removed Sir John's helmet and breastplate. Then the girl's own deft fingers unlaced his doublet and sleeves, pulled off his sweat-soaked shirt, stiff here and there with drying blood. Tamar dipped her cloths in the brimming basin and began to clean his wounds.

Don Fernando de Mendoza had left his own quarterdeck as soon as the last English carcass was dumped unceremoniously into the sea. There were his own casualties to be seen to, scores of dead and wounded. There were the ruined boarding nets to be repaired as best they could be, a fallen foretop yard to be cleared away. But Señor Salazar could manage that, Salazar and the captains of the soldiery. Don Fernando was a man of sixty, and he had been on his feet since daybreak. Shoulders aching under the heavy armor, legs unsteady with fatigue, the lord admiral descended the companion and closed his cabin door behind him.

The cabin was dim and stately, paneled in mahogany, lit by a silver candelabrum beside a polished table. A frugal meal waited for him there, bread and meat and red wine in a silver goblet. But he went down first upon his knees before the gilded crucifix that hung above his bed.

He prayed briefly, giving thanks. Then he sat and ate.

They had fought well, the English, he thought as he chewed his food. But then, the English always did fight well. The French, the Saracens were more dashing, the Dutch as doggedly persistent. But all things considered, the English were the most consistent. He thought of the great Armada of 'eighty-eight, and grimaced.

This time, at least, it would be different.

Tamar worked quickly over Sir John Burrow's injuries, head bent, not looking him in the face. She knew the enormity of what she was doing: tending the English commander on his own quarterdeck, his hands still reeking with the blood of her countrymen. But it was his battered body she saw, and trembled inwardly to see so brutalized. It was the great purple bruise under his heart that made her own heart ache, the welling gash across his forearm, the bloody cut above his eye that filled her with pity and fear. As in a dream, she labored over his hurts and never asked herself why.

John Burrow felt her hands move over him, firm but gentle, cleaning and binding. He sank without protest now into the chair she ordered up in her rapid, broken English. He would save his strength. God knew he would need it.

They would close and board again at once, of course. They would have to. The island of Corvo was well above the horizon now, and the shadows of evening were settling like a fine mist over the sea. Whether the carrack took refuge in the island or simply faded into the gathering dark, she would surely be beyond their reach by morning.

So they would board again—the *Roebuck* and the *Bonaventure* this time. Burrow had seen how the *Foresight*'s boarders had been cut to pieces on the Spaniard's decks the last time. They would be in no condition to fight again that day. So it must be the battered, sluggish *Susan Bonaventure*. Captain Thynne was old and paunchy, and half his crew were hurt or ailing, but they would have to be sent in nonetheless. Burrow had no reserves left him. He must throw all he had into this final desperate gamble.

A crude plan, thought Burrow ruefully, but the best he could do now. Master Adam must hail and tell them. And he himself must husband what strength was left him for what was to come. His back, he realized, would feel uncommonly bare to his enemies with the big Welshman gone.

He did not let himself think more than that.

"You will not fight again?"

Tamar stood before him still, a slim, wide-skirted silhouette against the flaming western sky.

"You will not fight again?" she repeated sharply.

"There is naught for it, my lady," he answered her, "but we must fight."

"Your hurts have not yet stopped bleeding," she said shakily, "and you will go back there again?" Her face was a pale oval looking up at him, her eyes wide and dark.

"There is no choice, my lady."

"There is always a choice!" she flared at him out of the dimness. "You are a fool, Capitán John Burrow—a fool! *There is always a choice!*" She caught up her skirts and fled, across the quarterdeck toward her cabin door.

John Burrow watched her go with a dull sense of wonder. His solidly practical countryman's mind knew he was right, that it was fight now or die. But he had never seen such bitterness in young eyes, heard such certainty in a defiant young voice.

Neither Burrow nor Tamar nor anyone else in the English fleet saw something that would have put an end to any thought of further fight that day—or that voyage—if they had seen it. For their eyes were all to the south and west, squinting into the setting sun after the lumbering mass of the great carrack. None saw, emerging from behind the volcanic crags of Corvo to the north, the shapes of other ships. There, dark and lean and deadly, moving under topsails only, the first of the Vera Cruz galleons slid silently into view.

DON DIEGO AGUILAR STOOD TO HAVE HIS STEEL CORSELET strapped on. He accepted his rapier and dagger from Ensign Barba's hands. Only the helmet remained, an ordinary infantryman's morion, distinguished by a scarlet plume. Don Diego took the helmet under his left arm and nodded. Barba swung open the cabin door and Aguilar stepped with the slightest of swaggers out upon the deck.

The English squadron was closer now, much closer.

The privateers were clustered to windward of the carrack, three war galleons, as his were three. But there the similarity ended. The corsairs were older vessels, worn by a long Atlantic crossing and half a voyage back. All three were badly battered by the day's exchange of shot with the *Madre de Dios*. No match, thought Aguilar, for his fresh men and sleek new ships.

And there was the carrack itself, its mizzen shot away, its bulwarks splintered, but awesome still in its vast size, in the slumbering power of its guns. The great ship was creeping eastward, the corsairs keeping pace with her, holding the weather gauge to windward. The *Madre de Dios* might play its part as well, thought Aguilar. If he could take the Englishmen between his own fleet and the carrack—

"It is they, all right," said Barba, squat and grinning, at his master's side. "All that is left of the ships that stormed Havana. That one yonder"—he pointed with a stubby finger—"that one with the leaping deer for figurehead was the first to shell the Fuerza."

"It will be Burrow's, then," said Aguilar. That one, he thought, would be his own particular concern.

"They have not seen us yet," observed the Basque lieutenant with satisfaction.

"It is almost dark," said Aguilar thoughtfully, "and we

are moving with the darkness of the island behind us. If we do not light the lanterns, we may come quite close upon them unobserved."

The English guns were booming now, and the carrack's answering. Two of the privateersmen were closing slowly on the *Mother of God* once more. It was time for action.

Don Diego placed his plumed morion on his head and mounted to the aftercastle.

Barba followed, grinning still. He had never seen his chief more avid for the fray.

To the Lord Admiral Don Fernando de Mendoza, the privateersmen looked like ghost ships as they came at him out of the gloaming, the *Roebuck* first, the *Susan Bonaventure* after. The leading vessel moved sluggishly now, listing noticeably to larboard. The *Bonaventure* had lost half her foremast and they had not even taken time to clear away the tumbled spars and rigging.

Truly, Don Fernando told himself, these English corsairs must be mad.

Then the privateers' cannon spoke, fingers of fire in the thickening dusk, and the *Mother of God* shuddered once more under the impact of the English shot. The lord admiral braced himself against the stem of the great gilded lantern and waited for his own guns to answer.

They did, first the barking stern chasers, then the booming culverins and demiculverins of the broadside, row on row. Even above the rolling clouds of smoke, Admiral Mendoza could see the mastheads of the *Roebuck* jolted by the weight of iron that crashed into her waist, her swaying castles. But when the smoke dissipated, he saw her still coming on. She was within half a musket shot now. A musket ball pinged off the metal fitting of the lantern above the lord admiral's head.

My God, he thought, *they are going to board again!*

On the *Roebuck*'s gun deck, Murrain Pikestaff drove his men like a man possessed as the ship came on that last time.

He poured every ounce of his burning hatred of the Spaniard into that last fight. His face was black as a demon's with powder smoke as he swabbed and loaded, sighted and fired the long brass culverins. There was gunpowder and to spare, in casks ranged down the center of the long, low-raftered deck. Tubs of water steamed, swab handles broke, men and boys rushed frantically about. And everywhere the gritty smoke swirled, leaving skin smarting, throats hot and dry, eyes that burned like the pit.

But if the *Roebuck* pounded her foe unmercifully, she took a brutal pounding in return. And she had already felt the crushing broadsides of the *Madre de Dios* that day. Her shrouds and sheets and ratlines were shot to pieces, half her sails flapping loose and windless as she drifted in to board once more. Her bulwarks were stove in in a dozen places. The hurt and slain lay untended on her decks.

And then came that last tremendous broadside from the *Mother of God.*

Spanish round shot slammed into the English flagship from waterline to poop, all those tiers of guns roaring almost at one moment. And the worst of it came crashing into the long, low gun deck where Murrain Pikestaff labored to prepare a final broadside of their own. Guns slewed round, men went down screaming among splintered timbers and flying round shot. The gun deck was devastated, turned in seconds from the efficient engine of destruction it had been into a charnel house.

But there were guns on the deck above still. Murrain Pikestaff, clutching a burning match cord in one shaking hand, stumbled out of the carnage and up the companion-way. There were long guns on the open main deck above that might still be functional, that might yet hurl an answer at the dons. Long jaw working, deep-set eyes blinking, he emerged into the wreckage of the ship's waist.

Broken bulwarks, slewed guns and guns knocked off their carriages, fallen spars, a tangle of ropes and flapping sail, the moaning wounded and the dead greeted his eye. There was a crackle of musketry and a swirl of smoke, and through it all the great bulk of the *Madre de Dios* loomed closer above the broken railing.

On the high forecastle, the quarterdeck, and the poop cf the *Roebuck*, boarding parties gathered. But the ruined waist was deserted except for the master gunner, picking his way toward the culverins on the far side of the ship, facing away from the carrack. These guns were charged and ready too. If he could get men to swing them round, he would open a path for the boarders with a vengeance.

It was he who first saw the oncoming Spanish galleons, dark now against the fading grey of the island. All other eyes were fixed on the *Mother of God,* heaving momently closer through the eddying smoke of that last broadside. Pikestaff's jaw dropped in astonishment, his mouth opened to shout a warning.

At that instant a musket ball crashed through the back of his skull and buried itself in his brain. The long burning match cord he carried forgotten in one hand had made a mark for a musketeer on the *Madre de Dios.* He had fired high, but he had not missed his target. Murrain Pikestaff fell forward across the brass mountings of the nearest culverin and lay still.

Then the *Roebuck* came crashing in under the forward quarter of the great carrack, and the last battle began.

The shock of the impact knocked Burrow and half his company off their feet. But they were up again at once, snatching up their swords and pikes, some flinging themselves upon the Spaniard's netting, others clambering over her rails or leaping into her fore-chains. Shouts of "God and Saint George for England—a Burrow—a Burrow!" burst hoarsely from a hundred throats as they fought their way once more into the floating fortress that was the *Mother of God.*

The *Susan Bonaventure* came next, gliding up on the leeward side preceded by a rattle of arquebus and musket fire, flinging out grappling irons to lock like a mastiff to the great ship's after quarter. "God help us all," puffed Captain Thynne as he swung his belly over his own forecastle rail and hauled himself into the shredded nets of the carrack. Followed by every seaman, pikeman, and musketeer that was fit to hold a weapon, he charged into battle like a boy, shouting "A Burrow, and Saint George for England!"

Howls of *"Santiago!"* met them once more as they came. But the shouts seemed fewer now, and mixed with cries in Portuguese and more exotic Eastern tongues.

Portuguese and heathen, thought Sir John Burrow as he waded into his foes. Good—we've thinned out the Spaniards then. And the Spaniards were the best of them, he knew. But he did not smile when he thought it.

There was no exaltation anywhere that night, as the freebooters carved their way across those slippery decks, cluttered with the injured and the slain. There was only red fury and naked terror. Only the fury of the freebooters, the terror of their foes.

For suddenly, mysteriously, it was clear to both sides that the English were going to win.

Don Fernando de Mendoza, Lord Admiral of the Malabar Carracks, commander of the *Madre de Dios*, was the first to see it.

He saw it in the wavering eyes of his officers, in the frightened faces of his men. The crews of two privateersmen were pouring across his decks. His Spanish soldiers were mostly dead or wounded, his Portuguese and Lascars seeking shelter belowdecks from the English fury. Don Fernando himself was reeling with fatigue, his arm scarce able to lift his long Toledo sword. He knew that it was over, and that he had lost.

He felt no fear, or even much regret. He had made his peace with God, and it had been many years since he had been afraid of dying. And he felt only a momentary pang at the thought of falling to a plebeian corsair blade.

But the face that burst suddenly out of the struggling mob

of shadows before him was not plebeian. It was a face that he had had pointed out to him more than once during that day of battle.

"*El capitán* Burrow." He raised a gauntleted left hand, as he had done that afternoon. But his eyes were watchful beneath the tufted white brows, and he kept his point high, poised for thrust or parry.

"Don Fernando de Mendoza," the black-bearded man before him responded. His voice was hard. There was cold murder in that long, scarred face, those haggard eyes. The tall Englishman's shoulders flexed, his rapier shot out.

Don Fernando, to his own astonishment, deflected that first thrust successfully. The English corsair, he thought, must be as tired almost as he.

"*Para su Majestad de Inglaterra?*" the Spanish commander could not forbear to gibe. Somehow this did not look to him like a man passionate to die and kill for Queen and country, as the English said.

"*Para mi amigo!*" snapped John Burrow. "For my friend!" His point lashed out once more.

Don Fernando de Mendoza reeled back against the heavy teakwood rail. His sword hilt clanged on the loose-hanging rudder far below, then splashed into the sea. The old man himself was pinioned against the railing, his left hand clawing shakily at a dislocated shoulder. He felt the warmth of his own blood oozing over his fingers. His eyes were fixed upon the Englishman's rapier point, trembling very slightly now, no more than an inch from his face.

For his friend, Don Fernando thought, *he will do it.*

For one unending moment, John Burrow stood there at the highest point of the great ship's towering aftercastle, while the battle swirled behind him. His arm was flung back, his grey steel rapier poised to plunge into that pulsing throat. The tendons of his wrist and forearm grew taut for the stroke.

But he saw the dark blood welling from the old man's shoulder over that spidery white hand. And he heard

Tamar's voice, as he had heard it on his own quarterdeck that night: *There is always a choice, John Burrow! There is always a choice!*

That was when he saw her.

She stood straight and still in the lurid jungle that was the *Roebuck*'s waist, her face and figure lit up by the newly kindled fires that rose through the companionway from the gun deck below. But the girl paid no heed to the flames. Her eyes were fixed upon the dark figures locked in combat on the Spaniard's decks, seeking, seeking for a tall familiar figure in her turn.

There is always a choice.

Sir John Burrow turned up his sword blade and slashed through the halyard that held the great banner of Castile, flapping heavily in the darkness overhead. The flag curled and fell, fluttering like a great bird, off into the darkness. The lord admiral slumped with a stifled groan, still clutching his ruined shoulder. Burrow, his mouth and eyes expressionless in the flaring light of the fires from his own shattered flagship, felt suddenly utterly exhausted. He sheathed his sword with a clang and turned wearily away, into the wild shouts of his victorious company.

It was at that moment of triumph and exhaustion that he heard, inexplicably, incredibly, rolling flat and hard over the cheers of his men, a renewed crash of artillery out of the darkness.

CHAPTER

37

THE HOPES AND FEARS OF TAMAR DE LA BARCA HAD CAREENED wildly from one extreme to the other during that interminable day. Her heart had pounded with panic fear during the great bombardments. Yet she had been calm and firm enough when she had gone out onto the quarterdeck to bind up Sir John Burrow's wounds. She had begun the day with an unreasoning surge of hope that salvation from all her anguished uncertainties might be at hand, that the famous lord admiral might take her home and her old life begin again. She ended the day in desperate fear once more —fear not for herself, but for the life of the English pirate who had carried her away.

She had been ashamed of her terror that morning, as she had been ashamed during the English raid upon Havana. As the day progressed, however, her shame had passed. She had heard the groans and cries of the corsairs themselves as the guns thundered and the *Roebuck* shuddered to the impact of Spanish shot. If even these hardened men-at-arms shook with fear in the face of battle, surely there was nothing shameful in the trembling limbs of a gently bred girl, however noble her Castilian blood.

With her shame, she felt the fear itself fade too. Her knees still trembled, her breath still caught in her throat when the guns crashed beneath her feet, or when the glass from the mullioned windows exploded across the room. But her spirit stood apart from the battle, apart from her own shaken body. And when she needed to, she found that her spirit could master even the terrors of the flesh and move her to action in the face of fear.

So it was as the *Roebuck* grated up alongside the *Madre de Dios* for the last time and the English freebooters swarmed aboard once more.

"My lady," said Marina gruffly, plucking at her sleeve. The two women crouched in a corner of their cabin, listening to the shouting and the clang of weapons beyond its wooden walls. "My lady, there is fire."

The acrid smell of smoke was clear in the low-raftered room, littered with broken furniture and glass, torn hangings and scattered clothing. There was a different smell to it, no longer the saltpeter stench of gunpowder, but the cleaner, far more frightening odor of burning tar and wood. It was the ship itself that was burning.

"We will go out on the deck," said Tamar firmly, "and see."

In fact, she felt remarkably unconcerned with the fate of the ship, though her own destiny was clearly bound up with that of this battered wooden hulk. What took her out onto the *Roebuck*'s precariously canting deck while the fight still raged on the greater vessel grappled close against hers was not a concern for her own safety at all. It was, quite simply, a visceral need to know how it fared with John Burrow.

"My lady—here!" Marina called in a low, guttural voice, taking temporary shelter in the shadow of the longboat, now knocked loose from its davits and fallen askew across the sloping deck. "Come here, out of the firelight!"

But Tamar paid no attention. With her eyes fixed on the high pooped carrack beyond the *Roebuck*'s splintered bulwarks, she picked her way out into the jungle of the ship's waist. As the flames rose higher behind her, she strained to make out the tall, familiar figure of the corsair chief amid the bang of Spanish muskets and the flash and clang of steel.

She moved slowly among the tangle of rigging and broken spars, the dismounted guns and the torn bodies of the dead. She had paused beside the corpse of the master gunner, sprawled over the trunnions of a long brass culverin with a still-sputtering match grotesquely clutched in one clenched fist. Then she heard the voice of her duenna once more.

"My lady!" the old woman called again. There was a new

note in her voice, a note of amazement more than fear, that turned Tamar's head at last.

She turned and followed the Indian woman's outstretched hand. And she stared in stupefaction at what she saw.

There, not twenty yards away in the flame-lit darkness, a ship was slowly detaching itself from the gloom. There was another behind it, and the shadow of yet a third. But it was the first and nearest, looming so miraculously close across the oily swells, that transfixed the Governor of Cuba's daughter.

For it was a Spanish vessel. The banner of the royal house of Castile fluttered at her poop, where the name *Trinidad* glowed dully. The troops who crouched expectant at her rails were Spanish soldiers, their plumed morions and axe-headed halberds clearly visible in the light of the leaping fires around the Spanish girl. And there, at the angle of the quarterdeck, with his squat Basque ensign Barba like some diabolical familiar at his elbow, stood Don Diego Aguilar.

Aguilar saw the ships locked together, drifting toward him through the shredding smoke of that last broadside. The *Roebuck* was clearly listing badly, riddled below the water-line. Smoke was funneling out of her battered forecastle, flames licking up from the gun deck aft. Not one cannon in three still jutted from her gunports, and her littered decks seemed almost deserted, every man committed to the struggle aboard the carrack. Of the other English privateer, grappled to the *Madre de Dios* on the other side, he could see nothing but masts and tattered sails.

For a moment he thought of circling around the combatants to get at the other ship, so obviously was the *Roebuck* doomed. But this was the English flagship, and he was gluttonous of honor.

At that instant, Don Diego had no thought at all of the lady he had been sent to rescue, the girl whose body in marriage he had all but contracted for with the Governor of Cuba. His strange, lashless eyes were shining with excitement, his swarthy face dark with enthusiasm for the coming conflict. He felt the hunter's exultation as he slipped silently up on his unsuspecting prey. His throat was husky, his palms dry with the joy of vengeance about to be consummated in the destruction of the tall Englishman whom he, like Tamar, strove to single out from the shadowy figures locked in combat who thronged the carrack's deck.

But of Tamar de la Barca, the lovely girl who had fallen beneath his hands one drunken night seven weeks before, he had no thought at all.

Then he saw her.

Barba muttered an imprecation at his elbow, touched his arm, and pointed. Aguilar lowered his eyes from the shadowy bulk of the *Madre de Dios* to the waist of the nearer vessel. In the lurid glare of the flames gouting up from the aft companionway, he saw her. The sight of her struck him like a physical blow.

The girl's slender body and lovely face were lit dramatically from one side by the fires. The delicacy of her throat and shoulders, the compact thrust of a breast, even the shadows that played around her eyes and cheeks and mouth were sharply defined in that red light. His heart gave a mighty throb at the sight, and his throat was dry with more than a lust for vengeance.

Quite simply and totally, he wanted her. At this moment of impending violence, of battle and vengeance and a golden future to be won or lost, Don Diego was swept by the passionate hunger that this beautiful, softly scented daughter of Castile had aroused in him from the beginning. With his rapier half drawn, with the order to his musketeers to open fire on his lips, he was shaken by a spasm of lust such as he had not felt since Tamar's struggling body had writhed under his in his mean rooftop shanty in the Cerro.

The fight was ending on the *Madre de Dios*, and scattered English cheers were blending into a roar of victory. Don Diego scarcely noticed.

For the girl had seen him now.

Even at twenty yards and in the unsteady light, he could see the shock on her face, and then the horror. He saw her start forward on the slanting deck, and then seem to fall. She disappeared, at any rate, behind the slewed cannon with the corpse of the English seaman fallen across it.

But he had seen the horror in her face. Horror of him. The same revulsion that had twisted up her face that night on his rude pallet. He had seen, and in an instant rage mounted in his soul, mingling with the lust behind his eyes.

"By God, Barba," he said shakily, his voice thick with passion, "but I'll have the bitch before cockcrow! Aye, take her spread-eagled over the big Englishman's corpse, damn both their souls to hell!"

Barba grinned maliciously, showing broken teeth. His master, he thought, was capable of the most amazing notions.

Then Tamar was standing once more.

But the shock and the horror were gone from her face now. There was no fear there at all. There was, to the eternal confounding of Don Diego Aguilar, only a cold anger in those dark eyes, hardening that young mouth. Anger and resolution, a determination as single-minded as that which had brought Aguilar himself so far across the sea.

In total disbelief, the Spanish Commander saw the Governor's daughter of Cuba push the mariner's corpse off the long brass culverin before her, reach forward with her right hand, and thrust the tip of a flickering artilleryman's match full into the touchhole.

38

THE LONG-BARRELED CULVERIN NORMALLY FIRED AN EIGHTEEN-pound ball, and could hurl it a mile or more. But as the *Roebuck* closed with the *Madre de Dios*, all the cannon and culverins on the open deck had been stuffed half the length of the bore with improvised canister instead. Stones, nails, broken chain, bits of metal of all sorts had been rammed down the muzzles of the guns in hopes of sweeping the Spaniard's railings clean before the English boarded. The crushing Spanish broadside had torn loose the tackle that held this gun—had actually swung it around to face almost diametrically away from the carrack. Which meant that its long, ugly barrel was leveled straight at the crowded waist and quarterdeck of the *Trinidad* as it emerged from the darkness on the other side.

Fired point-blank at less than twenty yards, the havoc that single culverin wrought on the decks of the Spanish flagship was unbelievable.

The improvised grapeshot scythed through shrouds and ratlines, and through the close-packed men beyond. It cut a wide swathe through them, shredding leather and cloth and tearing through human flesh. Half the Spanish boarding party was struck down by that single blind-luck shot. And the very center of that whirring hail of death was the angle of the waist and quarterdeck where Don Diego Aguilar stood with his grinning ensign, halfway down the companion ladder, his rapier half drawn.

An instant before, at least, he had stood there. When he saw what the madwoman on the English privateer was about to do, he had flung himself desperately off the ladder, lunging for safety behind the bulwarks of the ship's waist, four or five feet below.

He had one blurred vision of the rounded railing, the

tarry ratlines, the armored backs and shoulders of the halberdiers, starting back themselves as the English gun belched black powder smoke and orange flame. One glimpse of the protecting shadow of the ship's stout bulwarks which no canister could penetrate.

One last flashing vision of safety, so close beneath him. Then the hail of flying metal caught him in midair.

The tight, hard-muscled body of the Spanish captain jerked like a rag doll and somersaulted backward into the ladder. His rapier arched through space and vanished into the darkness. His helmet clanged against the cabin wall and fell among the surge of screaming men below. Aguilar himself jolted off the companion ladder and slid forward, facedown on the deck, leaving a smear of shining red behind him. He lay, palms up, his head twisted around at an impossible angle, half his face shot away. The short, powerful fingers of his left hand still twitched convulsively, and blood bubbled from two terrible wounds in the belly underneath.

Ensign Barba stood where he had been, at his master's side on the ladder to the quarterdeck, staring appalled at his commander's quivering corpse and the bloody remnants of the boarding party. He was completely untouched by the shower of English shot which had splintered the gilded wood around him and had all but cut Don Diego Aguilar in two.

Sir John Burrow, high on the poop deck of the *Madre de Dios,* had been turning into the cheers of his freebooters, scattered over the decks of the great carrack below, when the culverin went off. He took all of it in in one stunned moment: the dark ships looming out of the night, the slim girlish figure, bending now over the huge gun, the gout of flame and powder smoke that turned the waist of the approaching *Trinidad* into a shambles in an instant. And he saw too what happened to the girl herself—what must happen to her in the wake of that tremendous artillery discharge.

The culverin's ground tackle had been torn loose by the Spanish broadside that had slewed it around and driven it halfway across the deck. Without these huge restraining cables, the gun's recoil jolted it backward, back across the ship's littered waist, caroming off the mast, bounding over dead and wounded mariners, till it crashed into the broken railings on the other side of the deck.

The girl who had been bending over the gun's breech to thrust the flickering splint home was flung violently to one side. From where Sir John stood, she vanished completely in the clutter of spars and cordage and fallen sail, the backward eddy of black smoke.

Burrow vaulted the poop-deck rail, took the quarterdeck and the half deck in a dozen strides, and vaulted down once more. In seconds, he had thrust his way through victors and vanquished alike, had leaped from the carrack's rail into the waist of his own burning vessel, and was fighting his way through the wreckage toward the place where he had seen Tamar's flung body disappear.

"*Aquí, inglés,*" a harsh voice called from the lee of the stove-in longboat. "*Aquí está!*"

He saw the Indian woman crouching, tugging at something. Then he himself was flinging aside fallen timbering, the whitewashed handle of the great pump, clawing amid the crackle of the flames and the reek of powder smoke for the torn gown and soft, unmoving body of Tamar de la Barca.

Consciousness came back in fits and starts, brief intermittent flickers of awareness between longer spans of darkness and oblivion.

Tamar's first memory after the glowing splint vanished into the touchhole and the great brass cascabel of the gun leaped up and back and struck her was the feel of John Burrow's arms around her, and the hard metal of his corselet against her breast. His voice was speaking close to her ear, speaking urgently and passionately, asking her something. But his Spanish was garbled and unclear to her, and the world wheeled around her in great circles and then faded out once more.

Then she was lying in bed, a large, mustily curtained, miraculously undamaged bed in the cabin of a ship. She had seen this room before, she thought vaguely, with its heavy furniture of teak and ebony, its silver fittings and the crucifix above her head. It was the lord admiral's quarters on the great carrack, that she had visited that Sunday so infinitely long ago.

For a moment, she thought she was back in Havana harbor once again. Then she heard the English voices, talking around the dark polished table across from her.

"They've veered off, but they'll return," the slack-bellied old captain called Thynne was saying. "Three of 'em, and his Majesty of Spain's best war galleons too, from what I saw."

Tamar, whose English was still only rudimentary, caught no more than every other word. But she lay there and listened nonetheless, letting the words make patterns in her mind.

"They'll come," replied the crisp voice of Master Adam, "and we shall be ready for them when they do."

"How so, sir? With the *Roebuck* afire and sinking beside us, the *Foresight* and the *Bonaventure* scarce mustering half their companies—"

"Aye," said the only voice the half-conscious girl wanted to hear in all the world, "aye, but Master Adam speaks truth nonetheless. For we have more than three broken privateers to meet the Spaniards with. We have the biggest ship in the world beneath our feet this moment!"

There were shouts on deck, the creak of ancient timbers and the sound of a distant gun. The girl felt the world slipping away from her once more.

"We'll cut the *Roebuck* free to swim or founder as she will, and use her company to man this great carrack of Spain ourselves. Send us your best gunners as well, gentlemen, and we'll set some of these Portugees to manning their own guns for us. And then by God we'll give the dons a taste of what we've had this day!"

Then the whirlpool of darkness rose up once more and enveloped Tamar de la Barca.

The first crash of the *Madre de Dios'* guns jolted her awake, shaking the cabin, bringing her bolt upright in the bed. She felt her own aching body, clad only in her shift, and found no more than cuts and swollen bruises in the blackness. But the act of sitting up itself brought a wave of giddiness, and she sank back as another tier of guns boomed somewhere in the bowels of the ship below her, and then another.

She heard the artillery thereafter, but only sporadically, in confused snatches interspersed with longer spells of unconsciousness or near-delirium.

It all mingled in her mind with distorted memories of the corsair guns over Havana, of the daylong battle with the great carrack where she now lay, and with the cannon she herself had fired—into the faces of her own people. She saw those faces still, saw jaws dropping and arms raised in disbelief as she rolled the dead corsair off the gun and drove home the burning splint. She saw and groaned in her sleep at the sight. But one face she did not see. One face she somehow knew she would never see again even in her most fevered dreams—the face that had made her nights terrible for so long.

When Tamar finally came fully awake, it was long after midnight, and the guns were still. Candles glimmered in a wall sconce across the room once more. And John Burrow stood there beside her, his sword and breastplate set aside, his heavy countryman's hands stretched out to her at last.

THE FIGHT OF THE ENGLISH FREEBOOTERS AND THE VERA Cruz galleons lasted little more than three hours. The Spanish war galleons tacked expertly about their huddled foes, exchanging artillery fire at a prudent distance under the westering moon. They were testing the English weariness and will to fight, rather than seeking to do serious damage. For the Spaniards' own will to engage was low indeed.

They were no cowards, the dark-eyed, darkly bearded men of the *Santa Clara* and the *Santa Cruz*, the survivors of the *Trinidad*. The Spaniards and *mestizos* who manned them, the elegantly dressed Castilian officers who commanded were men of honor and high resolve. They had followed Don Diego Aguilar willingly enough, eager to serve under so aggressive and bold a commander. The captain the island aristocracy had so contemptuously dismissed as impetuous and crude was a coming man to the officers of the Vera Cruz squadron. A man who might lead them all to fame and glory in the service of their King.

Instead, he had led them to a double setback that left them stunned.

For two hours, the dazed Spaniards circled the English uncertainly, probing at their defenses, finding them unyielding. No shortage of powder and shot could be detected, nor any lack of vigor as their long guns boomed. And the immense broadsides of the *Madre de Dios* were a thing to marvel at. They had never bargained for this.

Still less had they expected the loss of their bold commander at the first onset.

The captains of both the other Spanish vessels crossed to the demoralized *Trinidad* to see it with their own eyes. They stared down at the bloody corpse, at the sagging jaw and the single dead eye staring up at them, and shook their heads. They heard the wounded sailing master's insistence that his ship was ruined, that he had but half a crew and must put back for refitting at the nearest port. And they gazed up at the massive, battered but still formidable flanks of the great carrack, wondering what sort of men these English corsairs must be, that had dared to scale those decks.

Shortly after midnight, they broke off the action and put back toward Flores.

Sir John Burrow watched them go from the heights of the carrack's poop deck, in the shadow of the great lantern. They were hull down over the sea already, mere shadows in the starlight now that the moon was gone. By morning the Spanish ships would be anchored in the roadstead at Flores, and the English would be safely on their way.

It was over.

Burrow turned heavily away, ignoring the rising shouts and laughter of the men around him as they abandoned their places by the guns and laid aside their weapons at last. His freebooters had fought for twenty hours without rest. They had had a day and a night of killing, bleeding, dying for this moment. There would be no controlling them after that.

He knew he should try. But not now. There was something else he must do now.

With a heart beating faster than it had all that day, John Burrow descended to the quarterdeck and the heavy teakwood door where old Marina squatted cross-legged on the deck. The tall Englishman looked at her, and she rose and went away. Without a backward glance, he pushed open the door and stepped inside.

Behind him, over all the decks and levels of the great ship, the Saturnalia was beginning.

The open decks of the *Mother of God* were a butcher's shambles. Dead and dying men lay everywhere, sprawled, contorted, curled in the shadows or quivering still in the lurid torchlight. About the great helm, where a dozen men at a time had labored to steer the giant ship, the dead lay in heaps, cut down again and again by the English guns.

The groans of the wounded, the lamentations of the captives rivaled the shouts and drunken laughter of the victors. For rough hands had already broached casks of Spanish wine, and the potent liquor passed rapidly from hand to hand. Nor were many drafts required to intoxicate such utterly exhausted men as the English privateers were that night.

Up shadowy companionways, down into the pitch-black holds, torches and candles flared. Drunken freebooters burst out upon the decks draped in glowing silks and calicoes, lapped in exotic ornaments of silver and beaten gold. The looting had begun.

In the small but tastefully appointed cabin assigned to Don Ricardo de Olid, the looters were more than a little disappointed. The terrified servant, Manuel, stood in a corner beside a clothespress, watching the English pirates tear the place apart. One of them had his late master's best fustian coat about his shoulders, another Don Ricardo's gold chain across his naked, hairy chest. But the rest found little to content them as they ransacked the chests and other baggage the young courtier had brought aboard in Havana harbor.

"Papers, God's death—no more nor papers here!" a greasy-bearded villain swore as he pried open the teakwood casket which the dead cavalier's uncles had so carefully entrusted to him the very night they sailed from Cuba. He flung the casket and its contents down in disgust.

Another disappointed corsair set a candle to the half-filled chest. Less drunken comrades cried out in alarm, kicked out the cabin's single small window, and pitched the casket and its smoldering contents out into the sea.

After that the lot of them trooped on out, more than one of them cuffing Manuel in passing as a general expression of their disappointment.

Manuel saw the last of them out before he slid Don Ricardo's slim gilt rapier out from behind the clothespress. He knew a number of sentimental ladies in Madrid and

Seville and even in Lisbon who would bid well for such a memento of the slain hero. Wiping the blood off his mouth, he wondered if he ought not to allow his dead master's lady mother to make the first offer?

In the depths of the aftercastle, two levels below the lord admiral's cabin, Master Adam directed a more disciplined search. Behind bales of silks and silk brocades, casks of pungent spices and East Indian tea, they had found a low, shadowy doorway.

The door had been locked when they found it. It lay split and battered, off its hinges now. Flickering candles lit a small room, piled to the roof around three sides with boxes and chests. Master Adam surveyed them, then nodded and stepped back. A pair of brawny seamen, naked to the waist, hauled the nearest ironbound chest out and took their axes to it.

The sailing master's tidy soul was affronted as he watched the axes rise and fall, their shadows moving grotesquely across the candlelit walls. But the chests would all be triple-locked, and one of the keys at least would be held by the Council of the Indies in Seville. And even the meticulous sailing master was in no mood to play at locksmith now.

The axe blades bit deep, the echo of the blows filled the low, paneled room. In less than a minute, the lid fell away in two halves. Master Adam approached once more, holding a flaming stub above his head. A dull luster glinted back at him.

He had two more of the heavy chests broken open at random before he was satisfied. Two of the three were packed with brick-sized silver ingots, still dull with the dust of a jungle trail in Panama. The third was filled with neatly stacked bars of Indian gold. And the strong room was lined around three sides with ironbound chests and boxes.

It was a sight old Matthew Morgan would have reveled in, thought Adam with a sigh. And then: *A sight the captain general should have been the first to see.* This was the point of it, the end of it, what they had come so far to find. And where was Sir John Burrow now?

With a crease between his dark, reflective eyes, Master Adam strolled across the strong room and mounted the ladder to the deck.

In the sumptuous cabin of the Lord Admiral of the Fleet, Sir John Burrow drew back the bed-curtains and looked down. He saw Tamar, her small body clad only in a linen shift, her hair loose among the cushions on the bolster. Her eyes were open and shining in the candlelight, gazing up at him.

"My lady is somewhat recovered?" he heard himself say in his clearest formal Spanish.

"I am, sir," she answered in an unsteady voice. "And—and you, John Burrow?"

He shrugged slightly, and winced in spite of himself. The wounds she had bound up that afternoon had bled once more since then, in the thrust and parry of the taking of the carrack. And he had taken more cuts in that fray too. His usual quota of wounds and injuries, he thought wryly. The reward as much of clumsiness as of courage. The consequence, above all, of the wretched ill fortune that dogged his footsteps through the long wars, past and present and to come.

"But you *are* hurt," the girl protested, reaching out to touch one of his hands, square and flat, with a fresh cut across the back of it. "And your face—"

She sat up in dismay, raising gentle fingers to a swelling purple patch that mantled the whole left side of his head beneath the old scar and the thick black hair. She was genuinely alarmed at the injury. And genuinely astonished once more—so preoccupied was she with his hurts—when the English corsair sat down beside her on the bed, gathered her small body up in his arms, and pressed his mouth on hers.

40

SHE WAS HER FATHER'S DAUGHTER STILL, AND HE AN ENGLISH
pirate. And none of it seemed to matter a bit!

Over the weeks since she had been carried off from Cuba,
Tamar de la Barca had longed for many things that could
not be. She had yearned for home and for her life to be as
it had been before, though that home could never be hers
again, nor life as it had been. She had secretly desired the
Sir John Burrow of her daydreams, the kind and laughing
man of those weeks at sea, as though he could somehow be
dissociated from the privateer whose eyes had first fixed
hers, grey and hard as granite, in the Plaza de Armas at
Havana. She had longed for so many things that were not, as
though the imperious will of the Governor's daughter could
make them so simply by wishing it. And she had wept tears
of vexation when the world did not transform itself to suit
her desires.

But that day of terror had brought a growing sense of the
realities of things. And when she had thrust home that glowing match and hurled an avalanche of flying metal into the
face that had haunted her nightmares for so long, she had
blown away the last of her own delusions too. She knew the
world for what it was now, a savage place, the jungle of
Marina's childhood and her own people's past. And she knew
herself for what she was—as much a part of that savage world
as the corsair who had come for her at last.

Tamar longed for only one thing now: for the man seated
beside her on that slowly swaying bed. Not for some romantic
dream of chivalry, but for the flesh-and-blood man himself,
with all the scars upon his body and his soul. For the eyes
that could be as hard in battle as they were tender and full
of love at this moment.

Through his stiff doublet and sleeves, through the thinness

of her shift, the man and the woman felt the warmth of each other's body. For a long time, they simply held each other close, and did not speak.

Around them, the *Madre de Dios* was given over wholly to revelry and looting now. There would be the devil to pay for the plundering, John Burrow knew, when they got back to England. Those of us that are going back, he thought. For there was a raw place still in his heart for Matthew Morgan, who would not be going home this time.

Then he surrendered himself to the miracle of this moment. To the small hands that held him, the lips beneath his. To the eyes that searched his even as her mouth melted beneath his own. The eyes that wanted to know if she should be ashamed.

It was the final measure of their separateness—the shamefastness of the Spanish girl, the corsair with his mind still dark with war and plunder. But they pressed more tightly together still, striving to obliterate that separateness by the sheer closeness of their embrace. And then Burrow laid the girl back upon the bed and rose to pull off his half-laced doublet.

"My lord," said Tamar in an unsteady voice. "Please—" She knew she should say, *Please don't.* But she whispered only, as the last of his clothing fell away and he came down to her, "Please be gentle."

Their bodies were so strange together, she thought. His heavy-muscled, bandaged and perspiring still from that day of horror. Hers so small and smooth and trembling there beside him on the bed. His hands were big and frighteningly unfamiliar as they stroked her nakedness in the linen shift. Only the low, tired voice in her ear and the somber eyes in the candlelight were familiar to her now.

The sea breeze buffeted at the mullioned panes with the coats of arms of Castile and Aragon engraved upon them, dimming the sounds of shouts and laughter from the ship around them. They lay very close, in silence now, exploring each other's bodies while the distance that divided them still slowly shrank away.

John Burrow felt the small-boned slenderness of her, the gracious curve of flank and thigh. He felt no boyish surge of lust to possess her yet. They were together, he told himself, and they would always be together now.

He knew better.

On the weary, practical surface of his mind, he knew that this was madness. He knew that while he lay there, the prize he had labored for so long was being stripped and looted by other men. He knew he should be there, forcing order on that chaos.

And for this girl in his arms, why, she would be home with her people in the spring. And he—a man of substance at the Queen's Majesty's court, perhaps? Havana raped, a great treasure ship sailed home in triumph—would it be enough to buy an end to the wars for him at last?

With the top of his mind, he thought about it still. But the throb of the blood beat louder in him now, drowning out the dreams and scheming of a dozen years, carrying him back to an earlier time. Caressing the body of the girl beside him, he thought of how the blood had throbbed in his veins when he swung the great scythe in his father's fields under an August sun. He remembered the heave and thrust of the pitchfork in those half-forgotten years when there were no wars to fight.

The urgency was mounting in him now, rising like the sun of those vanished years. He stroked the underside of her breasts and kissed her nipples and heard her sigh. He came over on top of her at last, and his swollen manhood probed her restless thighs.

Tamar's mind was a tumble of brightly colored images as she felt his body over hers, as she cried out and clutched him passionately to her. She saw macaws flutter among the palms, and purple flowers spilling over whitewashed walls. She heard the bells of the Franciscans and felt cool raindrops on her cheeks, as she had felt them at her window the night the great carrack sailed. And she trembled with the delirium she had felt then for the first time, the fevers no rain could cool. The fever that consumed her still, here in this bed, with this man.

Burrow felt the heat of her lips, the ardor of her body moving under his.

"Oh, my love—please, my love—" she whispered.

Fiercely, tenderly, with a groan of relief and joy, he thrust into her heaving loins.

In that moment, her past, his future vanished utterly. Havana and London were no more. They were two bodies joined, two mouths together, hair in each other's faces, sweat mingling in the twisted sheets. They had cast their identities away with stays and slops and petticoats. They were two bodies, young and slender, older, scarred, fused in the annihilating unity of love.

They were two bodies become one. And though they scarcely knew it, there in the creaking cabin under the night wind, over the wash of the sea, they were two souls fused into one as well.

BOOK V

FORTUNE

AND

MEN'S EYES

When, in disgrace with fortune and men's eyes,
I all alone beweep my outcast state,
And trouble deaf heaven with my bootless cries,
And look upon myself, and curse my fate . . .

Haply I think on thee, and then my state,
Like to the lark at break of day arising
From sullen earth, sings hymns at heaven's gate;

For thy sweet love remember'd such wealth brings
That then I scorn to change my state with kings.

—WILLIAM SHAKESPEARE,
Sonnet XXIX

CHAPTER

41

SLEET BEAT UPON THE HIGH ARCHED WINDOWS. IT WAS A DIRTY autumn night at Westminster, and the Queen's Council was in session after supper once again.

The lords of the Council—small-eyed, pasty-faced men with rings on their fingers—sat rather more alertly than usual about the long table. They pulled their lower lips or stroked their beards, listening intently as the last of a long list was read out by a clerk with a monotonous tenor voice:

"Spices, viz., pepper, cloves, mace, cinnamon, nutmeg, and ginger, to the value of one hundred and one thousand, five hundred seventy-eight pounds, eleven shillings, and fourpence.

"Drugs of sundry sorts, viz., benjamin, frankincense, *Aloe succotrina,* and others, to the value of ten thousand, seven hundred and four pounds, five shillings.

"Silks, wrought and unwrought, viz., damasks, taffetas, China silk, sleeved silk, white twisted silk, cloth of gold, all to the value of forty-four thousand, one hundred eight pounds, eight shillings, and threepence.

"The sum and total value of all these goods, received at the Leaden Hall this fifteenth November *anno* fifteen hundred ninety-seven, is in the amount of two hundred and forty-one thousand and two hundred pounds."

There was a moment's silence, in which the rattle of the sleet on the windowpanes sounded clearly in the room.

"Add to that," interjected Sir Walter Raleigh coolly, "the value of the gold and silver bullion deposited in the Tower, and invoiced as I understand it at a million and a half in Spanish pesos—and it is a tidy sum indeed to divide, gentlemen."

"Her gracious Majesty, of course," said Sir Robert Cecil quickly, "has a fifth for her customary share, a tenth or more for her own particular investment, and lastly a third of the whole, out of which she must pay the seamen's wages for the voyage. Said wages," he added, "should come to some six thousand pounds by my estimate."

"And vastly too much for them too," growled Lord Admiral Howard. "A passel of thieves, by God. A passel of damned thieves."

Raleigh leaned forward, but white-bearded old Lord Treasurer Burghley silenced him with the tap of a gold ring on the table.

"You shall have your hundred thousand, Sir Walter," he croaked. "And my lord of Cumberland his. But there are others whose claims must be met as well. Others who will not come off so profitably." He glanced down at a sheet of foolscap before him, narrowing his eyes. "There is Master Henry Colethrust and Company, for their ship the *Lark*, for which they claim two thousand pounds' prize share and the same again, value of the ship that was lost. There is Alderman Saltanstalle, for the use of the *Susan Bonaventure*, claiming three thousand five hundred pounds. And there is my lord of Westmorland yonder"—he inclined his head gravely toward the young nobleman, standing at the far end of the table, his hat in his hand and Catesby by his side—"who claims no less than forty thousand pounds for his share as Vice Admiral of the Fleet, nominate if not in fact, thanks to the usurpation of Sir John Burrow. And so on, gentlemen. Not so very much, this famous great carrack, when all the claims are in."

"If I may speak to that, my lords," said the Earl of Westmorland, stepping forward with a bow and an elegant leg. "It is the usurpation of my rightful share of due authority that most galls upon me, your lordships. More so even than the loss of my fair share of the prize money." The pale young gentleman's face glowed self-righteously: he had quite convinced himself that he believed it. "For if I had had my say in ship's council, and my views been duly heeded—as prescribed in your lordships' second commission—I flatter myself that my voice and Master Catesby's might have saved her

Majesty a ship or two, aye and the lost loot of Havana too!"

"Of course," said Raleigh mildly, "it is perhaps understandable that this second commission of which my lord speaks was never heeded by Sir John—since it never came into his hands, but arrived in Plymouth three days after his fleet had sailed!"

"The Council's will," said Burghley severely, "is the Council's will. If Sir John chooses to sail before receiving due communication of it, he does so at his peril!"

"Sir John," said Paymaster Catesby, stepping forward in his turn, "is no respecter of persons or due authority, if I may say so, my lords. His flouting of my lord of Westmorland's opinions, and of my own humble but well-intended views, shows this again and again. As we have deposed in writing, and set our signatures thereto."

"We have your depositions, Master Catesby," said Cecil, with a look that said clearly, *and we are well aware of your own interests therein.* But it was not an unfriendly look.

Sir Robert Cecil was an ambitious man himself: he could use so shrewd a conniver as Nicholas Catesby. And he could see no use at all in the military skills and piratical impulses of the Walter Raleighs and the John Burrows of this world.

" 'Tis not Sir John's usurpations I hear so much about," said Lord Howard grumpily, "as his secret booties. Perhaps his lordship of Westmorland can tell us something of that as well, eh?"

"Aye, secret shares, secret booty!" protested another grey-bearded lord of the Council. "Every seaman and ship's boy of 'em has stolen a royal ransom from the carrack before she ever reached port! Rubies, diamonds, pearls! Silver plate, porcelains, tapestries, cloth o' gold, aye, and golden ingots for all we know!"

"You hear of it on every hand," another fretted angrily. "Where was this famous Sir John Burrow while all this plundering went forward on his own prize, eh?"

Even Sir Walter Raleigh looked uncomfortably down his nose at this.

"It appears from our reports," said Robert Cecil primly, "that Sir John was otherwise occupied that night."

"Indeed," snorted Lord Howard, "and every night after, from what I hear. Every night and half the day—wantoning with a Spanish strumpet!"

"No strumpet, I think, my lord," said Cecil, "but a lady of high degree. Own daughter to the *adelantado* of New Spain, is it not?"

"The Governor of Cuba," said Raleigh. "But it will make no difference to the Queen, whose firm strictures on such matters are well-known." Sir Walter spoke wryly, from unhappy experience. He had himself been consigned to the Tower of London once for getting a lady of quality with child—and he had even married the lady!

Whether it was her own vaunted chastity or some more plebeian jealousy, the Virgin Queen of England was bitterly unforgiving of such moral lapses by her handsome courtiers.

"No strumpet, certainly," said Lord Burghley grimly. "We have in fact numerous representations here from the most noble house of de la Barca, in Cuba and in Castile, offering substantial ransoms for the lady Sir John took from her father's house in Havana." The Lord Treasurer looked round the table. "And can anyone tell me what has become of her, then?" he demanded petulantly.

"Sir John," said Raleigh, "freed not only the Spanish admiral Mendoza, but all his Spanish captives of quality without any ransom at all, as I understand. Aye, and put the very crew of the carrack ashore at St. Michael's. Handsomely done, I should say, and at some considerable risk to himself too."

"No doubt," said Burghley dryly. "But the chivalrous Sir John does not seem to have set this particular lady of quality —this Lady Isabel de la Barca—free at St. Michael's or anywhere else. Where is she then?

"And where, for that matter, is Sir John himself? Has any

man seen *him,* since he sailed into Dartmouth with his prize? Where has *he* got to?"

No one answered. No one knew.

"Most unusual," grumped Burghley, shuffling his papers, "most unusual indeed."

"Unheard-of" would have been a better phrase. The Lord Treasurer could not remember when a victorious commander had omitted to come up to London, to hover about the court and the closets of the great to guarantee his own exorbitant share of the loot. Well, Sir John Burrow would learn the cost of his omission!

"If it please you, then, gentlemen," Lord Burghley concluded without a trace of irony, "I shall myself take in hand the distribution of the prize money in this case. Doing my best, of course, to meet all just demands and claims made upon it." All demands, in sum, except those of Sir John Burrow, Knight, Captain General of the Fleet.

"Fortune's fool, Sir John, and always was," murmured Raleigh, strolling out of the Council chamber in company with Sir Robert Cecil. "He has brought home the richest prize of the war—the people hail him in the street for another Francis Drake—and he's a ruined man!"

"The court is full of Machiavels," said Cecil, "as none should know better than you and I," he added cheerfully. "For have we not both suffered, even as Sir John does, from politicians and detractors?" The two men passed out into the antechamber arm in arm.

Sir Walter Raleigh and little Robert Cecil—Robert the Devil, his enemies called him—were among the bitterest rivals and most violent intriguers at Queen Elizabeth's court. But at least they knew how to play the game.

42

THE GREY STONE MANOR HOUSE ON THE HIGH FELLS WAS NOT so great as the family mansion at Gainsborough, where Lord Thomas ruled over the family estates, but it was sizable enough. It was built of roughhewn stone, roofed with thick slabs of thatch. It was in the high country of the West Riding, a country of vast distances and far-off hills. And it was Sir John Burrow's only hold in all of England.

It was here that he came that cold November, when all was done and over with.

"A land of thieves and Border lords, my lady," he told the girl who rode beside him, wrapped close against the raw wind from the north. "They say in the dales that the high fells 'breed tall men, and hard of nature.' "

Tamar smiled up at him, but did not speak. Her lips trembled with the cold. For the first time in her life, she had seen her own breath made visible, hovering as a tiny mist in the air before her face.

"Shrewder landlords than I am," said Burrow, "run sheep on these bare slopes, and cattle in the dales. But I will still raise horses here, as my fathers did."

Horses, thought old Marina glumly, hunched on her placid mule behind her mistress's grey mare. She hated the monstrous brutes—she almost thought, *from beyond the sea.* But she was beyond the sea now herself, for all of what years were left her. She shook her head, her dark, hawk-featured face expressionless at the ways the gods dealt with mortals.

They rounded the last steep upward curve in the hillside track, and came in sight of the manor, a high-roofed silhouette against a grey and tumbled.sky.

Tamar looked up at it, thinking of her father's tile-roofed house in the park of palms, with its gardens of tamarind and mango. She knew there would be no tropical flowers here, nor any of the life and color of the streets of Havana, bright with gaudy fabrics, dark and perspiring with skins of half a dozen hues. It would all be very different indeed, living in this land of strange crops and pastures, under this tall grey northern sky.

She found herself shivering with sheer excitement at the prospect.

"Ah, but ye're cold, lass," said Burrow, laying his heavy arm about her shoulders. "And it's a cold welcome we'll have this day, I fear," he added ruefully, "for I've warned neither the cottagers nor the serving folk up yonder of our coming. But old Wat and his Kate will have the house warm enough by nightfall. Ye'll like them both. And the tenants will be around soon enough, to do their duty by the new lady of the manor."

Tamar laughed aloud then, surprised at the tinkling of her own laughter in this thinner northern air. "I shall expect them pleasantly, John," she said in her still uncertain English, "your Wat and your Kate, and the rest of them."

"And there will be spring coming, lass," said Sir John, brightening in his turn, his quiet eyes smiling down at her. "Ye must wait for the sun in England, Tamar—it is not like your summer islands of the south. But spring in England is worth waiting for."

And John Burrow would wait too, though armies marched and galleons sailed that and every spring. For he had made his choice, that moment on the carrack's poop, when he had held his rapier point an inch from an old man's throat, and stayed his hand. Had not this girl beside him told him that there is always a choice?

Riding up the last few yards toward the grey walls and thick oak doors of her new home, Tamar knew that she had made her choice too. And she was happier than she had ever been, for all the chill wind blowing.